# Closed Casket

## by
Deany Ray

# Chapter One

JOINING THE WITNESS PROTECTION PROGRAM is like winning a lottery you never wanted to enter. Your prize? A brand-new life! But if you make one goof, you're not just going to get kicked out. No, you would be part of a disappearing act even Houdini would envy.

Chewing my gum and staring at that casket as I elbowed my way through the St. Paul's Church for a funeral—with Edie in tow—I couldn't help but think that could have been me in there, or even Gran. Being so close to death made me ponder. Living with the knowledge that our lives were in perpetual danger was a bitter pill to swallow.

WITSEC—the witness security program—didn't exactly offer a life of ease. It was far from being a picnic. There was no lemonade, no cake and definitely no cookies. If the wrong people were to locate Gran and me here, we'd definitely end up in that casket. By "here" I meant the absolute worst place I could have chosen for us to relocate. It was sticky, steamy, humid, and swarming with bizarre creatures and bugs. In good old Florida, where you broke a sweat the moment you stepped out of the shower and needed to get back in there.

And how do you end up in witness protection? Mostly you did some bad stuff, you got caught, then you're testifying against individuals in your own group who have committed even worse stuff, put them in jail and get yourself a free ticket into a new life, but then you need protection from those very people and their cohorts, who are now rightfully blaming you for throwing them in the slammer.

In our case, Gran got busted for tax evasion and money laundering, putting everything into motion. Not that I was an innocent lamb, I was just lucky enough to dodge their radar. Gran was given a deal: spill the beans on our organization's members, and the government would tuck her away somewhere the organization wouldn't sniff her out. Since I lived with Gran and was close to her, we had to stick together. I needed to be by her side so that said organization couldn't use me to get to her, threatening her through me.

The trial and relocation chewed up thirteen months of our lives. We skulked in various motels across the country, babysat by the US marshals, guarding our safety and relocation. Thirteen months of flipping through daytime TV channels and tipping back drinks.

Then, as the cherry on top of the cake of taking away our lives as we knew it, the marshals plonked us into a retirement complex in the oh-so-scintillating Bitter End in Florida, expecting us to blend in seamlessly, like nothing had happened. Like we weren't the sorest thumb in what we perceived as a lame-o community. Yes, we were now living in a town named Bitter End. It felt more like a cosmic joke; a name that resonated with our current sentiments more than we'd cared to admit.

I wouldn't have ever chosen to live here but the alternative was daring to voluntarily step out of witness protection and praying not to get caught by our organization or remaining in witness protection and getting caught up in some dodgy hustle, and landing in jail.

So, I decided to make this an oddly fulfilling experience. Well, mostly. Because the internal turmoil was more than real.

Surprisingly, one thing that diverted my mind from the constant churn of this witness protection gig and the unattainability of returning home, was our new neighbor, Edith Donovan. We all called her Edie.

She was the absolute opposite of Gran and me. She was the yin to our yang. And sometimes the other way around. She was five foot one with perfectly arched white curls and she had a thing for polka-dot dresses that kind of hurt my corneas. Yet, somehow, we were drawn to each other.

Although she was what we'd term a regular civilian, she had this knack for embroiling us in trouble. Wrap your head around that—us, the seasoned criminals, getting into trouble thanks to an average civilian. If Edie knew our true origins, and the organization we were part of, her perfectly coiffed locks would hit the floor faster than you can say "witness protection."

Gran and I were part of the Oregon Falcons, an exclusive motorcycle club with rules that swerved far from the legal lanes. The Falcons spanned across the United States, but the Oregon branch stood out as the most prosperous. I only knew life being part of the Oregon Falcons. Gran was already a member when I came into this world. Both my parents, also Oregon Falcons, had died in an airplane crash shortly after I was born. It was one of those small airplanes flying over the Oregon mountains, and the fog was just too thick. From that moment on, Gran, my paternal grandmother, took me into her care.

# CLOSED CASKET

It was me and my Gran in our hometown in Oregon. We had the house to ourselves, Gran on the ground floor and me upstairs, and we had our Harleys. Our beloved Harleys. Every crisp Oregon morning, we revved through the woods, by the lakes, and over the mountains. That was pure freedom. Well, that and having the local PD in our pockets. The Falcons had that kind of pull.

Needless to say, we had to leave everything behind—our house, our money, our bikes, our lives, even our souls—to relocate to Florida. Our Falcons logo tattoo on our ankle had to be erased too; they were too much of a trademark, too recognizable. Despite being miles away from our previous life, WITSEC left no room for risk, eliminating any possibility of recognition. At times, I caught a glimpse of my ankle and was briefly startled to find my tattoo gone. I was certain Gran felt the same, but her being tough as nails, she rarely expressed the emotional weight this experience carried for her.

WITSEC offered us therapy, thinking it would smooth things over. That lasted an hour before the therapist ran out in tears. If we could break a government shrink in under an hour, WITSEC seriously needed an upgrade.

It was early November, marking over two months since we settled into the retirement complex. The holiday season loomed, but we were far from thrilled. We were dreading it, actually. There was no cheerful anticipation to celebrate; instead, it felt more like a reminder of our distant home that we could never return to. Last year, our celebration amounted to holing up in a motel room somewhere in the heart of we-couldn't-care-less-how-about-just-shoot-us-now New Mexico. And by celebration, I meant Gran and I poured ourselves an extra glass of rum.

This year, we anticipated the potential coercion of our neighbors in dragging us into their festivities, so we decided to counterattack first. For Halloween, we had told them we were heading back to Idaho—yet another fabrication courtesy of our fake identities—for a supposed relative's birthday. In reality, we rented a room in a neighboring town.

We planned on doing the same for Thanksgiving and Christmas and New Year's as well. While normal people were gearing up for parties and joyful gatherings, Gran's and my mood was more aligned with the emotional intensity of undergoing a root canal.

# CLOSED CASKET

It all boiled down to, we felt invincible in our old lives, and we now felt as fragile as a snowman in Florida. Where we actually lived now. That was extremely unsettling.

As unsettling as the sight of that casket up front next to the altar. Too many thoughts of mortality swirled through my mind. Also, being in a church gave me the creeps. I didn't exactly consider myself a religious person. That would kind of clash with my life spent treading on the wrong side of the law.

"Man, this place is packed," Edie said and wiped some sweat from her forehead. For the funeral she wore a black dress, but I swear I could see even blacker polka dots on it.

"I still don't get why I'm here," I said, chewing my gum vigorously, while a person elbowed me to get ahead. "Hey, watch it." The old Piper wouldn't have had any patience for this kind of nonsense, especially older folks elbowing me. That Piper might have taken them down with force. I definitely had some anger issues back then, way back then, especially in my teen years. These days, I tried my best to keep it in check. Which only worked out sometimes.

"You're here because you're my ride," Edie said. "I can't drive my car here for the funeral. That would be tacky."

It was funny how Edie always found a reason for me to be her own personal chauffeur. Her car, a 1967 candy-apple-red Chevrolet Impala barely saw the light of day, lounging in her garage most of the time. Apparently, the car was too fragile for mundane tasks like grocery shopping, let alone anything else.

"You could have driven here with any of the other three hundred residents," I pointed out, scanning the crowded church where more than half the seats were occupied by folks from the Till the Bitter End Independent Living.

Edie waved away the suggestion. "Yeah, but then all I would hear is conversations about the deceased, death in general, and the reminder that we are old as well and close to the grave and blah blah blah. That would only get me depressed."

I almost choked on my own saliva. If Edie had known what had been going on in my head, she would have more than welcomed those conversations with the others.

"I think you could have handled it," I said.

"Maybe," Edie replied. "But every available ride was already booked. Everybody hitched a ride here with somebody."

I found it hard to believe that Edie couldn't get a ride with anybody. She was like the MVP of the retirement complex.

"Nobody had room for future Prom queen?" I teased.

Edie blushed but didn't say anything.

The seniors were throwing a senior Prom night on Saturday. Yes, an actual senior Prom night. When I first heard about it, I wasn't sure if it was a joke or not. Turns out, no joke. The seniors were dead serious about their parties. Yet another reason to skip out on all the holiday festivities. If they were putting this much effort into a non-holiday party, nobody could tell what they'd do for a holiday one.

About a week and a half ago, they held preliminary voting for Prom king and Prom queen. Yes, I couldn't believe that either. What were the criteria for that? Loose skin, cataracts, and swollen joints? Was that what retired life was like? Was that what I was meant to look forward to at that age?

We had been at the dining hall post-dinner when the Prom committee unveiled the nominees. For the men, it was Harvey Benson, Arthur Gretch, and Theodore Lawrence. Theodore's nomination didn't surprise me; he was the most coveted bachelor in the entire retirement complex. I really liked him. It was too bad he wasn't about forty years younger.

Then came the announcement of the nominees for Prom queen.

The three women and two men from the Prom committee sported wide grins as they read the nominees. The first one was Edie, which was no surprise there. I could see she wasn't surprised either. She rose from her seat and graciously acknowledged the applause. That woman was born to entertain crowds.

The second nominee was Lucretia Barnett, whom I endearingly dubbed Sourpuss. Her nickname said it all. Her nomination was a mystery since I was convinced she had a heart of stone. If she made the nomination list, I wouldn't be shocked if it was due to some unfair play.

"How on earth did that happen?" Edie asked loudly after Sourpuss's name was called out.

Sourpuss shot a venomous look toward Edie.

"I would have gotten rid of her long ago if I were you," Gran had said to Edie.

"You keep saying that, but I don't know what it means," Edie replied. "What would you do? You can't off her or anything."

Gran stared at Edie like she didn't understand those words.

"You know what?" Edie said. "I don't even wanna know."

"Then stop complaining about her if you're not going to do anything about it," Gran said.

Edie opened her mouth, but I put my hand up. "Guys, please," I said. "I just had a delicious dinner and it already got ruined solely by the mention of Sourpuss's name. So can we please drop it? It's bad enough that—"

"—and the third nominee is Dorothy Harris," a loud voice had rung out.

All three of us stopped talking. As did everybody else. It took me a second to process the information. By the look on Gran's face, she needed more than a second. And it wasn't just the fact that she was nominated for Prom queen—something I could never say out loud without bursting into laugher. It was also the name thing. Whenever someone called out for Piper Harris or Dorothy Harris, we still took a beat longer to respond. We had to change our last names due to WITSEC rules, but we still struggled to identify with the last name Harris.

"What just happened here?" Gran murmured.

All eyes were fixed on us. Then clapping erupted.

Gran whipped her head at Edie and me in a desperate look.

"You just got nominated for...Prom queen," I said with my bottom lip quivering.

"Don't be ridiculous," Gran scoffed. "Someone's playing a prank on me." She narrowed her eyes. "Edie, is this your doing?" Then she looked at me. "Piper, was that you? No, let me guess. You both plotted against me."

"Gee, Dorothy, paranoid much?" Edie said, applauding along. "I welcome some good, healthy competition, especially from a fellow resident that I like." She gestured toward Sourpuss. "Not like that shrew."

"So how many nominees are there?" I asked.

"Three," Edie said.

"So it's you, Gran, and Sourpuss?" I shook my head. "This is going to be wild."

"Let the games begin," Edie had said.

Now, at the funeral, I glanced around the church.

"Tell me again why the whole complex is here?" I said to Edie. I even spotted Sourpuss somewhere in the crowd.

"I told you, the guy was our dentist," she replied matter-of-factly. As if that explanation should clarify everything. Seeing my puzzled face, she continued, "Do you know how important dental health is at our age? Dr. Stephen Curtis was the maestro of molars around here."

"The maestro of molars?" I asked, cringing.

"Yeah, the grand poobah of pearly whites," Edie said.

"You mean, more like the grand wizard of dentures."

"That's what I said," Edie replied. "Anyway, Dr. Curtis was not even sixty and had a heart attack. We're here to pay our respects. Plus, it looks good for me to attend the funeral when nearly everyone from the complex is here."

Ah. Why of course. Now I got it. This was all politics. A future Prom queen needed to act in certain ways, and "not caring" about the dentist wasn't one of them. Edie needed to show up at this funeral where her potential voters were, display compassion, and all that jazz. Now it made sense why Sourpuss was here too. She and Edie were smart cookies about this one. Gran was not. She wasn't here. Then again, maybe *she* was the smartest. This was probably one of the rare occasions where she had the whole complex mostly to herself. No nosy neighbor intrusions! She could stage a shooting range at the complex and nobody would care.

While the church was still filling up and Edie and I got sandwiched in the crowd, she leaned in and whispered, "That's Dr. Curtis' wife over there, Eleanor." I scanned the front and spotted a woman in her fifties, donning an all-black ensemble, including a massive hat that made me think of British royalty. She had dark blond hair and a slim figure. She was dabbing at her eyes, but her tears somehow didn't come off as heartfelt.

Edie revealed that Eleanor Curtis ran a clothing store in downtown Bitter End. Then she pointed out the woman in the "not-so-appropriate" tight black pants as Eleanor's sister, and the man beside them as their bother, who lived near Savannah and drove here for the funeral.

The group of men in black suits clustered nearby, almost identical in their attire and demeanor, were Dr. Curtis' high-achieving buddies. Lawyers, tax consultants, doctors—the whole suite. They were today's pallbearers.

"We've been joking around at the complex, calling them the Casa Nostra," Edie snickered under her breath, trying to keep a straight face.

I gulped nervously and chewed my gum even harder.

"You know . . . like the mafia," Edie continued.

*Chew, chew, chew.*

"Yeah, I wouldn't know anything about that," I said.

"Nonsense, surely you've heard of it," Edie persisted. "You know, Casa Nostra, like—" She then mimicked a throat-slitting gesture.

I almost swallowed my gum.

"Edie!" I said a bit too loudly. I so needed this to stop.

"What?" she said, innocently. "I'm just trying to lighten up the mood."

I stared at her. "At a funeral?"

She shrugged.

"Could we move on?" I asked.

Edie sighed. "Fine."

She then proceeded to tell me that the deceased and his wife did not have any children and most of Dr. Curtis' relatives were also non-existent. Also, Eleanor Curtis would sell her husband's dental practice, since the boss was now dead.

So now I was all caught up with gossip I didn't need to know, didn't want to know, and couldn't have cared less about.

During the sermon, my mind wandered to the concept of Casa Nostra and their code of conduct. That was exactly what I didn't need to think about right now. I watched the group of men looking all solemn and thought about what Edie just said. They did have that air of wealth and power, were probably influential people, entitled almost. Hopefully none of them was in the business of . . . throat-slitting.

An eternity later, the sermon was done, the eulogy was done, and I was also done and just wanted to get this over with. People shuffled outside to get into the cars and drive to the cemetery for the burial. I let out a breath while I shielded my face from the sun. Why didn't I just stay at the house? I didn't have any business being at the funeral of a stranger. Then again, it was not like I had any other pressing business today.

"Okay, men, let's lift," the funeral director said, as the other men aligned themselves on both sides of the casket. He squeezed in between them to help carry the casket.

# CLOSED CASKET

They hoisted the casket and began their descent down the church stairs. Fortunately, Florida decided to tone it down a bit in November. We were dealing with around eighty degrees instead of a hundred. Funny how perspectives shift. Who would've guessed I'd be downright ecstatic about eighty degrees, calling it a relief from the scorching heat. Nonetheless, the humidity here made everything worse. I was practically sweating buckets nonstop.

On the plus side, I finally got to wear an all-black outfit, despite the sun. It was a funeral, after all. My wavy, long, dark-brown hair was up in a ponytail, as it was most of the time here.

I zoned out while Edie shook hands and chatted away. She somehow managed to be the MVP at a funeral too.

Then we queued behind the casket and the pallbearers. That gave me heart palpitations and I couldn't wait to get this whole shindig over with. I gnawed harder on my gum like it held the secrets to calm me down.

As I ruminated on life and death, I noticed the men struggling to bear the weight of the casket. Gee, how heavy was that dentist?

The guys broke into a sweat and wore twisted expressions on their faces. One guy's knees buckled, and he said, "I can't hold it any longer." One second later, the casket slipped from his hands, and from there, the scene turned into a slow-motion disaster.

As the other men lost their grip, the casket began its rolling descent down the stairs. Gasps echoed, hands flew to cover mouths, and eyes widened as the casket glided down around fifty feet of stairs. It struck the final step, causing the lid to slide off with a thud.

I stood there, mouth agape, feeling like I was watching a movie. Maybe this funeral had a silver lining after all.

Nobody moved for several seconds. Then everyone dashed down the stairs like they were giving out freebies, circling the casket. What unfolded before our eyes wasn't exactly what we expected. Sure, there was a dead guy in the casket, the presumed Emperor of Grillz. But alongside him, a half-naked young red-haired woman, wrapped in a sheet, tumbled out as well.

My gum almost fell out of my mouth.

Where was my popcorn?

# Chapter Two

EDIE MADE THE SIGN OF THE CROSS, and I swear some women nearly passed out. This wasn't what I had signed up for when Edie talked me into coming to this funeral.

I bit down on my gum with more vigor, probably not realizing the loud sound I was making. A few folks shot me dirty looks.

"Would you please?" Edie said to me, eyeing my jaw.

"Sorry," I said and continued chewing silently.

I was surprised Edie hadn't fainted.

"Are you okay?" I asked her.

She stared down at the scene before us and nodded. "I think so. I may need a bit to process this."

I could never predict Edie's reactions, at least most of the time. She was an odd mix of scaredy-cat and overly brave, always catching me off guard with her different sides. Just when I expected her to freak out, she found the humor in the situation. Or the other way around. Or maybe she'd spent too much time around Gran and me.

Oh, Gran. Too bad she wasn't here. She would have loved this.

After another few seconds of stunned silence, the crowd began to react. The widow, wearing her oversized black hat, was now sobbing uncontrollably, throwing herself over her husband's body. Now she did that? Her shocked siblings tried to comfort her, while other mourners looked appalled and scrambled to do something.

I stared at the red-haired woman, although my view wasn't optimal. I couldn't help but wonder how she ended up in the guy's casket. This was probably the question on everyone's mind. Did the woman have any connection to the deceased?

What timing. She was close to disappearing forever. Once they had buried that casket, nobody would have found her. But as I mulled it over, I realized that someone had tried to pull the old coffin trick. From my past life in Oregon, I'd picked up a few tips on making someone . . . let's say, vanish. It was nearly impossible to pin a murder on someone if the body was never found. And this girl right here definitely didn't land in the guy's casket by accident. How would that even work? Did someone ever say, "Oops, placed the body in the wrong casket, right on top of another dead body?" Nobody gets into a situation like that, not even in a drunken stupor.

20

Someone wanted to make this woman disappear.

She lay there lifeless on the last step of the church, draped in a white-ish sheet. She had a slender figure and her red hair cascaded down her neck. I think I spotted a small tattoo on her calf, or maybe it was on her ankle. I couldn't see clearly. Shaking my head, I dismissed it. A tattoo on the ankle only reminded me of my own past and I was sure I was just seeing things.

Someone hurriedly covered her up, so I didn't have time to inspect for any visible wounds on her body, aside from what was exposed. Not that I cared, it was more a reflex.

All in all, she was an attractive woman and seeing her lifeless body lying there like that, so undignified, made me a bit sad.

Someone clearly called the cops, as expected, because I heard sirens approaching.

That was my cue to leave.

Cops and I, we were not exactly on friendly terms. Never have been and never would be. Back in Oregon, our organization practically had the cops wrapped around our fingers. It wasn't like we plundered the town like Vikings on a spree, we still had to watch our backs around the cops, but all in all, they knew who we were, and we always did that dance around the whole arrest scenario.

The Falcons ran our town, and our only hassle was dealing with rival groups. Cops were mostly an obstruction. Once, an old-timer from the Falcons, Billy Bob, got pulled over for speeding on the highway right outside our turf. The cop, a rookie, hadn't learned the ropes yet and charged Billy Bob for resisting arrest.

Two hours later, probably when the rookie cop realized his mistake, he released Billy Bob with shaking hands and a tear in his eye. I didn't want to know how the cop found out about his error.

"Okay, party's over," I said to Edie. "I'm driving back."

"You're always so uncomfortable when the police come near you," Edie said with a frown. "What's the deal?"

"Nothing is the deal," I said and smacked my gum. "Why would anything be the deal? I just don't like the cops, okay?"

Edie laughed. "What are you, a fugitive or something?"

I almost swallowed my gum again. Few things got under my skin, but ever since I landed in Bitter End, something shifted. I felt uneasy, oddly self-aware, and exposed. Which I kind of was. The cozy shield the Falcons once offered was history. Now, it was all about the WITSEC rules, which was like comparing a security blanket to a paper napkin. I'd like my blankie back, thank you very much.

"A fugitive, good one," I said and forced a laugh. If only she'd knew how close she was to the truth. "So? Are you coming with me or are you staying?"

"You're seriously going?" Edie asked.

"Yes," I said. "What's the point in sticking around? The cops are going to close the area, so you're not going to see much, they're going to question us and that could take hours, and I can't handle the wife's wailing much longer."

Edie rolled her eyes. "Gee, you really know how to kill a vibe."

"Vibe? Did you say vibe?" I asked. "Remember how it was when you found Edgar on your front lawn?"

About two and a half months ago, shortly after Gran and I arrived at the retirement complex, we had found Edie hovering over a dead body in her front yard. Somehow, she got us involved in solving that murder and that led to a whirlwind of antics. I've had more run-ins with dead bodies in this retirement gig than in my entire previous life. And that was saying something.

"Of course I remember," Edie said blushing, shuffling her feet in front of her. "But that one concerned *me*, with emphasis on me. This one just doesn't feel that . . ."

"Personal?" I asked.

Edie nodded. "Well, yeah. I don't want to sound insensitive but . . ."

I smiled. "I know what you mean."

Boy, did I understand.

Interestingly enough, when I first met Edie, she seemed like your run-of-the-mill old lady, baking pies and gossiping. She was still all that, but she was also full of surprises with her flashes of brilliance and unfiltered honesty that sometimes came off as naive but were smarter than she seemed.

Then there were those times when Edie jumped into things without thinking and dragged Gran and me along, expecting us to pull off a rescue mission.

Edie decided to stick around—funny how it was no problem to get a ride back—, so I hustled back to the car before the sun torched a hole in my black clothes. I threw out my gum and slipped into the silver Ford Taurus—an older-model car I was still sharing with Gran—then headed back to the retirement center. I cranked up the AC and took my sweet time driving because, to be honest, I wasn't in a hurry to get back to the whole lot of nothingness that had become my life.

Since I was plucked out of my regular life and thrown into this witness protection ordeal, I've sort of been drifting. The good folks at WITSEC expected me to find a job to sustain myself. Gran and I still received monthly subsistence checks, but that wouldn't last forever. Gran was forced to sell the house and the cabin near Mount Hood in Oregon, our second home. Gran was now pretty much set up and could afford to live in the retirement complex in the new house when the government money stopped. It was not like she would be entering the job market again at her age, especially since she's never worked a regular gig in her whole life. She was running a trucking company that was a front for money laundering.

I, on the other hand, was working behind the bar at Choppers, the local watering hole in our hometown. I also handled the books, and let's just say I had a way with numbers—creatively speaking. Sadly, those accounting skills weren't exactly on the legal job list anymore. It was made crystal clear that Gran and I weren't allowed to tiptoe into anything illegal. We could've, sure, but if WITSEC caught wind of it, then it was game over.

Only that was exactly the thrill we'd longed for. We *could* start a little side gig and play the "don't get caught" game. We would thrive on the adrenaline rush. On the real excitement. For god's sake, that was our whole life. How did they expect us to switch gears so fast? Or ever, for that matter.

So, with that itch for thrills and my current humdrum life in Florida, I've been stuck in neutral, job-wise. Life-wise. Emotional-wise. Everything-wise. I had a brief stint at another bar here in Bitter End a few weeks back but what do you know, it ended with another corpse and the bar getting shut down.

So I had to start from scratch again.

Or not.

During my last dead body adventure at the bar, I bumped into this private investigator who was just as gruff and unapologetic as I was. At least, as I was deep inside my soul. He was even shadier than a palm tree in Florida. But, in his own way, I was sure there was a hint of goodness hiding behind his rough exterior. Sometimes.

We teamed up to crack the murder case at said bar. He then offered me a job, like a consultant of sorts, for the cases he got as a PI.

I couldn't give him an answer right away. He totally caught me off guard and I hated being caught off guard. I was still kind of wrestling with my inertia and this inability to make a solid decision. Or did I wallow in those feelings? I had no idea. But honestly, who the hell wouldn't be depressed in a situation like this?

I rolled by the sign that read *Welcome to Till the Bitter End Independent Living. Where your tropical dreams come true.*

Oh, joy. If only I had any *tropical* dreams.

If someone had told me I'd end up in a Florida retirement complex, I'd have laughed in their face. But the marshals brought Gran here, and I had to tag along. The initial plan was to stay temporarily with her and then find my own place. As with my job hunt, finding an apartment gave me the same feeling of analysis paralysis.

Luckily, the administration gave me the nod to stay with Gran until the end of this year, so about two more months. I should've been on the hunt for my own place, especially since Gran's house was a one-bedroom setup where I crashed on the living room couch that I resented with my whole being. That couch has become my nemesis. Gran's entire house wasn't exactly what we had chosen for ourselves. It was a gray painted bungalow, with an equally gray colored roof and a wide porch. The garish yellow carpet, the ugly green curtains and the brown nemesis-couch, complete with one of those CRT television sets made you think you stepped into a time machine and got out in 1972.

Come to think of it, I wasn't sure if I *did* prefer this style of house décor since every other home in the retirement complex was way too cutesy for my taste, and definitely way too cutesy for Gran's taste too. Each house was painted in pastel colors and had these colorful gnomes in the front yard that made us cringe every time we passed them. The accompanying cheerful potted plants only added insult to injury.

I parked the car at the curb in front of Gran's house, turned off the engine, and leaned back, letting out a sigh. I glanced at the golf cart parked in front of Gran's garage. That's when the usual wave of nostalgia hit. I missed my bike and Gran missed her bike. We switched from a Harley to a golf cart. It was like Cinderella but in reverse.

Then my eyes landed on Gran's front lawn and that lifted my spirits a bit. There were seven naughty-looking gnomes just chilling in the grass. A few weeks ago, Edie got us wrapped up in this prank with Sourpuss where we swapped her real gnomes with these, well, let's say, colorful ones.

One had his pants down, exposing his privates, another one was exposing his backside, as if mooning someone. Another gnome was seated on the toilet reading a newspaper, while still another had both hands up in a devilish rock 'n' roll gesture and their tongue sticking out. There was even one that was entirely nude, yet hiding behind a surfboard with his hand over his mouth that was shaped like an O, seemingly embarrassed to be seen au naturel. One gnome was dressed up like Santa Claus with dark sunglasses and puffing away on a Cuban cigar.

Then there was the biker gnome dressed appropriately in black leather and mirrored shades, who had some sort of firearm attached to his belt, and was showing his middle finger.

When the gig was up, we had to switch them back but the store didn't take them back. Gran's house was the only spot where these gnomes kinda fit—not to mention, it fit with her too—and after a lot of convincing, she finally caved and reluctantly agreed to host them.

It must have dawned on Gran that this place didn't really resonate with her as much as her old home in Oregon did. That was probably why neither of us bothered much about making this place homey. So throw junk on the lawn? Sure! We'd just leave it there.

The funny twist was: those lewd gnomes somehow boosted Gran's status in the retirement community. She was all about not fitting in. She stuck to her biker gear despite the scorching Florida sun, donning her boots, denim jeans, and the classic white top with her black aviators, giving off her "don't mess with me" vibe. She had a knack for speaking her mind, giving soft threats, and taking zero crap. But despite her attitude, she became a community favorite. Evidence for that was her nomination for Prom queen. I still had to chuckle even thinking that. Gran. A Prom queen. More improbable than us landing in witness protection.

I felt glued to my car seat as I still watched the house. I didn't need to hurry anywhere. I could just stay here in the car for hours if I wanted to. Just like apparently, I still wanted to stay in Gran's house. That was my norm. The only norm I knew. It might sound lame for a thirty-year-old to not be thrilled about living solo and having their own space, but hey, that was just how life rolled sometimes. Maybe deep down, that was why I wasn't rushing to pack my bags. Moving out meant leaving Gran behind, and after a whirlwind of changes over the past fifteen months, I wasn't exactly itching for another big shift.

Edie was the one who really fought for me to stay. She beamed with pride as she dropped the bombshell that there was a loophole in the system. As it turned out, the law and the community contract let persons under fifty-five stay if there was at least one person in the household who was over the threshold. That would be Gran and me in the setup.

I had to admit, my heart skipped a beat when Edie shared the news. There was only one big issue. Space. The house had one bedroom. If I had to sleep on that couch forever and always, I would beg Gran to shoot me and end my misery.

Edie dismissed my concern and said we'll find a way around it.

"How?" I had asked. "Magic? Build a new wing?"

Edie snapped her fingers. "You're right. I should look into that. I'll see if it's doable, construction-wise and all."

If searching for a job and sprucing up the house was already pushing my limits, slapping on an extra wing—as if we were talking about a castle—was kind of like asking me to climb Mount Everest. Without an oxygen tank.

I finally got out of the car and headed for the front door. It was noon, so I should hurry for my nap. Gran was probably snoring on the couch already. Just as I reached for my keys, voices drifted from inside. I distinguished a male voice, but the words were all mushed up, so no clue what he said.

My heart rate skyrocketed.

In moments like this, paranoia took over, logic was thrown out the window and my brain started playing out every worst-case scenario possible.

This was it. The Falcons had found us.

# Chapter Three

GRAN HAVING COMPANY immediately set off alarm bells in my head. It had to be the Falcons, right? Maybe their top-notch hitman had found his way into Gran's place, holding her hostage, and waiting for me to show up so he could finish us both.

The panic-induced sweat fest didn't help with the mental meltdown I felt at that moment.

What to do? What to do?

I shook my head. I had to do what I've always done.

Survive.

I pressed my ear against the door, but it was all muffled chatter. Obviously I recognized Gran's voice. I would recognize it anytime. But I couldn't make out what the conversation was about. Was it tension I sensed? Did the man in there just threatened Gran?

This was what my life has come to. Welcome to Paranoia Central. Population: Me. Witness protection felt more like The Fear Olympics. I had never before truly felt fear like this. Being in witness protection meant we were living always looking over our shoulder. Normal human interactions always had that hint of suspicion and small things could trigger the "The Falcons are here!" alarm in my brain.

So while it might have been just Gran now having a chat with a neighbor, my brain still went into overdrive and my survival instinct kicked in.

I had to save Gran.

Sucky for me, I didn't have my weapon of choice with me. My knife. Another thing that changed since living in Florida. I felt like I was missing a limb without my knife. But where the hell would I hide one while wearing Florida-appropriate clothing? I was wearing stretchy black pants without any pockets and the ugliest black sneakers known to humanity right now. Come to think of it, I could have stashed my knife at the rim of my pants somehow. But it was too late for that.

I had to do this without my knife.

First things first. I had to know who was inside the house and what their position was.

I moved away from the front door, with the porch letting out a squeak as if it wanted to blow my cover. I tip-toed around the house corner and crept closer to the living room window. My whole body was in stealth mode. Who would I even call if things went south? The cops? And tell them what? That our arch-nemeses were on our trail? That the people we were running from have found us? That would mean virtually ending Gran's life.

And what about Gran? How did she end up in this situation? She always knew how to take care of herself and she was always packing, witness protection or not.

Pressed against the wall, I leaned in for a sneaky peek through the window. The sun was glaring so I edged closer, hoping nobody would spot me. The window was shut tight, since we always had the AC running in the house.

I was squinting through the glass and was just about ready to give up and try another window, when a barrel of a gun popped up right into my face from inside the house.

"Oh, Jesus almighty," I yelped and instantly ducked. That was it. My life was over. The Falcons' hitmen were probably jumping out of bushes any second now.

Instead, the window cranked open, and Gran stuck her nose out, gun in hand.

"What the hell are you doing out here?" she asked. "I almost shot you."

"You think?" I said and straightened up. "The question is, what are you doing?"

"I sensed there was an intruder lurking around the house," Gran said. "I heard the porch screech."

Of course she did. If anyone would hear that, it was Gran.

"Why were you lurking around?" Gran asked.

I shook my head and said, "I'm coming around."

I strutted back to the porch, where Gran already held the door open. I got inside and saw Theodore lounging on the couch with a huge grin plastered across his face.

I let out a breath. I got this all wrong—again—confirming the kind of anxiety I was constantly living with. The irony of ironies would be a shootout between Gran and me, mistaking each other for the enemy.

"Theodore, it's just you," I said.

"Who did you expect, Piper?" he asked.

I shrugged. What could I say? That I expected a lineup of hitmen and assassins inside the house?

"Well, I . . . I heard voices and . . ." I began.

"And you didn't think that could mean Dorothy had visitors?"

Gran and I exchanged glances.

Theodore laughed. "You two are something else. That's why I like you so much." He gave Gran a wink. She showed him the cold shoulder by looking away.

That was a classic game between those two. Theodore has been pursuing Gran but she kept him at arm's length. Although, he was here now in the house, so that was odd.

Gran tucked her gun back inside her waist and took a seat at the kitchen table. I sat next to her and wiped off sweat from my forehead.

"Why weren't you on high alert just now?" I asked Theodore. "Obviously Gran suspected an intruder. You're still relaxing on the couch."

"Because I knew she was overreacting," Theodore said.

I thought about that for a second.

"But don't you still have that reflex for potential danger, that tendency to exaggerate from time to time?" I asked him. "Isn't that part of your wiring by now?"

Theodore was an ex-Navy Seal who had the rank of captain and who retired after serving thirty years in the service. Gran was extra careful around him, considering his background. An ex-military man, even in his seventies and retired for nearly two decades, would have sharp instincts like the ones taught in the service: capable of perceiving things civilians wouldn't. A.k.a. Gran's and my fake identities. But as much as we intended to stay away from Theodore—and from our whole community here in Florida, for that matter—we still collided together.

I'd wish Gran collided more with Theodore, although I was aware of the danger. He was six feet tall and had thinning gray hair. He had broad shoulders and a sturdy build and he was a complete gentleman. But most importantly, he took a liking to Gran.

Theodore glanced at me, his expression turning serious. "I had to unlearn that reflex after retiring. That kind of reflex can mess with your head. It can take over your life. You end up suspecting everyone and everything in your regular life. That's no way to live."

The silence that followed was heavy. I could feel Gran tensing up beside me and I was tensing up myself. Theodore's words hit home, sinking right into the core of us. Yes, I sure as heck knew what he was talking about. Only a minute ago I had my nose pressed against the window, convinced the Falcons had found us. But how does one get rid of those reflexes? Those very reflexes were what kept Gran and me alive. That was something Theodore didn't know and would never find out.

I cleared my throat. "I see."

That was the only thing that came out of my mouth.

I expected Theodore to question us about our reactions just now. Apparently, Gran whipped out her gun in front of him without a care in the world. But then again, that was very much like Gran. Half of the people here got wind of the fact that Gran was packing. Besides, her paranoia probably also took over, figuring there was danger outside the house, and decided it was better to be safe than sorry.

Theodore smiled widely at Gran and me. No questions. No inquiries. No nothing.

So I decided to change the subject.

"So what brings you by, Theodore?" I asked.

"Oh, I just came for a chat," he said, and his eyes cut to Gran. Did I just disturb them?

"I was also just asking Dorothy if she would join me at the senior's prom on Saturday," he said, smiling again.

I turned to Gran with a huge grin. "Oh, really?"

Gran rolled her eyes. "Yes, and I already told him I'm not the prom kind of gal. I don't belong there."

"Oh, I think you belong there more than you think," Theodore said. "You already got nominated for Prom queen."

I had to stifle a laugh.

Theodore continued. "Admit it, Dorothy. People like you. They enjoy your company, as charming as it is."

God, he was so good at teasing Gran.

"Theodore is right," I said. "I think it's a great idea you going to the prom with him. We could even do some dress shopping before. Maybe you'll even wear a corsage!" I couldn't help it; I was on the verge of bursting out with laughter. From riding a Harley to wearing a dress and a corsage, and nominated for Prom queen? Even with hitmen on the search for us and living in witness protection, this moment right here . . . totally worth it.

Gran narrowed her eyes, and I sensed a bubble of annoyance building. I only hoped she wouldn't pull her gun on me again. She turned to me. "You know, people here like you too."

My grin disappeared. Uh-oh. Something wasn't right.

"Well, of course," Theodore said. "People here love you, Piper. You're a breath of fresh air, just as Dorothy is. You have to come to the prom too."

Crap.

Gran put on a huge grin now and I was the one narrowing my eyes at her.

*Well played, Gran.*

"But this is a senior's prom," I said, trying to get out of it. "I don't belong there, this is your party."

"Nonsense," Theodore said. "You're practically one of us already. Saturday's shindig is a must. And hey, if you're worried about a date, we'll figure it out. I'm sure Edie can work some magic."

I almost fell off my chair while Gran busted out laughing.

"What do you mean, Edie can work some magic?" I asked, although I already knew his answer.

"I think you know what I'm talking about," Theodore said, shifting on the couch. "*He* would love to take you to the prom."

I knew exactly who Theodore was talking about and I was definitely not going there. I did not have the mental energy for it. "Theodore, I don't know what you're talking about." Then I mumbled under my breath, "Take me to the prom, huh. I can take *myself* to the prom."

"Then it's a deal," Theodore said, smiling. "You're both coming to the party."

Gran and I shared a look again. We wouldn't be able to get out of it. There was no escaping these people here. Edie would probably show up and drag us there herself.

41

"Alright, my work here is done," Theodore said and stood. "Dorothy, I'll swing by to pick you up on Saturday. But I'm sure we'll see each other before then too."

Just before leaving, he turned, his hand on the doorknob. "By the way, how was the funeral, Piper? I know you tagged along with Edie."

"Oh, the funeral," I said, scratching the back of my neck. "It was . . . interesting." I really liked Theodore, but telling a story about a corpse popping out of a casket would only drain me emotionally right now and he would find out soon enough either way. "Edie can tell you all about it, since she's still there."

"She's still there?" Theodore asked, surprised. "But didn't you drive there together?"

"I ran out of patience and came back early," I said, smiling.

"That I understand," he said. "I couldn't find the energy to even go there. I knew Dr. Curtis, but between you and me, after all those Navy-related funeral ceremonies, I couldn't muster up a ton of feelings for my dentist."

And that was why I liked Theodore so much.

After he left, I turned to Gran. "Well, gee, thanks a lot for that."

"You started it," she said. "You know I'm going to take you down with me."

I laughed. I knew she did.

"So why did you drive back without your best friend?" Gran asked.

My best friend. At thirty, my best friend was a septuagenarian.

"There was an incident at the funeral," I said.

Gran looked at me questioningly.

"Someone tried to pull the old coffin trick," I said, as I took off the sneakers and ambled to the fridge for a bottle of water.

Gran frowned. "The coffin trick? What do you mean, the coffin trick? Like, the coffin trick?"

I took a big gulp of water. "Yup. There was a second body in the casket. It was too heavy for the guys to carry so it slipped on the stairs in front of the church, then bounced around, slid down, the lid came off, and a woman popped out." I paused. "She was pretty. Red-haired."

Gran blinked at me twice. "You're kidding."

"Nope, no joke. Why would I joke about something like that?"

Gran shrugged. "I don't know. To make my life here more bearable maybe?"

"Ha, I think your life is more bearable than you think." I returned to the table, plopped down next to Gran, and let out a deep breath.

"So it really happened?" Gran asked and a smirk formed at the corner of her mouth. "A red-haired woman was inside the casket with that dentist guy?" She slapped her thigh in amusement. "Now this is more like it. Finally, some action here."

"Finally?" I glanced at her incredulously. "Haven't we had enough action since we got here? All the dead bodies we stumbled upon, getting mixed up in figuring out the murders, shooting at people and getting shot at, that was not enough action for you?"

Gran adjusted her gun tighter in her waistband. "That was just warming up."

I shook my head. "Well, I don't want that kind of drama around here. We're not home, remember? We're supposed to lay low and live a normal life." I winced as those words left my mouth. Who was I kidding? Gran? She knew me better than I knew myself. My reaction at seeing the second corpse at the funeral had been very similar. I felt excitement.

"You're one to talk," Gran said. "You're the one who got involved in all of that. Or better yet, you let yourself be dragged into it. You could have said no,

44

even if it meant leaving Edie in the lurch. You're not the type to be pushed around. So admit it. You got involved because you wanted to. You want to live a normal life? Then we could just go right ahead and shoot ourselves now. We don't do normal life. We're not cut out for that."

Damn it. She hit the nail on the head. I had no counterarguments.

I took some more gulps of water.

"So someone pulled the old coffin trick?" Gran asked.

"Seems that way," I said. "Someone definitely didn't want that girl to be found. It's clear she didn't die of natural causes then. I overheard some mourners saying there was a mix-up, and the poor girl ended up in the dentist's casket by mistake."

Gran laughed. "Yeah, right. As if you'd miss an extra body in there."

"Exactly," I said. "That was no accident."

Gran leaned back in her chair. "Well, it was either a crooked staff member at the funeral home who did it or someone broke in and put the body in there."

I thought about it. Sounded about right.

"After they murdered her," I added.

"Obviously," Gran said. "But they always make the same mistake with this trick."

"The weight issue," I said.

"Bingo," Gran said. "Even if the second body is a lightweight, it's still two bodies. The casket is heavier, and chances are good something like this happens."

I nodded along. Whoever did this must have been desperate or inexperienced to think they could pull it off. But that was not my problem. Looking into this mess was not my job.

\*\*\*

A couple of hours later Edie still wasn't back. I knew she would come straight to us to report on all the gossip. I kept glancing out the window towards her house, just checking if she really wasn't back yet, and every time, Gran shook her head. She knew I was getting curious.

I was on the couch with Gran and while she was already napping, I was teetering on the edge of dreamland myself.

Then came the loud knock on the door.

My eyes shot wide open while Gran jolted upright, her short honey-blonde bob all tousled as she blinked around, half-confused. Every time she did that, I was certain she was trying to figure out where the heck she was, expecting to wake up in her Oregon house. I totally got that.

"Why does she always do that?" Gran asked, and I knew she meant Edie. "It's like she's spying on us and waiting for the worst moment to come over."

Gran was right about that too. Edie had a knack for showing up when we were either snoozing or in mid-nap, which was basically all the time. That should have made me rethink our current lives, but I pushed that thought away, as I always did.

Gran got up and shuffled to the bathroom.

I opened the door. I expected Edie but it wasn't Edie. Funny how easily I've dropped that essential habit. You know, the whole "checking before opening the door" thing. When you're in witness protection and hitmen are after you, that should be Door Opening 101. Yet, there I was, not even throwing a glance through the peephole.

Before me stood a hairy chest landscape, giving off a scent of salami mixed with cheap cologne, and a toothpick bouncing up and down next to a Grand Canyon-sized tooth gap.

"Hey, kiddo, how's it going?" he asked.

47

Leonardi. Full name: Leo Leonardi. That's right. No joke there.

Leonardi was the private investigator I bumped into a few weeks back at the bar I was working at. He was the one proposing we should work together for the cases he got.

He had a Mediterranean complexion, and a deep, gruff voice in a Brooklyn accent. His clothing style made you reach for a fork to poke your eye out. Short-sleeved shirt in a busy pattern, the color of mustard and purple that was too tight for his protruding beer belly. Way too many buttons loose, always showing off his hairy cleavage. Slacks that never matched with his shirt color-wise. Pointy, shiny dress shoes. He wore his dark brown hair slicked back. He had a small, silver earring in his left lobe and a golden, chunky necklace around his neck. On his wrist he wore a shiny watch, and I was sure that was a real Rolex, although he pretended it was fake.

All in all, he looked like a pimp.

"Oh, hi," I said.

He looked behind him at the front lawn. "Nice décor. They really stand out."

"The gnomes? Oh yeah, just what we were aiming for."

48

"I like them," he said with a wide grin.

I scanned the area over his shoulder. "Where's your truck?"

You couldn't miss his truck. It was a beat-up, roaring beast that could probably be heard from outer space. How the cops hadn't pulled that clunker off the road was beyond me. That thing was a hazard. I learned it the hard way on my last adventure with Leonardi.

He still grinned, gnawing on that toothpick. "Parked it around the corner."

"So I wouldn't make an escape through the back window?" I asked.

"Maybe."

I rolled my eyes. "Okay, what's going on? I didn't exactly expect you."

"You should have," Leonardi said. "I'm not giving up so fast. Not with someone with your skill set."

"Yeah, about that . . ." I said. "I still don't know—"

Leonardi put his hand up. "Yeah, yeah, excuses upon excuses. Before you shut the door in my face, listen up. I have a case for you. Something easy." He pulled a photo out of his pocket and shoved it in my face. "I need you to find this woman."

I focused on the picture and blinked twice. She was a pretty one, smiling into the camera. She was somewhere on a beach. She looked to be having a good time. She had flowing red hair.

"You're right, it is easy," I said. "She's dead. Popped out of a casket this morning at St. Paul's Church."

Leonardi's jaw dropped, and his toothpick fell on the ground.

# Chapter Four

"WHAT DID YOU JUST SAY?" Leonardi asked, frowning.

I sighed. "Come on in."

Leonardi walked inside and nodded at Gran who just came out of the bathroom. She startled slightly, obviously expecting Edie.

Leonardi's eyes dropped to Gran's waist. He grinned. "You sleeping with that too?"

"Showering with it too," Gran shot back. That earned a loud laugh from Leonardi.

"You two are always making my day," he said.

Leonardi strode to the couch and sprawled across it, arms flung over the headrest, like he owned the place. His beer belly took center stage. He was a mix of irritating and fascinating at the same time.

"So again, what happened at what church today?" he asked me.

Gran and I settled at the kitchen table, deliberately marking our territory on one side, while Leonardi lounged carefree on the other. But I was sure he gave a tiny rat's ass about that.

I filled him in on today's funeral fiasco and the unexpected second body in the casket. Leonardi listened, nodding along. Then after I finished, he let out a breath and said, "I gotta tell ya, I'm rarely speechless."

"Tell me about it," I said. "Wasn't exactly the ending I was expecting."

"You sure it was her?" Leonardi asked, showing me the picture of the dead girl again.

"Positive," I said.

"So, murdered?" Leonardi asked.

"Well, what do you think?" I asked, rolling my eyes.

"Okay, chill," he said, putting his hands up in defense. "Just trying to wrap my mind around it. Do you know how she died?"

I shook my head. "No, didn't see anything visible on her body. Nothing that stuck out."

Leonardi rubbed his face and then glanced toward the kitchen area. "Got any beer or something? I know you always have something."

If even Leonardi knew about us always having a stash of "something", I should really reconsider some things in our lives.

"Got any more of that good rum here?" he asked.

"No," Gran said.

"You're lying," Leonardi replied. "You do have some."

Gran shifted nervously in her seat.

"Okay, before we have a shootout here because of rum, Gran had found a very nice and vintage rum bottle that she'll only open on special occasions," I said.

Leonardi opened his mouth but then I said, "No, this is not a special occasion."

"And here I was, thinking I was special," he said with a hint of sarcasm.

I got up and brought out three beers from the fridge. We cracked them open, and we each took a long, satisfying gulp.

"So there you have it," I said and placed the beer bottle on the table. "Case closed."

Leonardi made an appreciative sound after his gulp of beer, then fixed his eyes on me. I sighed. "It's not closed, is it?"

"What do you think?" he asked. "Isn't this right up your alley? You like a challenge."

"How do you know what I like?" I asked.

"Puh-lease," he said and laughed. "Hairdresser my butt. Found a job yet?"

I pursed my lips.

Shortly after Gran and I landed at the retirement complex, I was asked what I did for a living. Because Gran and I hadn't had our stories straight, I'd blurted out I was a hairdresser. Big mistake—as it turned out that being a hairdresser at a retirement complex was like suddenly becoming the savior of the world. But after I dyed one of the resident's hair purple, I announced I would be exiting the business.

Leonardi got the same version of my story but he was smart enough to question it.

"Thought so," he said.

Then he paused and I could tell he was processing the information I just relayed.

"First things first," he said and got up from the couch. "I need to call my client and report what happened. I'll take this outside."

"Tell your client it was my pleasure to crack the case and I only accept cash payments," I shouted after Leonardi as he opened the door.

I could sense him grinning again, though he didn't turn around.

He went outside and I peered out the window, watching him pacing around and talking vividly on the phone.

"This just got interesting," Gran said.

"How much more interesting can we handle?" I asked, my eyes still glued on Leonardi.

"It's only our lives we have to lose," Gran said. "But then again, we already kind of lost them."

Her words hit hard. In a way, we had already lost our lives.

Ten minutes later, Leonardi ended the call and headed inside again. I moved from the window and resumed my seat at the kitchen table next to Gran. Leonardi strolled back in, got comfortable back on the couch with a boyish grin plastered on his face.

"What are you so happy about?" I asked him.

"We need to find out what happened to that girl," Leonardi said with an air of triumph.

Okay, so he got the murder case from his client. That was almost expected.

"We?" I asked.

"Yeah, we. Consider this your job right here. It's a miracle you haven't come running to me already. If you keep this up, you'll end up drowning in depression here in silver city."

Gran took a gulp of beer to stifle a laugh.

I shot her a look. "What's so amusing?"

"I'm with him on this one," Gran said. "I don't know what you're waiting for."

I thought about it. What was I waiting for? There were so many things to consider that I didn't know where to start. Leonardi had mentioned I could work for him as a consultant. Consult him on his cases, which was a fancy way of saying I'd be a PI without a license. He would also have to pay me, like legally pay me. There had to be clean money coming in. He already knew that.

But what would I tell Brett Dillon?

Brett Dillon was the US marshal who'd gotten appointed to Gran and me. It was safe to say we made his life a living nightmare. He was in charge of Gran and me staying alive. And also, us not starting a side hustle that could get us kicked out of WITSEC. Me playing private detective—although legal—was still not something he would approve of. The nature of the job would have me too close to the real law enforcement scene. By butting my nose into murder cases, just like this one, I'd be dangerously close to exposing my real identity. One scan of my fingerprint, and they'd know something fishy was up with me.

Dillon expected me to land a typical job like a factory worker or nail technician. Boy, he would love it if I were a hairdresser for real.

If I turned down Leonardi's offer, though, he would be right. I would only sink further into my gloom. Luckily for me, he also made it clear that he didn't care how I went about solving the cases and honestly, that was the freedom I needed for my sanity. That was me at the core. This was where the struggle came from. I knew what I wanted to do, what I needed for my mental well-being, and that was exactly what I wasn't supposed to do.

Ugh.

*Screw it.*

"How much does it pay?" I asked.

Gran got up and high-fived Leonardi. I rolled my eyes.

"Two thousand for you," Leonardi said.

"As a retainer?" I asked. "And the hourly payment?"

Leonardi grinned. "As a whole package for you now. We can discuss an extra hourly pay for future gigs."

Okay, we were starting out slow. I kinda figured that. But still, he could do better.

"Two thousand for first-degree murder?" I said. "Because it sure looks like first-degree murder. You do know murder is pretty high up on the felony list, right?"

Leonardi let out a, "duh."

"Three thousand," he said. "And that's my final offer."

I rested my hands on my knees and took a breath. I looked Leonardi dead in the eye. "Five thousand. And that's *my* final offer."

The tension in the room could have cut through steel. I could almost hear my heartbeat and Gran's soft breathing. But even from the corner of my eye, I knew she was smiling ear to ear.

"Heck yeah, that's my granddaughter," she said. Then we high-fived.

Leonardi shouldn't have been surprised. He wanted someone with my skills, so I was going to give it to him.

"Fine, kiddo, we have a deal," he said. "Spit shake?"

I held my hand up. "Nah, I'm good. But maybe we can do a pinky swear." My hands would reek of salami for days.

Leonardi let out a loud laugh. "I'm good too, thanks."

"You know we need to do this by the book, right?" I asked. "It has to be legit."

"Yeah, I know," Leonardi said. "The money from me to you needs to take the legal way. I've already got your paperwork all set."

I blinked twice.

Leonardi flashed me his tooth gap. "Now I got you surprised, didn't I?"

"Heck, yeah."

"Damn straight."

Gran and I said in unison.

Then we all clinked our beer bottles.

"I'll come by your office soon about that paperwork," I said. "I'm surprised you don't have it with you."

"I wanted to leave room for a bit of suspense," he said.

"Okay, so who's the redhead and who's your client?" I asked Leonardi.

"The victim's name is Lola Duvall. She works as an escort girl and lives with a coworker of hers, Ruby Hansen. Ruby hired me to find Lola because she's been missing for two days."

"So she's MIA for two days and ends up dead in some other guy's casket," I said.

"And not by accident," Leonardi said.

Gran let out a snort. "Not if she fell, hit her head and took a nosedive right into the dead man's box."

"I gotta tell you," Leonardi said. "I've seen a lot of stuff in my life but even that seems improbable."

Gran nodded in agreement.

"How do you know your client?" I asked Leonardi. "Amherst Street?"

Amherst Street was in a not-so-fancy part of town. It was more cracked pavements and rundown buildings. It was the kind of place where shady dealings went down, sketchy bars were rough around the edges, and packing was probably a must. So right up my alley.

Leonardi's office was in the same part of town, only four blocks from Amherst Street.

He nodded. "We've been hanging around the same areas for some time now, so yes, we knew of each other."

"Did she go to the cops too?" I asked.

"She said she did, and the cops filed a missing person's report, but she felt that they wouldn't exactly hurry up to investigate, given her line of work," Leonardi said. "So she came to me."

"Got it," I said. "I wonder if the cops identified Lola. It's not like she had her ID with her, the way she was wrapped in that sheet."

"Well, probably they matched the body to the description in the missing person's report," Gran said.

I nodded. "Most likely." Then I asked Leonardi, "Did you know Lola personally?"

"I didn't," Leonardi said. "I remember seeing her a few times in a bar where I used to hang out in, but just as with Ruby, I only knew of her." He took a swig of beer. "What a waste. She had her whole life before her."

"How old was she?" I asked.

"Twenty-two," Leonardi said.

There was silence for a few beats. I could sense we were all reflecting on the possibilities and dreams that Lola couldn't live out. Then I reflected on the fact that Gran and I were still alive.

"Do you have any contacts in the Police Department?" I asked Leonardi. "At least if we find out how she was murdered, then we have a starting point."

Leonardi cracked his knuckles. "I may have some. I'll see what I can find out. So you didn't see anything on her body? Bruises? Wounds?"

"I wasn't really inspecting her, but nothing jumped out," I said. "There were no obvious bloodstains on the sheet she was wrapped in and there were no obvious bullet holes either, so I'm tipping on strangulation or blunt force trauma. Her long hair covered her neck so I couldn't really see any marks. It would be good if you got confirmation from the cops about how she died."

Leonardi flashed me his tooth gap and his eyes twinkled.

I frowned. "What?"

"I knew you were good," he said. "Your grandma is good too. Unfortunately, I can't afford to pay both of you."

I playfully slapped Gran on her shoulder and said, "That's not a problem, she'll do it for free."

Leonardi laughed. "I believe that."

Gran turned to me and gave me her signature death stare.

"Anyway," I continued, "I wonder why Lola was left naked and wrapped in a sheet."

"Well, she worked as an escort girl, so—" Leonardi said.

"—so we can assume she was doing stuff that went beyond her escorting and she was maybe in bed with a client? Maybe she had a fight with the client, and he went too far? Then he left her like that, put a sheet around her, dumped her clothes and purse somewhere, and figured another man's funeral was the best way to dispose of the body?"

"I agree," Leonardi said. "Which brings us to how she got into that guy's casket. Who was he anyway?"

I told him everything I knew about the dead guy. Which was not that much. The seniors' go-to dentist, left a wife behind, no kids, in his mid-fifties, ran a successful dental practice in Bitter End. As far as I had gathered, he was also born near Bitter End and grew up in the area.

Leonardi glanced into the direction of the fridge, then he asked, "Do we think there could be a connection between this dentist and Lola?"

Gran got up and brought Leonardi another bottle of beer.

I shrugged. "I have no idea. Maybe someone just dumped Lola's body into his casket out of convenience. Or maybe there is a connection. Given her profession, I think it's obvious what that connection could be."

"If that's the case, then you should look into the wife," Gran said, taking a chug of beer.

"That easy, huh?" Leonardi said.

Gran shrugged. "Most of the times, the answer's right under your nose."

"It might be smarter to find out first how Lola got into that casket without anybody detecting it," Leonardi said. "I'm thinking it was either a shady employee from the funeral home or someone broke in there and placed the body in the dentist's casket."

I chuckled and Gran shook her head in amusement.

Leonardi raised an eyebrow. "What? What did I say?"

I nodded toward Gran. "That's exactly what she said today."

Leonardi looked impressed.

"I told you she's doing it for free," I said and elbowed Gran jokingly.

"Will you two get off my back?" Gran said. "It's plain as day the body was placed in the casket at the funeral home. That's where you have most access to it. There's no way to do that after the casket leaves the home. Unless you think the church is a good place."

"Which home handled the funeral?" Leonardi asked.

I shrugged. "No idea."

"Weren't you at the funeral?" he asked.

"I didn't pay attention at the time," I said. "Not like I was working a case. I was too busy counting the seconds until I got out of there."

"But you're working a case now," he said. "For five thousand!"

"Well, I'm guessing you're getting paid too, so do your part," I replied.

Leonardi smiled. "Tough cookie is what you are."

"I'm the sweetest cookie you're ever gonna meet," I said grinning.

Leonardi slapped his thigh and laughed. "Yeah, I think you are." He cleared his throat. "Okay, finding out which funeral home it was is not an issue."

"You know you're the one who has to handle the data, names, addresses," I said. "You're the one with an office and resources, whatever they are."

Leonardi nodded and took another swig of beer.

"Okay, so we have the funeral home angle," I said, leaning in my seat. "Then we need to find out if there's any connection between the dentist and Lola. Not sure how to find that out since they're both dead. And assuming they had some kind of affair, and the wife found out, she would be our prime suspect. Problem is, she'd never talk to us."

"If there's a connection, there has to be a trail," Gran said. "And where do you find a trail?"

Leonardi and I exchanged glances.

"In his home."

"At his practice."

Leonardi and I spoke at the same time.

Gran put her beer down and nodded. "There you have it."

I felt a headache coming on just thinking about breaking and entering the dentist's home and workplace. That was exactly the reason why I was reluctant to work with Leonardi. If I got caught, then I'd be out of WITSEC. Or end up in jail. Or more likely both. I was aware of that, but I was still going to go through with it. I had to rely on my skills and the fact that I was good at what I did. I felt a buzz in my gut. This was just like old times; I felt like myself again. Except back then, working outside of the law was more like level ten. Now it was cranked up to level twenty. Getting arrested back in Oregon didn't remotely have the consequences it would have now. So the thrill was even higher.

"You know, if the dentist and Lola did have an affair," I said, "then the trail wouldn't be at the guy's home, where he lived with his wife. It would be at his workplace. Less chance of getting caught."

"You're right," Leonardi said. "Unless the wife worked with him at his practice."

"She doesn't," I said. "She owns a clothing store downtown."

"Then workplace it is," Leonardi said.

"We have to figure out how to go about it so his employees talk to us," I said. "As long as they're still there."

Edie had told me Eleanor Curtis would sell her husband's dental practice. The staff was probably still working, wrapping up loose ends with the patients.

I was curious about one thing, though.

"Tell me something," I said to Leonardi. "How come this roommate of Lola's is paying that much money to find out what happened to her? What's her interest in all this?"

"These girls watch out for each other," Leonardi said. "They have each other's backs. Most of them have rough family histories. That's how they usually end up doing what they're doing. So they lean on each other for support."

That much I figured already. We knew a couple of escort girls back home in Oregon and their family history was very similar.

"The cops probably won't put the girl's murder at the top of their priority list, considering her job," Gran added. "So the roommate has more incentive going to a PI to get some answers."

"Exactly," Leonardi said. "And speaking of which, are we sure the dentist died of natural causes?"

"As far as I know, yes," I said. "But then again, all of this just happened now, so anything's possible."

"I'm thinking the cops would look into the dentist's death first," Leonardi said. "To make sure there wasn't any foul play."

"I agree," I said. "He would be first on their list, being a person of standing in the community and—"

I heard a loud car door slam outside. I frowned and moved to the window. It was Edie, yakking and laughing with another resident who had dropped her off at home.

Uh-oh. I knew what was coming next. Edie would come over, she would find Leonardi here, and would want to know what was going on. Then she would find out about my supposed new job and lecture me about getting mixed up with folks like Leonardi. Then she would want to get involved herself. Edie was all contradictions.

I wanted to delay that chaos as long as possible. It was one thing to do this and put myself into danger, it was another thing to worry about Edie too.

"Oh," I said to Leonardi, "you need to leave through the bathroom window. Now."

Leonardi frowned and Gran immediately caught on. "It's Edie, isn't it?" she asked.

I nodded. "We have about thirty seconds."

Gran nodded in agreement, then said to Leonardi, "Don't worry, you'll fit through the window frame."

Leonardi looked from me to Gran and back. "You're kidding, right?"

I peeked through the window and saw Edie waving goodbye to her ride. Then she eyed Gran's house and started walking over.

"Twenty seconds," I said. "No, we're not kidding. It's a long story, but I'm trying to keep our neighbor out of it for as long as possible. She can't see you here or we'll never hear the end of it. She's not a fan of you either. So get up now and we'll talk tomorrow."

"Have you lost your mind?" Leonardi asked.

Okay, how to convince him to move right now? Then my glance landed on the kitchen cupboard.

"You can have the rum bottle," I said.

"What?" Gran whipped her head around. "No way!"

Leonardi smiled widely. "Seriously? You're that desperate?"

"I am," I said. "Now take it and go."

Leonardi jumped up from the couch, snatched the rum bottle as fast as he could while winking at Gran, then ran for the bathroom window in the back.

Edie knocked on the door.

I could hear Leonardi struggling in the bathroom.

Edie knocked again.

"In a minute," I yelled out then whispered to Gran, "What is he doing? Is it that hard to jump out?"

"I'll go see," Gran said. "I don't know how you always get me involved in such bull—" She mumbled something while heading to the bathroom.

The knock on the door got louder. What was Leonardi doing? I ran to the back to see Gran pushing Leonardi's butt out the window.

"Good god!" I said.

"Maybe lay off the salami for a while," Gran said to Leonardi. "You don't even fit through a window frame."

Finally, Leonardi landed with a thud on the ground. Then a muffled and annoyed voice came, and he said, "This rum better be good."

I ran back to the front door and opened it wide just as Edie was about to knock it down with her fists.

"What is going on in here?" she asked.

I tried to calm down my breathing. "Nothing. You just woke us up from our nap."

"Yeah, yeah," Edie said. "Like I always do."

## Chapter Five

WE WERE IN THE GOLF CART on our way to the dining hall for breakfast. It was about 9 a.m. Gran was sitting in the back, Edie in the passenger seat, and I was driving.

Gran was in her usual attire: black biker boots, blue denim jeans, and her white tank top, complete with her Aviators. She rocked the biker-chick vibe. Her refusal to wear Florida-appropriate outfits astonished me. How she managed in this humidity was beyond me.

I would have loved to wear my usual biker outfit too, like I did back home, but I reluctantly switched to flip-flops or white sneakers. I drew the line at sandals. They had way too many straps over my foot that kept rubbing against the skin, making them a nightmare to wear.

Today I wore khaki shorts, a blue T-shirt, dark sunglasses and the flip-flops. My skin was ghostly white. Sunbathing wasn't really my thing. I was not a lay-on-the-beach kind of gal. I was the drive-my-Harley-through-the-mountains one.

Edie had her own style too. Her white curls looked perfectly arched, like she slept standing up.

Today she wore her purple and pink polka dot dress and her usual chunky sandals. But something was different. Her sandals. They had a new look. Black, shiny, with leather straps. I stifled a laugh. Another month and she'd be Gran's clone.

As per usual, we looked like a girl band, each with our unique style, ready to take the retirement complex by storm.

When we got here in Bitter End, Gran and I didn't even think about dining out. That would have meant mingling and talking with other people who lived here, which we absolutely rejected. At least in theory. Our plans were to cook our meals at Gran's house or have it delivered. But things went in a different direction, especially when Edie became our next-door neighbor, and the other residents got thrown into the mix too.

Somehow, they took a liking to us. At least, I think they did. It felt odd. We all came from different worlds, and it was obvious Gran and I acted differently. But maybe that was the spice they were looking for.

We were now regulars at the dining hall.

"Man, I'm hungry," Edie said. "Could you drive faster?"

"Why didn't you eat something at home?" I asked her. "You know we're not starting our day that early."

"That's the understatement of the year," Edie said with a snort. "I don't even know when you're starting your day, it's like you're always sleeping or napping."

"What else is there to do around here?" I asked.

"Are you even kidding me?" Edie replied. "Do you want me to point out all the exciting things that are happening here? Like for example, the upcoming Prom night?"

Oh yeah, those kinds of things. The Prom night. Awesome. I had meant more like things that I could really get on board with, something that felt more like home. Well, except for all the dead bodies and me solving the crimes somehow. Okay, so maybe stuff *was* happening here.

"Fine, I'll take it back," I said. "This place is a madhouse."

"Don't think I don't get your sarcasm," Edie said. Then she turned to Gran who pretended not to be part of this conversation. "I heard you got asked out to the prom." She wiggled her eyebrows up and down.

"Of course you did," Gran said, rolling her eyes. "What, you bugged my place or something?"

Edie laughed. "Don't be silly." She paused, then said, "It's a hidden camera."

I chuckled. Edie was unfazed by Gran's attitude.

"Anyway, you two would make such a cute couple," Edie continued.

"Couple?" Gran said. "What are you talking about? We're not a couple and we're not going to be a couple. It's just two people going to the same event in the same direction."

"That sounds like a date to me," Edie said.

Edie really knew how to push Gran's buttons. Sometimes, I was afraid Gran would be too quick with her gun.

"If anyone should have a date, it's Piper," Gran said, and I could see her smiling wide in the rearview mirror.

I stopped abruptly at a red light, maybe a little too abruptly.

*Thanks, Gran, for using me to deflect from yourself.*

"Of course," Edie said. "She really needs a date and I know just exactly who to ask."

"Um, hello," I said, pushing my sunglasses further up my nose. "You're talking like I'm not here.

I don't need a date and I would really prefer if we just dropped this subject. Like forever."

"You're always saying that," Edie replied. "It's like you're a hundred years old. Look, even your grandmother has a date."

I could see Gran was torn between holding in laughter and jumping out of a moving golf cart.

"I am totally for my grandmother having a date," I said. "But that doesn't mean I should have one as well."

How could I even consider dating? How could I even begin to fathom the thought of meeting someone? How could I even talk to a new guy? I would have to feed him lie after lie. I would never be able to tell him about the real me, where I come from, what I did and why I was here in Florida. How could I build a relationship based on a completely false identity?

Back in Oregon, the guys I dated were part of the Falcons network. It made things simpler. None of us had to hide our real selves. Honestly, I'd never really contemplated what it would be like to date someone outside our community. But now, I was confronted with it a lot, especially since the residents here kept insisting on managing my love life—or lack thereof.

I couldn't tell Edie and I couldn't tell the others why I was so reluctant to date. I had to keep up the lie for them as well. Carrying this lie felt like a heavy burden on my shoulders and my soul all the time. Sometimes it became overwhelming, this constant pressure to hide the truth. There were moments when I wanted to shout it out loud right in the middle of rush hour at the dining hall.

"Okay," Edie said. "I'll drop it for now."

*How about forever?*

The light turned green, and I drove off.

"Change of subject, please," I said.

"Fine," Edie said and turned to Gran. "Dorothy, you really missed out yesterday. I thought I was seeing things when that girl fell out of Dr. Curtis's casket."

"Yeah, you already mentioned that yesterday when you gave us the full report," Gran said.

After Leonardi left Gran's house and Edie came over, she gave us a detailed rundown of the saga at the church following the casket incident.

The cops had arrived, closed everything down, and talked to everybody. They pretty much did exactly what I had expected and what I escaped from.

"You seem surprisingly chipper considering you saw a dead body again," Gran said. "I remember you reacting different before. As in, overreacting, if you ask me."

"Edie's been hanging around us too long, that's what it is," I chimed in.

"I think so too," Edie said, blushing. "Who wouldn't get hardened, after spending time with the two of you?"

"I'll take that as a compliment," Gran said.

We speculated yesterday about what could have happened with the girl from the casket. Edie wasn't foolish, she suspected foul play as well. Obviously, I didn't say anything to her about my conversation with Leonardi and the fact that I knew who the victim was now.

Edie gave us a very good clue, though. She overheard the detectives talking and apparently, Lola was dead for about thirty-six hours. Which lined up with Leonardi's information that Lola was missing for two days. So she was murdered, then the killer waited to dispose of her body. They either knew about the dentist's upcoming funeral or they picked the first one to be scheduled and the dentist happened to be it. It was still amazing how anyone could pull that off. Breaking and entering a funeral home while carrying a dead body was serious high-stakes maneuvering. Then again, when the incentive is high enough, everything is possible.

I, personally, would have a plan in place to get rid of a body because there were so many good options to do that. Rookies didn't have a plan in place and had to wing it. Especially when the murder wasn't planned. Which it kind of seemed like it wasn't.

Strangulation or blunt force trauma were usually crimes of passion, spur of the moment acts. Shooting or stabbing could be both planned and unplanned. Then there was poisoning. Now poisoning was really a beauty. You could plan those out for weeks, months or even years ahead. Depending on the proximity to your target, you could even poison them with a super low risk of it being labeled as murder.

I was still leaning towards strangulation or a wack in the head for Lola instead of poison. That was just my gut.

"I'm curious what the police will find out about the young girl and how she got in there," Edie said.

"Yeah, me too," I said absently.

The headwind was feeling good as I swerved on the streets of the community complex. We were like in a small village here. It took about ten minutes to drive from Gran's house to the dining hall. There were diamond lanes on the streets, meaning there were more golf carts driving around than cars.

I parked ours, and we walked on the path between the perfectly manicured lawns of the retirement complex, past the swimming pool, past the mini-golf course, past the rec hall, and headed to the dining hall.

As we were approaching the front doors, I saw a booth right out front to the side.

"Is that Sourpuss?" I asked, squinting.

You couldn't really miss her. Her tight bun was up in the air like an antenna and her sourish-looking face made you run for the woods. How she was nominated for Prom queen, I still didn't get.

"Yeah, that's her," Edie said. "According to my intel, she was gonna put up a booth here."

Just like Edie, Sourpuss was campaigning hard for her title as Prom queen. Was this life after retirement? If yes, someone just shoot me now.

"You people really need to get a life," Gran said.

"This *is* the life," Edie retorted. "Can't you see we're doing stuff? We're doing life. You're the one inside all day that has to be dragged to our events. If you ask me, *you* should get a life."

Ouch. That stung. Edie was right and Gran knew it. That's why she didn't have any comebacks. She just pursed her lips and looked away. Edie didn't notice it, but I saw the sadness across Gran's face. I was the only one who could see that. And the only one who knew what Gran meant. She wanted a life but this was not it. She and Edie had completely different definitions of what it meant to really be living.

Sourpuss was behind the booth and two other women were next to her. Edie, Gran and I gave them a dirty look, despite Gran and me wearing dark sunglasses.

The booth had the works. A table with merch that had Sourpuss's face on it and buttons to pin to your chest. It was like she was running for mayor. One of the other two women hollered out to every person entering the dining hall, "Get your 'I'm voting for Lucretia' button here!"

As we were passing by, I did a double take. There was a stash of flyers on the table that read, "Free foot powder for every voter."

I guessed Edie saw it too since she stopped abruptly and I bumped into her.

"What the heck, Piper?" she asked, turning around.

"Sorry, your brake lights were out," I said and pushed my sunglasses further up my nose.

"Well, if it isn't the Siamese twins," Sourpuss sneered in our direction.

Gran shot her a fierce look and her hand instinctively reached for the back of her waist. But she wouldn't find anything there. Frisking your own grandmother before leaving the house was quite the experience. I've been trying to convince her that we were living in a retirement complex now, not in a war zone. Although how many times had I wished I had my knife on me. But bottom line, Gran had to realize she couldn't just threaten people in their seventies and up. I mean, Sourpuss for sure was a threat but not the I'm-going-to-shoot-you one. At least, not yet.

"Is this some sick joke?" Edie asked and nodded toward the flyers. "Who's gonna want to take foot powder from you? Do you really want to poison everyone?"

Sourpuss shrugged. "Not if they vote for me."

There was a whole back story with the foot powder at the retirement complex. To this day I didn't understand what was the fascination with foot powder amongst the residents here. After losing a game of paintball, Sourpuss and the losing teams had to give out gift baskets to the winning teams containing foot powder. Soon afterward, a lot of people, including Edie, developed a rash on their feet. Everyone had a suspicion Sourpuss meddled with the foot powder. But as it often is in politics, Sourpuss denied it all, blaming Edie and her faction, and now she was here offering that damn thing again. People would believe anything. It didn't help that Gran used the same poisonous powder as revenge and smashed containers of it against Sourpuss's house. We still had a lot of foot powder stashed at Gran's house, because as Gran had put it, "You never know when you have an enemy, and you need it." So now we were counting guns, knives, *and* foot powder as our own personal weapons.

Edie jabbed a finger in Sourpuss's face. "You will fail, do you hear me? You will not win this thing, you prune."

Sourpuss moved closer and her nose was almost touching Edie's finger. "We'll just see about that, grandmama."

Gran yawned. "Could we move it along please? I'm hungry."

With one last dirty look towards Sourpuss, we entered the dining hall.

Edie whispered to me, "I really need to up my game with this campaigning stuff."

"Don't you have some kind of parade planned for today?" I asked her. I think she told me about it but to be honest I kind of blocked out the details because I still couldn't grasp the fact that this was my life.

"Yes, I have, and it will blow their minds," Edie said, smiling wide.

Oh, good god, maybe I shouldn't be around when that parade happens.

"What about you, Dorothy?" Edie asked Gran. "Aren't you going to do anything?"

What an interesting question. If Gran were to campaign for herself, she would hold the residents at gunpoint and make them vote for her.

"I'm better at doing stuff that would make them not vote for me," Gran said.

Edie rolled her eyes. "You're nominated for Prom queen. Just roll with it, don't be such a negative Nelly."

In the dining hall, we saw Beatrice and Theodore sitting at a table in the back. Beatrice waved at us, and we made our way to them.

"There you are, finally," Beatrice said to us. She always seemed to be anywhere before us and saving seats for us. Beatrice was the woman whose hair I dyed purple by accident. At first, I was worried she might have a heart attack, but Gran convinced her it was a good thing to stand out. So she kept the purple hair. Which was a good thing. It diverted attention from her lipstick that was always outside the lines.

"You know they're not morning people," Edie said, pointing at Gran and me.

"I know and I don't get it," Beatrice said, looking at us through her thick glasses. "There's so much to do around here, how can you sleep all day?"

I didn't have the energy for this again.

"Hello Dorothy, hello Piper," Theodore said, standing up and helping us into our seats. I caught a few glances from nearby tables, some envious looks aimed our way, from a group of women.

"There's only boring stuff to do around here," Gran said as she settled into her seat.

"How can you say that?" Beatrice asked, appalled. "We have our prom night coming up and there's all the preparations for that. Our parties are always epic."

"Tell me about it," Edie said, pouring herself some coffee. "Although I wish some people wouldn't even be a part of it." She nodded toward the booth outside.

Beatrice rolled her eyes. "I don't get how anyone could even support her. She must have had some tricks up her sleeve to snag that nominee spot for prom queen."

"It's what I'm thinking too," Edie said. "That's why it's vital for her not to win. I'm campaigning as hard as I can, but she does it too and people seem to like it."

"Dorothy, why aren't you campaigning?" Beatrice asked.

"Campaigning?" Gran said. "For Prom queen? I'd rather get shot in the leg."

Theodore laughed and Beatrice's hand flew over her chest. "Then how would people vote for you if you don't show them you are worthy of the title?"

"I don't even know why I was worthy of getting nominated," Gran said.

"Because we like you more than you think," Edie said.

Gran stared at her. "Hmph. I don't get that either."

"I do," Theodore said, winking at Gran.

I swear I saw Gran blushing.

"Could we please move on?" Gran said. "I don't get why we're making such a fuss over Prom queens.

What about Prom kings?" Gran looked at Theodore. "You're a nominee for Prom king. Why aren't you campaigning?"

Theodore shrugged. "Because nobody cares about the king. They only care about the queen."

"That's sexist," Gran huffed.

"I agree," Theodore said. "You should change that first thing after you get chosen Prom queen."

The whole table laughed, minus Gran.

"Okay, moving on to other subjects," Beatrice said. "How about that funeral yesterday?"

Theodore cut his eyes to me. "Yes, that funeral. Piper, you didn't even tell me yesterday what had happened when you came back."

I shrugged. "Honestly, I really didn't feel like it. You were going to find out about it sooner rather than later, so..."

"I can't believe you missed the whole thing," Beatrice said to Gran. "You weren't at the funeral."

"Why would I be there?" Gran asked. "I didn't even know the guy." She took one of the empty coffee cups from the table and poured herself some coffee.

"Well, this is the way to get people to vote for you," Theodore said, taunting Gran.

"You weren't at the funeral either," Gran shot back.

"I know and I stand by it," Theodore said. "Just like you."

"But you're not getting any heat for it," Gran said.

"It's the sexist thing, remember?" Theodore said.

Gran shook her head and mumbled something about people here living in the Stone Age.

"What do you think happened to that poor girl?" Beatrice asked. "How did she get into Dr. Curtis's casket? There had to be some foul play there."

As expected, the case of the young girl falling from the dentist's casket made waves at the retirement complex. Everyone was speculating about what had happened. We got food from the buffet, and I heard what Beatrice and Theodore snagged up, but it wasn't information that I didn't know nor one I could use.

"I'm ready for round two," Edie said and headed for the buffet again.

The others and I were still sipping our coffees.

Another resident came by and greeted us. Her hair was in a complicated updo, and some curls were falling down into her eyes.

"Melanie, how is your knee?" Beatrice asked her.

Melanie started to say something about the weather and thankfully, she lived in a warm climate, so I zoned out. But my eyes spotted a button pinned to her chest. It was one of Sourpuss's buttons. But as I took a closer look I saw that something was terribly wrong. The button read, "Lucretia is sour as a lemon."

What the hell?

"Where did you get that button?" I asked the woman.

"Oh, outside, from Lucretia," she said. "I'm not really fond of her, actually, but all this wooing for us is kind of fun." She tapped the button proudly as if she had just won a prize.

"Did you even see what that button says?" I asked.

"Not really," the woman said. "I don't have my reading glasses with me. But I'm guessing it says something good about Lucretia? Like to vote for her or something?"

Gran, Beatrice, and Theodore leaned in and squinted.

A second later they burst out laughing. Even Gran smiled wide.

"What? What?" the woman asked. She tried to look down at her button.

I looked around me in the dining hall and I saw a few more people with the same button. Then I shook my head. These were all people who needed reading glasses because they were blind like a bat without them.

But the question was, why did Lucretia hand out buttons like this? Unless . . . she herself didn't know what was on them. Meaning someone meddled with the buttons and gave her wrong ones. But who could have done it? I turned and my gaze landed on Edie, who was in front of the buffet talking to one of the residents while holding an oatmeal bowl in her hand.

Oh, Edie. You've done it again.

When Sourpuss finally sees those buttons, she would go nuts.

In that second, Sourpuss burst into the dining room like a tornado. The bun being the top of the tornado. She frantically looked around and her gaze landed on Edie as well.

"You!" She cried. "You did this!"

Everybody dropped their forks and there was silence. The person Edie was talking to slowly backed away. Uh-oh. This was so not good. Why do they always have to fight when there's food next to them? There have been food fights here before. So retirement means a lot of foot powder and food fights.

Edie turned to Sourpuss, frowning. "What? Did what?"

Sourpuss marched to Edie holding one of her buttons out. She almost threw the button in Edie's face. "This! This is what you did!"

Edie squinted and read the text. Then she started laughing. Tears were falling down her cheeks.

"You think this is funny, huh?" Sourpuss asked.

Edie wiped away a tear. "How could it not be funny? Are you kidding me? But I didn't do it."

"Of course you did," Sourpuss said. "You're playing dirty, but you won't get away with it."

Edie got serious again. "*I* am playing dirty? *I am*? Look who's talking. The foot powder queen."

Everyone was looking from Edie to Sourpuss like watching a ping-pong match.

Sourpuss jabbed a finger at Edie. "You'll be sorry you did this."

Edie narrowed her eyes. "But I didn't do it, you old shrew!"

The oatmeal bowl in Edie's hand—yes, still in her hand—was beginning to tremble. This was not good. Any second now, that oatmeal was going to land in Sourpuss's face.

Sourpuss smiled a wicked smile and said, "You're not worthy of any kind of queen."

Oh, crap.

That was the low blow.

I shook my head. And kind of wished Gran had her gun on her.

Then, as if in slow motion, I saw Edie lifting her bowl holding arm and swinging, but Sourpuss probably expected the move, and she ducked just in time.

Edie threw the oatmeal bowl right past Sourpuss's head and it landed on . . . Ryker.

Ryker?

When did he walk in?

## Chapter Six

Everybody gasped at once.

Edie threw her hand over her mouth.

Sourpuss jumped up and looked over her shoulder.

And Ryker was standing there, oatmeal all over his face and chest.

Funnily enough, the first thing that came to mind was that he looked good even covered in oatmeal.

Ryker Donovan was Edie's grandson. He was in his thirties, and he was a private investigator and owner of Donovan's Security and Investigations here in Bitter End.

He was six foot two, had short dark hair and a nice healthy tan that made his dark eyes sparkle even brighter. He wore light-blue jeans and a black T-shirt that was not super tight, but tight enough to hug his muscular upper body. Even from where I was sitting, I could make out the edges of his tattoo on his left arm, peeking out from under his sleeve: a skull with a bike helmet on, nestled between two pistols that crossed each other.

Ironically, he rode a black Fat Boy V-twin softail cruiser with solid-cast disc wheels, a Harley Davidson model I absolutely loved.

Ryker and I seemed to often bump heads, personally and professionally. Smart as he was, he kept on questioning Gran's and my stories about coming here to Florida and about me being a hairdresser. It didn't help that somehow, I ended up involved in solving murders and constantly had to be careful about Ryker not to get caught doing something illegal.

"Oh, Ryker," Edie said. "Where did you come from? I'm sorry, I didn't see you."

"What is going on here?" Ryker asked, wiping off oatmeal from his face.

"The usual madness, that's what's going on," Sourpuss said. "I'm out of here." She brushed her dress like *she* was the one getting food all over her. "But this is not over," she said to Edie, then turned and marched right out of the dining hall.

Everyone exhaled a collective sigh of relief, then they all resumed eating, the familiar background buzz filling up the room again.

Ryker grabbed a napkin and wiped his shirt. I couldn't help but gaze at his body a bit longer. One of the staff members came rushing, but Edie said she'd clean up.

Then, she got herself a new oatmeal bowl and walked back to our table with Ryker in tow. It was then that Ryker and I made eye contact and for a second, I felt something like a lightning bolt going through my body. Or was it more a tingling? It's been so long since I felt something like this, I couldn't tell anymore. I shook that feeling away. I must be imagining things.

Ryker got himself a chair and squeezed in between me and Beatrice. I inhaled his musky scent and I felt that tingling again. What the heck?

"Is trouble brewing on the horizon again?" Ryker asked us, smiling. But he turned and looked at me for a couple of seconds longer.

I put my hands up in defense. "What are you looking at me for? It's your grandmother who always starts the trouble."

"I don't start any trouble," Edie said in a high-pitched voice. We all turned and stared at her.

Edie cleared her throat. "Well, not this time at least. I didn't switch her stupid buttons. But now I wish I did. Those things are hilarious, and did you see how pissed she was?"

I laughed. Edie was indeed incorrigible.

"Do I want to know what's going on?" Ryker asked.

"Trust me, you don't," Gran said.

"You didn't switch the buttons?" I asked Edie.

"What, you don't believe me?" Edie asked. "You know I would have told you if it were me."

Hmm. She was right. She would have told me. But if Edie didn't switch the buttons, then who did?

I could tell everybody was asking themselves the same thing and we all turned our heads to Gran at the same time.

She placed her coffee cup down and straightened her shoulders. "What are you looking at me for? You think I had something to do with it? Like I give a damn."

"Besides Edie, it's you who would have something to gain," Beatrice said. "You could just admit you did it, I don't see the problem. You know your secret's safe with us."

"Yeah, you know we always enjoy messing with Lucretia," Edie said.

Theodore leaned forward and studied Gran. "We all know Dorothy doesn't really value these kinds of events around here. So she would be the last person to suspect. But then again, I think deep inside her, she cares about it and I think she is enjoying this kind of fun too. I wouldn't be surprised if it turned out Dorothy switched the buttons."

Gran narrowed her eyes at Theodore. "Too bad you don't know me and you're way off with your assumption."

Theodore smiled. "We'll see."

"So what are you doing here?" Edie asked Ryker.

He poured himself some coffee as he yawned.

"You're looking tired," Edie said. "Are you okay?"

Ryker shook it off. "I'm okay, Grams, I've just been working long hours."

"You poor thing," Edie said, patting his arm. "You need a break. You need to relax and let loose." Then she put on a wicked smile and exchanged glances with Beatrice and Theodore.

*Oh, please don't.*

"You know, Ryker," Edie said, "Piper here doesn't have a date for the prom."

I rolled my eyes so far away it hurt.

"Guys, please don't do this," I said and wanted to get up but somehow, I felt glued to my seat.

Ryker turned to me and smiled wide. "She doesn't?"

Of course Ryker knew everything about the prom, he was always up to date with the goings-on at the retirement complex. He was also responsible for security, although I had zero idea what that entailed. I haven't seen him secure anything around here.

I rubbed my temples and said to myself, "I'm not here, I'm not here."

Totally ignoring me, Beatrice continued. "And we thought you could be her date."

"That's the only honorable thing to do," Theodore chirped in.

*You as well, Brutus?*

"Ryker, please ignore them," I said to him. "You know they're just messing with us. If we ignore them, they'll stop."

"Or maybe they'll just push harder," Ryker said.

I looked him in the eye. "So?"

"I'm not sure I can live with them pushing harder," Ryker said. "I have a life, you know?"

"Well, I have a life too," I said, not looking away, despite my inner wince. I so did *not* have a life. Not the life I wanted, anyhow.

"But maybe you like them pushing harder," Ryker said. "Maybe you're just afraid they're going to be right and that you're really going to have fun at the seniors' party with a date."

"Excuse me?" I asked, feeling a volcano building up inside me.

Everybody at the table leaned back in their seats to get away from the line of fire.

Gran mumbled something like, "This is not good."

But Ryker didn't stop. "You heard me. I think you're afraid. These residents here are having more fun than anybody I know at *our* age. That's why I'm always coming to their parties. I don't care much about that whole club scene downtown and whatnot. And you are basically living here and avoiding any opportunity for socializing. So yes, I think it's because you're afraid."

"Afraid of what, may I ask?" I said, and already felt my nostrils flaring. How dare he?

"Afraid of actually having fun?" Ryker said. "Letting go of whatever it is you need to let go of and enjoy the present?"

There was silence at the table. All I could hear was the background chatter. I had no comebacks and I hated that.

I didn't give Ryker enough credit initially, but every so often, he'd catch me off guard by almost reading my mind. He had no clue about my past and who I really was, but he could pick up on certain things fast. It felt unsettling.

Still, he poked at my stubborn side, and no one gets away with that, no matter how observant.

I sat up straighter while I poured myself some more coffee. "I know what you're doing, that you're trying to manipulate me for some reason, but just for the record, I'm not afraid," I said. "And I never really said that I'm not going to the party."

"So you are going?" Beatrice asked.

I paused, clenched my jaw, then answered, "Yes, I am."

"With Ryker as your date?" Edie asked, all beaming. "You know you need a date."

I narrowed my eyes at her. "Are they scanning us at the entrance for dates or something?"

"Actually, they do," Beatrice said, and I wasn't sure if she was kidding or not.

I narrowed my eyes at her too. At all of them, really. Then I said through gritted teeth, "Fine, with Ryker as my date."

"I like that," he said, all smiling.

Everybody let out a long breath. Edie and Beatrice high-fived and Theodore said, "Then we can all go together. Like a double date."

I almost spit my coffee out. Gran stopped with her coffee cup in midair. Things were going downhill fast around here.

"So, Ryker, you didn't tell us why you stopped by," Beatrice said. "Just for a chat?"

Thank goodness for the subject change.

"Mostly for a chat but I also wanted to check in on all of you and see how you're doing after yesterday's funeral," Ryker said.

I immediately perked up. This shouldn't have come as a surprise to me. As a well-connected PI, surely he found out about it.

"It was so surreal seeing how another person just slipped out of the casket," Edie said, wide-eyed.

Beatrice chimed in and shared Edie's feelings. Ryker found out that Gran and Theodore didn't attend the funeral and that I left shortly after the second body popped out.

I groaned inwardly. I knew Ryker was going to give me a hard time about it. Mostly he gave me a hard time about everything I did. He would question why I didn't stick around because everything I did was suspicious to him. The funny thing was, Ryker was suspicious of me because of his own good instincts, not because he knew who I really was. And his instinct told him something wasn't right. I often felt like I needed to put my guard up high when interacting with him.

He turned to me and nodded. "I hope it wasn't too disturbing for you to see that."

I waited for whatever came next, but he just stared at me. Oh, really? That was the game we were playing?

I was just about to say that everything was fine when Edie added, "Oh, come on, I wouldn't worry about Piper. She's totally unfazed with these things. Like she's seen it all her life."

Mental forehead smack.

Edie has done it again. Just when I thought I had it under control, Edie came out of nowhere and put me even more on the spot.

"Yes, I realized that as well," Ryker said.

"I'm sorry I can't get emotionally involved with people dying that I didn't even know personally," I said. "We've been here before. Can we move on, please?"

I was really tired having the same conversation all over again. It was somehow expected of me to totally freak out and behave like a little wuss girl, all sensitive. They had no idea who they were dealing with.

"What about Theodore?" I asked Ryker. "He doesn't freak out. Why don't you ask him why he's not more upset about this?"

"Theodore is an ex-Navy Seal," Ryker said. "He's seen worse. Are you ex-military?"

"No, I am a—" I said but stopped just in time.

Gran's eyes turned wide.

"You are what?" Ryker said and all eyes were on me.

I cleared my throat. I caught myself just in time. But it kind of hurt not to say what I really was. This was one of the times I really wanted to shout it out into the world. Instead, I said, "I'm a tough chick, that's what I am."

Everybody at the table laughed.

"You tell him, Piper," Theodore said.

"The toughest, I would say," Beatrice added.

"I'm so happy I have you as a neighbor," Edie said and reached out to pat my arm which kind of made my heart melt. But then she added, "You really don't take any crap from anybody."

"Grams!" Ryker said to Edie.

"What?" Edie said. "I can be rough around the edges too."

"That, I already know," Ryker said, smiling warmly at her.

Sometimes I envied the relationship between Edie and Ryker. They both loved each other and treated each other with warmth, but they also gave each other space to be who they were. Well, for the most part, at least. For the other part, Ryker had no idea what Edie was up to. And she intended to make it stay that way.

I was burning with curiosity about whether Ryker would be doing any investigation regarding our surprise corpse, Lola. But I couldn't just ask him outright. That would be again suspicious and would raise questions about why I was so invested.

Then it hit me. Not only would I have to tell Edie eventually about my partnership with Leonardi, but I also had to clue Ryker in. Ugh. Ryker and Leonardi did not get along, to put it mildly. Supposedly, it was a matter of different approaches to this job, one too by-the-book, the other too off-the-grid. But I had a feeling there was more to it, something more personal. I didn't push for the full story, figuring it would eventually come out. Yet, I mentally saved this potential tidbit that there could be something more to their animosity.

I would be having a real job with Leonardi. Legal and all. Yuck. So actually, I wouldn't be doing anything wrong. Well, except for not having a PI license and that could cause trouble with Ryker. Not to mention the cops, but I already decided I would take that risk for my own mental sanity.

With this consultant position, we would circumvent the "not having a PI license" issue. Leonardi wouldn't hire me as a PI, he would hire me as a consultant. Different job description that offered some coverage over my actual duties.

Only Ryker was not stupid. Not at all. He would give me grief again when he found out. Especially if his grandmother got involved too.

So I decided to postpone telling him.

Not that I even had to tell him anything about my life. It was more out of courtesy because of Edie. And because I wanted to be left in peace.

"So are you involved in that case, somehow?" Beatrice asked Ryker.

*Thank you, Beatrice!*

I was this close to telling her I could dye her hair purple anytime again.

I leaned in, trying not to give my nervousness away.

Ryker waited for a couple of beats while everyone at the table seemed to anxiously wait for his answer.

"Yes, I am," he finally said and there came a wave of "aah" and "ooh" from everyone except Gran and me.

Crap.

I exchanged glances with Gran. I knew what she was thinking. The same as I was. Trouble was brewing on the horizon.

"In what capacity are you involved?" Edie asked, sipping some coffee.

"That is client confidentiality," Ryker said.

Edie rolled her eyes. "Client confidentiality my butt. I'm your grandmother. I'm family!"

Ryker smiled. "You are family, Grams, and I love you, but I still can't divulge every aspect of my job. Not when I'm specifically hired for one. It's different when I'm investigating for my own interest."

Edie blew a raspberry. "It's still not fair."

Ryker squeezed her arm. "I know, Grams, I think so too."

Wow. So much warmth. So much patience that Ryker had with Edie. The relationship between Gran and I was totally different. Although we were also family, cared deeply for each other, and had an unspoken understanding, warm and touchy interactions weren't our style. We wouldn't even know how to act like that. We had our unique bond that others might envy for its depth, yet now and then, I couldn't help but wish I could hold Gran's hand without her looking at me like I was crazy.

I pushed that thought away and tried to process what Ryker had just said. What could his involvement be in this case? He was probably hired by the widow to find out why Lola was in her husband's casket. If I were her, my first concern would be whether my husband was having an affair with Lola. Even if they were both dead now and she wouldn't be able to kill them again for their affair, I would still want to know what happened.

"I hope you don't get involved in this one," Ryker said to me and woke me out of my thoughts. Then turned to Edie. "You too, Grams."

It was already too late for one of us, but Ryker didn't know that.

I felt my nostrils flaring again. "Really? Did you really say that to me?"

Ryker sighed. "Why of course. How could I even think of that? Me telling you what to do." He shook his head but smiled at me. That took me by surprise. I didn't know why, but he was kind of . . . adorable in that very moment. I smiled back against all my better judgement. If this was what we were playing—catch your opponent off guard—then I could play that game too. I changed gears and asked in my softest voice, "You're just looking out for me, aren't you?"

Everybody at the table dropped their jaws.

Ryker blushed. He really, really blushed. For a second, he was speechless.

*Booyah! Gotcha.*

He cleared his throat. "I'm looking out for *everybody*. Or at least, I'm trying to."

Edie elbowed his grandson. "But especially Piper, huh?"

Ryker almost went dark red. I loved it!

But then he caught himself in time.

"I know Piper can take care of herself, but I still wish she would be more careful," he said very diplomatically.

He sure knew by now how well I took care of things. Hostage situations, solving murders, you name it, I've already done it in the last two months since I've arrived in Florida. That was more action than I had back at home in one whole year.

*I* should have been the one saying, "Be careful, here I come."

## Chapter Seven

WE WERE FINISHED WITH breakfast and chatting at about eleven thirty a.m., so Gran and I headed back to the house. Ryker stayed behind and was still engaged in chats with others at different tables. I tried to discreetly observe him moving between tables, talking with the residents, without him noticing me. It was clear he was well-liked. I even caught a few starry-eyed glances from some female residents. One woman at a nearby table, part of the Sourpuss Resident Evil gang, couldn't help but gush about Ryker's bike. She called it a "sexy bike". I nearly choked on my last piece of rye imagining her perched on the bike behind Ryker, holding on for dear life as he maneuvered through the streets.

But Ryker seemed unfazed by the attention. He didn't seem to judge nor did he shrug off the attention. Instead, he responded with polite and diplomatic answers, handling the situation smoothly.

Weirdly, he gained my respect.

Edie remained with the others to talk about some prom whatnots. Decorations, food, activities, so all the things that Gran and I hated. Edie said she would get a ride back to her house with someone else.

"Okay, spit it out," I said to Gran while we were in the golf cart on the way to the house. "What did you do with those buttons?"

"What are you talking about?" Gran asked, pushing her Aviators further up her nose.

"You know very well what I'm talking about," I said. "Sourpuss's buttons. You did that. You made new ones and switched them with hers. You did the garden gnomes switcheroo all over again, only this time with her campaign buttons."

"May I remind you that the gnomes switcheroo was not my idea in the first place, and that you dragged me there like you always do?" Gran said.

I paused. And waited. Nothing else came.

"You didn't answer my question," I said.

"What question was that?" Gran said and I think I saw the corners of her mouth just slightly twitching upwards.

"What did you do with Sourpuss's buttons?" I asked again.

"Oh, that," Gran said. "That is a ridiculous question, and you know it."

I shook my head. "And still, you did not answer the question."

"I don't understand what you want from me," Gran said and I could see the corners of her mouth now really quivering. I could sense she wanted hard to keep it together.

Gran was a master at this. She could have become a courtroom lawyer. She could defend any criminal. But then, besides her being one, we'd have too many criminals roaming free out there in the world.

As soon as we got into the house, I texted Leonardi about the next steps. We didn't agree on anything specific yesterday, what with him needing to flee Gran's house so fast. We had talked about the funeral home and the widow and all, but it was obvious we had to talk to the roommate first, Ruby Hansen, Leonardi's client. She was the person closest to Lola so she could tell us about her life thus providing us with our next clue. We needed to know which angle to work best.

Leonardi gave me Ruby's address and I left Gran at the kitchen table counting her cards.

She seemed almost disappointed I was leaving without her. "Are you gonna be okay?" I asked.

"Of course I am," she replied.

That was such a big lie not even Gran could have hidden it. "Are you meeting with your poker buddies?"

Gran was a poker enthusiast and used to play it regularly. She was so good, Vegas should ban her from flying into town. High-stakes games were often held in the backroom of Choppers, or she hosted games at her own house with other members of the Falcons gang.

WITSEC wouldn't exactly approve of Gran still playing; they frowned upon ex-criminals doing that. They were weird like that. Still, poker remained Gran's last link to her past, after having to give up so much. She began teaching poker to seniors here at the retirement complex, using toothpicks as chips. I couldn't force Gran to stop and I did understand the drive behind it, so I just kept my eye on it and hoped Gran wouldn't take this too far.

"Could be," she said. "Later on." Then she looked me in the eye. "Please don't worry about me, okay? You have a lot on your plate either way. I'm going to be fine, you understand that?"

Oh wow. I was totally taken aback. I didn't expect such profound honesty from Gran.

"Um . . . okay, I understand," I said, and I almost walked over to her to touch her hand.

But then I didn't.

***

I was on my way to 71 Cocoanut Drive.

Interesting street name.

It was located in the east part of Bitter End and was the opposite of Amherst Street. It was a residential area with palm-fringed streets and immaculate sidewalks, well-manicured lawns and Spanish-style houses, painted in pastel hues—of course pastel, what else?—with terracotta roofs that gleamed under the sunshine. The area was one of suburban comfort and I couldn't help but wonder how two escort girls could afford to live in this region.

I parked across the street and cut the engine. Here I was, contemplating about potential jobs while I could make a career doing what Lola and Ruby did. Clearly, it was worth it. Unfortunately, that whole industry was not for me. I was way too wild and harsh to take crap from any client, just because he paid me.

Then I thought of my new consulting job. At least it would be legit. Well, on paper anyhow. In reality, I would be doing whatever I wanted as long as I wouldn't get caught. I didn't sign any papers yet and it was not like there was no coming back. It still bugged me, though. Everything bugged me since going into witness protection. My instinct radar was all wonky and I couldn't tell anymore what felt right and what felt wrong. Especially since those two words just began to have a totally different meaning to me than it did all my life.

Working with Leonardi would get me out of my funk. Or at least half out of my funk. The way I saw it now, I couldn't even imagine getting out of my funk ever. I couldn't imagine burying my former life and making peace with the fact that it would never be the same again.

A loud rumbling up on the street jolted me out of my thoughts.

I looked in the rearview mirror. What else could it be than Leonardi's truck.

He parked behind me, then we both got out of our cars.

"How did you ever think of doing proper investigative work when everybody can hear you from a mile away?" I asked.

His tooth gap appeared. "That's because I'm not into doing proper investigative work, I'm only interested in the end result. And it worked until now."

I looked him up and down. With his pimp-like outfit that he always wore and his slicked-back hair and brute demeanor, his truck was indeed the least of his problems.

"Fine, then let's see about this end result," I said and marched to the house.

"Ruby's expecting us," Leonardi said and caught me glancing at the beautiful house. "Not too shabby, right?"

"I had just thought I should change careers," I said with a laugh.

"It's not for you," Leonardi said as we walked the few steps on the porch. "You're more like me. Tough and aggressive."

"Thank you," I said. "Guess that's a compliment."

"I just compared you to myself, damn straight it's a compliment," Leonardi said, laughing. Then he got all serious. "Oh, by the way, I found out the cause of death. Lola's been strangled."

I gulped down hard. That's a sad way to go. But then again, every way to go was sad.

"So she was dead before she was placed in the casket," I said. "As suspected."

Leonardi nodded. "There's more. The dentist was dead before she died."

"Again, as suspected," I said. "My gut is telling me that guy really died of a heart attack."

"Same here," Leonardi said and just as he reached for the doorbell, the door opened, and a young woman appeared in the door frame.

She looked to be in her twenties too, just like Lola. She had short brown hair that was brushed perfectly, and immaculate skin, and wore a silky blue long robe. It was hard to imagine this person hanging out on Amherst Street.

"Ruby, thanks for seeing us," Leonardi said and stepped inside. "I told you about Piper, my apprentice."

I gazed at Leonardi, and he grinned at me. Apprentice? Is he serious?

I turned to Ruby and shook her hand. "I'm Piper Harris. I'm the Sherlock Holmes of internships."

Ruby shook my hand, but she didn't etch any expression on her face. "Nice to meet you. Please come in."

I entered and immediately saw Leonardi already sitting comfortably on the cream-colored, most likely very expensive couch in the spacious living room, that resembled more a huge foyer. I shook my head. How did this guy even get clients?

But funnily, Ruby didn't seem to be bothered by it.

I looked around and was in awe about the lavish, yet tasteful, décor of the house. A glittering chandelier adorned the ceiling, casting a golden glow over the lush carpets in neutral tones of cream and taupe. God, was I jealous! What I wouldn't give for this carpeting instead of the ugly, yellowi-ish carpeting at Gran's.

A sweeping staircase with wrought iron railings led to the bedrooms. I could see the open kitchen area to the side. The arrangement of pots and pans, the array of condiments on the counter, and other kitchen knick-knacks hinted at someone's love for cooking in this space.

"Are you cooking a lot?" I asked Ruby, still studying the beautiful kitchen.

Ruby moved to the ottoman across the couch. "It was mostly Lola who cooked. She preferred home-cooked meals over takeouts. I, of course, got a good deal with that, since she often cooked for both of us."

I perched on the edge of the couch next to Leonardi, cautious not to pollute this pristine place.

"I still can't believe she's gone," Ruby said, and a sadness crossed her pretty face.

"Were you close?" I inquired. Leonardi hadn't given me any prior details, which was a good call. That left me unbiased and open to Ruby's perspective on their relationship.

Ruby crossed her legs and tried to look poised. "As close as you can get in this business. There's a strong bond when your background is similar. We both come from broken homes, foster care, and just trying to make a living. Our professions are often undervalued and misunderstood."

"Ruby is working for Elite Companions," Leonardi explained. "Lola was working there too."

"Is that where you two met?" I asked.

Ruby nodded. "No, we met at a bar about two and a half years ago. I had just been fired from my job as a waitress. I had zero prospects and was also facing eviction from my older apartment. So I took this job. And Lola offered me the room up there." She pointed to the upper level.

"So it was just the two of you living here?" I asked.

Ruby nodded.

I thought about the life these women had led. Somehow, they stumbled into it, went down this path and then what? They could do this when they were twenty, but they had to know this industry was merciless and they would be dropped as soon as they didn't look young and fresh anymore.

As if reading my mind, Ruby said, "We didn't want to do this forever, you know? But we know how much money there is in this industry, so we were thinking of opening our own company down the road."

I smiled. I liked what I was hearing.

Ruby smiled back.

"I like her," she said to Leonardi. "She's not judgmental about what we do."

"I know," Leonardi said. "That's why I know she's a good addition to my company."

"Exactly," I said smirking. "And who knows, after learning the ropes I might as well just open up my own investigative company down the road."

Leonardi laughed. "See? What did I just say?"

Ruby laughed with us, and I had a feeling it may have been the first since Lola's passing.

"Oh, I'm sorry," Ruby jumped up. "I didn't even offer you any refreshments. I have coffee, tea, orange juice . . ."

I cut my eyes to Leonardi. I hoped he wouldn't ask for hard liquor. He must have sensed my gaze on him, because he put his hand up and said, "Thanks, we're good."

"Do you know how . . . how Lola . . . um . . ." Ruby couldn't get the words out.

Leonardi said in a soft voice that I've never heard before, "She was strangled. I'm so sorry."

Ruby tried to compose herself.

We gave her a minute.

She shook it off, then she said, "How can I help?"

"What can you tell us about Lola?" I asked. "How was her life? Did she have enemies? We're trying to figure out who could have done this to her and obviously, we have to start with her line of work."

"I understand," Ruby said.

We found out that Lola moved to Bitter End from Miami. She found this lifestyle of being an escort girl and living in this part of town totally fit her. She didn't want to go back. Ruby said that business was mostly their lives, and it was hard to form friendships with people outside this industry. That, I totally got.

Lola's clients, as well as Ruby's, were mostly high-profile clients. They didn't have any mentionable issues with any of the clients and Elite Companions took good care of them.

"Is this the way to go?" I asked. "Working for a company instead of freelancing?"

"With freelancing you don't have any securities put in place," Ruby said. "You'd have to vet your clients for yourself. That could put you in really unsafe situations."

I thought about it. I remembered Kathleen Riverbanks, who worked at a brothel back home in Oregon. She was not an official Falcon member. She was a freelancer and worked on her own terms. Gran and I respected that. The brothel acted more like the liaison between the client and the worker. I knew there was a lot of money swirling around in that industry and that Kathleen couldn't complain. That was the thing with people in that industry. They held a distinct set of ethics. As did I. Power, money and manipulation were all that really mattered.

Too bad I had lost them all.

Gran and I never ventured into that industry. Not because of some moral code—that we lacked either way—but because we found better prospects elsewhere. Most regular folks, taxpayers, and people pleasers have no clue about the many good opportunities out there. That whole office routine, working in a cubicle from nine to five for a paycheck that can barely keep you afloat, was just not my MO.

Ironically, my life right now living off of subsistence checks from the government was even worse than the cubicle life.

Ruby had told us that there was no one Lola had beef with, and that everything was going well.

"Well, except for . . ." Ruby said.

"Except for what?" I asked.

"I have a feeling Lola was seeing someone," Ruby said.

"You don't know for sure?" Leonardi asked.

Ruby shook her head. "She was secretive about that. She didn't tell me about any potential guy."

"Then how do you figure she was seeing someone?" I asked.

"You can just tell, you know? She went out in the evenings and would say she had to take care of something, and she was more sensitive somehow. It's been going on for about three months now."

"Okay," I said and thought about it. "But is that bad? That she was seeing someone?"

"I'm not sure it was good," Ruby said. "She wasn't the type to fall in love."

I frowned. "Um, wasn't the type to fall in love?"

"What does that mean?" Leonardi added.

"It means she was focused on business," Ruby said. "She was a pro in her work and if she did seek men, they were wealthy and provided for her. She was not out to look for love. We are not the 'search for real love and bullshit like that' kind of people. We're survivors and we want to thrive. Love only holds you back, hindering your full potential. Love makes your brain foggy."

I crossed my arms over my chest. She wasn't completely wrong. I knew exactly what she meant.

With my former boyfriends, I wasn't even sure I felt that feeling of love for them. It was more chemistry and a common lifestyle. But isn't that what they say? If you're unsure if you've ever truly loved, then the answer was probably no.

What I did know was that Ruby was right about the foggy brain and the not thinking straight. You do stuff while in a relationship and then you're blaming the other person for the things you chose to do yourself, when in fact, nobody had put a gun to your head. Well, except for when the Falcons literally put a gun to someone's head. That was a different story, though.

"Is there any way to find out who she was seeing?" I asked.

Ruby shrugged. "If she didn't tell me, then I'm guessing she didn't tell anyone else."

"Could it be a client?" Leonardi asked. "That's the most likely scenario."

"Anything is possible, I guess," Ruby said. "Although we swore we would never cross that line."

"I'm guessing we can't get her clients' names from the company?" I asked.

Ruby laughed. "Not a chance. They would only give those out over a solid warrant. That is, when the cops feel like looking into it."

"Why didn't she confide in you if she had a guy?" I asked Ruby.

"She was probably feeling guilty," Ruby said. "We didn't want to fall in love. We wanted to do our own thing. If I were her . . . I would feel ashamed too."

Wow. Feeling shame about loving someone was a whole other level of being emotionally broken. I felt for Lola and for Ruby.

"Okay, we're just going to have to figure out how to find out who the guy is," I said.

Leonardi nodded. "And on that note, did Lola know Dr. Stephen Curtis?"

"Was that the dentist?" Ruby asked and Leonardi nodded.

"I have no idea," Ruby said. "We didn't talk about each other's clients in detail, only when something was fishy. But he would certainly fit the bill."

"For being her client?" I asked.

Ruby nodded.

"How so?" I asked.

"White, middle-aged, married, higher income bracket," Ruby said. "That's mostly our clientele."

"Would he fit the bill as her love interest too?" Leonardi asked.

Ruby cringed a bit. "I hope not. Why get involved romantically, like genuinely romantically, with someone like that? Married and a couple of decades older than you? And now he's dead too."

We let that sink in.

At this point, anything was possible.

"So Lola never had any men over?" I asked.

Ruby shook her head. "Never. Neither of us. We would meet our clients mostly in hotels. I'm really hoping Lola was not seeing a client personally. I hope it was a regular guy, her age, who was okay with her job and she just needed some time until she could confide in me." Then she paused. "But I guess I'll never know how it would have turned out."

I wondered if this mystery man even knew about Lola's passing. It was only yesterday that she emerged from the casket and assuming the man wasn't her killer, there was a good chance he didn't even find out about it.

"When exactly did Lola disappear?" Leonardi asked. "You already told me it was Sunday, but do you have any specifics for us?"

Ruby nodded. "It was Sunday in the afternoon when she said she had to run an errand. I already figured that was the code for meeting with him. But honestly, I didn't think much of it. Not if I'd known what would happen. She didn't come back home that night, but that was okay, obviously I assumed she was with her fellow. But then on Monday she still hadn't shown up. I tried calling her, but her cell was turned off."

I asked Ruby for Lola's phone number. I could try reaching her, just in case. You never knew if someone did answer.

I dialed her number on speakerphone, and we waited.

The automated response came on. Her cell was turned off.

Like I had already suspected, the murderer must have gotten rid of her belongings.

"Were the cops here to search Lola's room?" Leonardi asked.

Ruby rolled her eyes. "What do you think?"

"I'm thinking no," Leonardi said. Then he added with a tone of sarcasm, "Why would they? It's only yesterday that she was found dead."

"Look at it this way," I said. "We have first dibs." I turned to Ruby. "Is that all right with you?" The last question was more out of curtesy.

"Knock yourselves out," Ruby said. "I'm going to make some tea."

Leonardi and I stood, and Ruby pointed to Lola's bedroom upstairs. We walked up the stairs, and before opening Lola's bedroom door, Leonardi produced two sets of latex gloves out of his pocket. I had made sure he would provide us with gloves before I left Gran's house.

Now I was sorry I didn't bring my own. His looked kind of used.

I grimaced as he handed me a pair. "Are these used?"

Leonardi frowned and looked closely at the gloves. "Um, not sure. Could be." Then he took an even closer look. "You know, I think they are. Must have forgotten to throw them out last time I did the—"

I put my hand up. "No. I don't want to know what you did last time with these gloves. Don't you have clean ones?"

Leonardi patted his pockets then flashed me a sheepish smile.

I rolled my eyes. "Jesus, you really are disgusting sometimes."

"By whose standards?" Leonardi asked.

I put my hand on my hip. "Civilized people."

Leonardi waved that away. "Oh those. They don't matter to me."

"Clearly," I said and donned the disgusting gloves, trying not to think of where they've been.

I'd rather wear the questionable gloves than have my fingerprints all over Lola's room. The cops may still show up, even if they're late. I suspected they started investigating the dentist's affairs first and if he really died of natural causes. Dentists first, call girls second. That was just the way things worked in this world. Which often made it simpler for the latter. There was more time to meddle with evidence this way.

We entered Lola's bedroom. It looked like a mix between modern elegance and cozy comfort. A queen-sized bed with plush pillows and a tufted headboard centered the room. Delicate sheer curtains framed the large window. I thought of Gran's old green-ish curtains and shook my head. There was a small seating area by the corner next to the window. A few art pieces hung on the walls. A wide desk was on the side opposite the window and the pièce de résistance was the walk-in closet that I could have killed for.

"Look at this!" I said as I flicked on the light in the closet room. Designer clothes, bags and shoes were neatly arranged on shelves and on golden hangers. "I'm mesmerized."

"You can use the money from this gig for something like that," Leonardi said, laughing.

At Gran's house? Sure. Then we would need to add two more wings.

I snapped back to reality.

If Lola was seeing someone, surely there'd be evidence of it. Love notes, gifts, candy leftovers. For me personally, an engraved knife would be the ultimate proof of love. A sharp one, compact enough to fit into my biker boots. Only I barely wore biker boots anymore, so maybe someone could create a knife small enough for my flip-flops, if that was even possible. Where would I stash it? Under a strap?

Leonardi and I got to work. We looked through her desk, drawers, under the bed. Everything was so neat and so in order. We didn't find anything that could have been a clue, but we hit pay dirt in the trash bin. There were some crumbled pieces of paper in there. I carefully took some out and unfolded them. There were the usual shopping lists and whatnot. Apparently, some people still used pen and paper for it instead of a phone.

One of the papers had a Dr. Stephen Curtis dentist office logo in the upper corner.

Leonardi and I exchanged glances. Then we high-fived.

"There's your connection," I said.

Leonardi nodded. "Just like expected."

So Lola did know the good old doctor. And apparently she was in his practice too. Lola must have grabbed the stationery while she was there.

"Let's see if we can find anything else," Leonardi said.

It felt exciting to search Lola's perfect closet space. The fabrics of her clothing felt soft and expensive. The leather of her shoes was shiny and clean. Maybe I could be a call girl. It was a skill I could learn, right?

In the bottom drawer on the far side I found a small cardboard box. I pulled it out and opened it. There were pictures inside, a necklace, stuff that looked like commemorative souvenirs, some older movie theatre stubs, and some loose marbles. Literally.

This was definitely a keepsake box.

I took out the pictures. There was Lola with a bunch of other people having a blast at the beach. She looked a couple of years younger. More like in her late teens. She was smiling wide. In one of the pictures, she was sitting on the same beach flanked by two guys, sharing laughter while pointing at something off-camera. I had to smile too. Those were nice memories she has had.

Then I saw another picture, obviously from the same beach trip. It was a clear profile shot of Lola, head to toe. My eyes cut to the tattoo on her ankle. I squinted at the image.

Then I froze and I felt a cold shiver running through my body.

Was that a . . . Falcon tattoo?

# Chapter Eight

I WAS CLOSE TO FAINTING.

A Falcons tattoo? Lola? A Falcon?

My mind was swirling with the worst scenarios possible. How could this be? No, it couldn't be.

I squinted at the image again.

There was a tattoo on her ankle, yes. I was looking for an image of a falcon with the name of a location beneath it. Mine had been Oregon. Lola's must have been Florida, if she really came from here.

There was indeed a bird-like image but it was too small to confirm it was a falcon. The details were hard to decipher due to the scale of the tattoo in that picture. I couldn't determine if there was another word beneath the bird image.

Still, I was in alarm mode.

This couldn't be happening. I tried not to hyperventilate.

I didn't come all the way here to freaking Florida, running away from the Falcons, only to bump into them again. I felt like the picture I was holding in my hand was burning, and I felt like any second now, the Falcons would march right in and get me.

Just to make sure, I checked all the pictures to see if any other person in it was sporting an ankle tattoo. They didn't. But then again, the pictures only showed most of them from the waist up.

"Are you okay?" Leonardi asked, snapping me back to reality. "You look like you've seen a ghost."

I have.

But I had to pull it together now. I would process this later.

I cleared my throat. "No, I'm fine. I just found this stuff in the box. Some personal items of Lola's."

"And?" Leonardi asked.

"Nothing worth mentioning," I said. "Seems to be stuff from years ago."

Leonardi got back to searching Lola's room, and I saw him tap beneath her desk. He was good. Most people, even in the investigative field, wouldn't think to look underneath furniture. There were a lot of people taping stuff beneath surfaces. It provided a good hiding place with easy access.

With my eyes on Leonardi, I slipped the picture of Lola in the back pocket of my shorts. I put the other pictures back in the box, then I closed the box and placed it in the drawer again.

We finished searching Lola's room and Leonardi had hoped to find more than just Dr.

Curtis's stationery. Little did he know, that was not even remotely the most spectacular thing we'd found.

We went downstairs where Ruby was back on the ottoman, sipping tea.

"Did you find anything useful?" she asked.

We showed Ruby the crumbled piece of paper.

Her eyebrows shot up. "Oh, so she was seeing the dentist?"

"Apparently so," Leonardi said. "We can't say if he was just her client or even more. But obviously, she's been to his dental practice."

I watched Ruby intently. She seemed genuinely surprised. No one was to say she didn't have anything to do with Lola's death. Just because she hired a PI didn't mean she was clean. If there was one thing I learned in my previous life, well, except for how to use a knife as a weapon, cook the books and threaten people, it was to never put anything past anyone.

"But, if Lola has been seeing the dentist, can we assume he had something to do with her dying?" Ruby asked, tears in her eyes.

"We don't know that," I said. "This is just a clue and something to get us started. But since the dentist died before Lola, he couldn't have murdered her."

Ruby shuddered. "I see." Then she looked at us. "But if the dentist didn't do it and Lola was seeing him, then it had to be . . ."

"The wife," I added.

Although only I knew about the window of opportunities that had just opened and that it could have been very well the Falcons. Still, if Lola had been seeing the dentist, the wife just became our prime suspect. But strangulation implied a man more than a woman. But hey, I wouldn't put it past any woman to have that strength in her.

Then a thought crossed my mind. The potential Falcon tattoo. Could Ruby be one too? I sneaked a peek at her bare ankles just to be sure. With her wearing the silk robe, I would have noticed a tattoo before, but needed to make sure. Just the thought of being with one of the Falcons in the same room gave me the shivers.

I couldn't believe that was really my life. I lived among the Falcons for thirty-one years and now I was petrified that I could be in the same room with one.

Luckily for me, though, I couldn't spot any tattoos on Ruby's ankle.

But I needed to ask her about Lola's.

"So Lola came here from Miami?" I asked. I had to phrase it in such a way that it wouldn't be suspicious with neither Ruby, nor Leonardi.

"Yes, she said she lived in Miami before coming to Bitter End."

"Do you know why exactly she left Miami?" I asked further. "I mean, it's Miami. Who wants to give that up for living here?"

Ruby tilted her head to the side and Leonardi stared at me incredulously.

"You mean just like *you* moved here?" Leonardi said.

Damn it.

"But I . . . didn't live in Miami, one of the hottest cities in the country," I said. "And I came here with my grandmother. That's totally different."

"Yeah, whatever you say," Leonardi said. Then turned back to Ruby. "Piper's question isn't that bad actually. Why would a young girl exchange the Miami lifestyle for the Bitter End one?"

Ruby shrugged. "Lola said she wanted to get out of that foster home she was in. She hated it. But she didn't talk much about it either. I had the feeling she wanted to put her past behind her. And for the record, the Miami lifestyle is so overestimated. It's not for everyone. Sure, the supply of clients would be amazing in Miami, but Bitter End isn't all that bad either." She paused. "I grew up around here and I'm not interested in moving to Miami."

"Interesting," Leonardi said. "What if she had beef with someone from her past, maybe someone from foster care. Maybe her past came back to haunt her."

I shivered inside. Those words held so much truth for me, I could feel it in my bones.

"People often have some kind of connection to the past, something that they keep around," I said. "I found a box with some private belongings of Lola's. Did you see that box before?"

"Oh, you mean that cardboard one?" Ruby asked. "Sure, she showed it to me once, I think. Don't we all have a box like that?"

I shivered again. No, not all people have the luxury of taking with them such a box. How I wish I could have taken such a box with me.

"Haven't seen the box in a while, though," Ruby said.

"Let me show you then," I said and ran back up to Lola's room, grabbed the box, pulled the picture from my pocket and threw it back in the box, then brought the box downstairs, opened it, and showed her the items.

"Have you already seen all this or is there something new here?" I asked Ruby. The tattoo was the only thing on my agenda now, but might as well find out if Lola has put anything in here recently that could be connected to the guy she was seeing and if that guy was indeed the dentist.

Ruby browsed through the items, but by the look on her face, nothing jumped out. "I've seen all this before, yes."

"Too bad," Leonardi said then turned to me. "But it was a good try, kid."

I pretended to think about it. "If there was someone from her past making a comeback, would there be a way to find out more about her past? How about that . . . ankle tattoo?"

I felt my heartrate going up.

"The tattoo?" Ruby asked, frowning.

"Yes, there is a small tattoo on Lola's ankle," I said and showed it to Ruby.

For normal people, having a tattoo on the ankle was nothing spectacular. For me, it meant the world right now.

Leonardi seemed to have caught on because he asked, "Do you know if that tattoo had a specific meaning for Lola? Did she say anything about it? How she got it? Was any other person involved?"

I could have kissed Leonardi!

Ruby squinted at the picture. "That thing? No, I don't think so. I mean, it's just a tattoo. Big deal, right? It's not like she was a tattoo fanatic. She just had the one, as far as I know. And it's not like we hung around the table and talked about tattoos. So no idea if that was supposed to mean anything."

I took in a deep breath as I asked nonchalantly, "Is that some kind of bird?"

Leonardi and Ruby both squinted at the picture again.

"It was some type of bird, but I couldn't tell you what kind," Ruby said. "Again, it's not like we extensively talked about this. The tattoo was on her leg too. It wasn't visible that much."

"Did the tattoo also contain a word?" I asked Ruby and hoped I wouldn't raise any suspicions with my detailed questions about that tattoo.

"A word?" Ruby frowned. "No, there was no word. What makes you think that?"

"Um . . ." I said, "I can make out a thin line just beneath the bird tattoo. But maybe I'm wrong."

Ruby looked at the picture again. "Yes, it does look that way, but there was just the bird."

I let out a small breath. I was still not out of the woods. Who knew what kind of tattoos the Falcons had here in Florida? I wasn't all up to date with the other Falcons branches throughout the US. I just assumed every state had the same tattoo of a falcon with their state name etched underneath. But maybe the Florida Falcons had only the falcon, no state name. Or maybe Ruby had been mistaken.

I wanted to talk more about the tattoo, but I knew that would be way too suspicious. I also felt extremely self-conscious in my shorts, with my own ankle out in the open. My tattoo was gone, but my own paranoia made me question how visible the spot was. In that moment, I felt it burn.

"I think the tattoo is a dead end," Leonardi said.

"I think so too," I said, letting out a breath. "Sorry, no stone unturned."

"So what now?" Ruby asked.

"We're going to look into the connection to the dentist and get back to you," Leonardi said.

\*\*\*

It was about 2 p.m. when Leonardi and I left Ruby's place.

# CLOSED CASKET

On the way to our cars, we talked about what we just found out. Leonardi suggested we visit the dentist's workplace to see if any of the staff recognized Lola. Dr. Curtis's employees most probably attended his funeral and had seen Lola pop out of the casket. If they've already seen Lola at the practice, then they would have recognized her. Most likely, they wouldn't talk to us about that, though. I had a feeling nobody would want to smear the good dentist's reputation. It would worth a try, still. You never knew when someone was going to talk.

Leonardi also suggested we go to the funeral home to see what happened there, if the staffers saw something suspicious before the casket was brought to the church.

". . . and just see if we can find out something there," Leonardi said. Then he paused. "Are you even listening?"

It was only then I realized I was on autopilot. I registered that Leonardi was talking to me and what he was saying but my mind was absolutely somewhere else. I still had the tattoo on my mind. Was Lola really a Falcon? It was just too ironic to move all the way from the other side of the country and still have the past haunt you.

I had brought back Lola's keepsake box into her closet and had snatched the picture again, hiding it in my pocket.

If Lola told the truth and she really came from Miami, I hoped the Falcons had their headquarters there and not in Bitter End. Which would make more sense, Miami being a bigger city. On the other hand, my hometown in Oregon wasn't a metropole and the Falcons were settled there.

All I knew was that if Lola really was one of the Falcons, then I would be so out of this investigation. No money in the world could make me investigate further and put my life and Gran's life at stake. But Leonardi didn't know that.

What I needed most now was to talk to Gran.

Leonardi was still staring at me and waiting for an answer.

"Yeah, sure, you're right," I said. "But you know what? I forgot I needed to . . . help around the retirement complex today."

"Huh?" Leonardi frowned. "Help around the retirement complex? What the heck is that supposed to mean?"

"There's this event on Saturday, you see, and I already promised I'd help my neighbor prepare for it," I said. "And it has to get done this afternoon, so I need to call it a day."

"What kind of event?" Leonardi asked, narrowing his eyes at me.

"It's a . . . um . . . prom night event," I said and could barely look him in the eye.

He flashed me his tooth gap. "A prom event? You mean like a high school prom night?"

"Yeah," I said, gulping. "I know how it sounds but it's a senior prom night. It's a whole big thing at the retirement complex and don't ask me how, but I always get involved somehow."

Leonardi broke out in a full-on laughter. "You know, I've heard a lot in my life, but this just tops it off." He bent over and held his stomach laughing.

I put my hands on my hips and narrowed my eyes at him. "Well, you don't have to mock it." I was kind of surprised that I took offense to his reaction although I shared his views about how lame the idea for the event was. But now, I found myself almost protective of the seniors, of my neighbors.

"So this is what you have to do today?" Leonardi asked. "Help around with a senior prom night? Instead of doing your job, the one you're getting paid for?"

I crossed my arms over my chest. "Yes, that is what I am going to do today. As far as I know, we haven't decided on me having certain work hours. We've said flexible hours. Besides, if I back out of it now and don't help, then I would never hear the end of it. You wouldn't have a partner to work with because they would lynch me. Those seniors are not something to be taken lightly. When you say you're going to be there, you have to be there."

Wow. What a speech.

Leonardi scratched the back of his head. "Yeah, okay, that I can see. Those seniors are scary. You don't kid around with them."

"We did good today, what with the talk with Ruby," I said. "Let's regroup tomorrow."

# Chapter Nine

I GOT INTO MY CAR and drove back to the house. I had no idea if Leonardi thought my actions were suspicious but there was no other way. I couldn't do this. I couldn't do this if the Falcons were involved. My mind swirled. What did this all mean? And what would I do now? I needed to stop investigating or else I would be getting too close to the Falcons.

Even now in the car, I felt like getting Falcon cooties all over me.

There wasn't a way for them to know instantly who I was, but it would still be too close for comfort. Then, if they found out who I was and that I was snooping around Lola's death, what would they do?

For all I knew, Lola could have been killed by the Falcons themselves.

I thought more about Lola and her past. Did she come here from Miami because she was on the run from the Falcons? Why voluntarily leave the Falcons network in Miami and move to Bitter End? Nobody wanted to *not* be in their network. Well, except for Gran and me, but that was the exception. So basically, why the hell would anyone want to defect voluntarily? It was a pretty sweet life living with the Falcons. It was a sucky life living without them.

But maybe Lola had some sort of fallout with them and decided that was not the life for her. Maybe she had more of a conscience. Good god. That was so weak. Being with the Falcons meant having power and having money. Screw conscience problems. Life was just too good being a Falcon.

I drove on autopilot to the retirement complex. It was early afternoon when I pulled the car to the curb. I couldn't wait to talk to Gran about it. She was always my go-to for seeking out advice, even if it often came off way out there. Still, there was always some kind of truth in her words that stuck with me.

I couldn't imagine my life without Gran. Which brought me back to the thought that I should move out of the house. That brought me further to thinking how the hell was I supposed to separate my life from Gran's? Ugh. Once again, I pushed that thought away.

My hopes were shot pretty quickly when I realized Gran was not at the house. The golf cart was missing too.

Damn it.

She was probably at the rec hall playing poker with her gang. Gran and I were both doing stuff that could get us kicked out of witness protection. Honestly, we were like ticking bombs just waiting to blow up.

Well, with Gran not being here right now, I had some time for myself to think things out. I cranked up the AC, although probably for the first time since I got here, I didn't care about being too hot.

I plopped down on the couch, leaned my head on the headrest and closed my eyes. I took a deep breath and tried to think of something else but thoughts of Lola kept swirling in my head and I couldn't disconnect. Now I was thinking about her connection to Dr. Stephen Curtis and the wife as a suspect. Spouses often found out about the extracurricular activities of their partner and then sought out revenge. But did the wife have so much strength to strangle Lola? I saw her at the funeral, she was slim. Strangulation required physical strength. But again, I wouldn't put it past her just because of statistics.

However, it clashed with the typical Falcon method of eliminating targets. Strangling was personal and left too much DNA. The Falcons operated on business motives. Usually, it involved shooting. From a distance.

So there it was. As of then, the suspects were either the wife or the Falcons. What a drastic contrast! If the Falcons did it, then good riddance to charging any of them, let alone make an arrest. We would never find the killer then. I knew that but I couldn't tell Leonardi anything. What I did know was that I could be poking around and waking up the bear but without uncovering the murderer. Those odds were not in my favor and I wasn't ready to gamble with them.

After about half an hour of deep breathing, I got up from the couch, headed for the fridge, and took out a nice cold bottle of beer. Just as I was about to open the bottle, there was a knock on the door.

I groaned. Seriously? I couldn't even drink my beer in peace.

This time I looked through the peephole. Edie, who else. I opened the door and saw her frowning.

"Where have you been?" she asked.

"Where have I been?" I replied. "What do you mean? I've been around. Why?"

"It was just odd you weren't home," Edie said. "I've been waiting for you to come back."

"Edie, you can't expect me to run my whole day by you," I said.

I knew she was going to find out eventually about me partnering with Leonardi, but I still wasn't ready to open up that Pandora's box right now. Especially since that would get back to Ryker. And with the latest development on the Falcons front, I wasn't even sure I would keep the partnership with Leonardi.

Edie sighed. "Fine, you're right, but I do need your help."

I frowned. I already knew by now what this meant, and it was never good. This smelled like trouble. "To do what?"

"I need your help with the Prom queen parade."

Oh, crap. That.

"What would that imply?" I asked, dying to take a huge gulp out of my beer.

"You know, decorating the golf cart and driving around," Edie said. "My constituency is waiting for me." She moved her eyebrows up and down.

That was it. Now I've heard it all.

"I have so many questions, I don't know where to start," I said.

"Then I'll tell you all about it," Edie said.

***

An hour and a half later, I was in the golf cart with Edie.

It was *her* golf cart for a change.

But I was her driver, as always.

Edie's idea was to have a prom queen parade leading through the retirement complex in a pimped-up golf cart. She was going to hand out flyers, advertising her as future Prom queen. We decorated her golf cart with tinsel and whatnots, and it basically looked like a Christmas tree.

I even installed some small speakers in the corners of the golf cart. They were wireless but obviously we needed my cell phone to connect to them and play some sounds, since Edie's phone was a brick that she barely used.

The sun was shining as I was slowly driving through the streets of the retirement complex while the soundtrack of "Rocky" spilled out of the speakers. Edie, wearing a silver tiara in her curls and a sash over her chest with the words "Prom queen Bitter End" written on it waived to the people as if she were the queen of England.

I didn't know if I should cry, run away, or shoot myself. I opted for the fourth option. I could use the distraction right now because I felt like going nuts thinking about the whole Lola and Falcons and dentist story.

"How much did this all cost you anyway?" I asked Edie pointing to all the decorations.

"It cost a bit," Edie said, waving to a resident that just left her house and who winked back. "But what am I supposed to spend my money on? I have enough in savings but who knows how long I'll live. I'm not going to just stash my money and not get any use out of it. I need to live."

What a change in mindset. Maybe Gran and I should be thankful we got Edie as our neighbor. She was the one who inadvertently dragged us out of our mental misery. Edie was all about life while we were all about sorrow.

"Yeah, I guess you're right," I said. Then in a teasing voice, I added, "So you decided to spend a chunk of your savings on campaigning to be Prom queen?"

"You're being sarcastic again," Edie said, turning to me. "You know I always get that. But of course I'm not spending *all* of my savings on this. There's something I learned when I got older and that is, we work and we work and we work our whole lives and we put every penny aside and then you get to be my age and you ask yourself, what did I do in my life? What pleasures did I indulge in? The advice to put everything in savings to really live life at sixty or seventy or even beyond that and then have the other people questioning you for that really sucks."

Edie took a deep breath.

Whoa. Ouch. That felt like a lightning strike. Only Edie could have done that. She could transition from her usual head-in-the-clouds demeanor to something so profound in an instant.

"Yeah, okay, I get your point," I said. "But apparently, it's not only money you put into this, it's also time. You planned this parade, and those flyers weren't made just today. You had those made. That takes planning."

Edie grinned. "Of course I planned it. What do you think? That I'm just going to wing it? As soon as I found out Sourpuss was one of the nominees too, I dove into planning mode."

"Funny you didn't mention anything to me," I said. "Just something about a parade but no details."

"I still like to have that mystery air to me," Edie said, taking a whole stack of flyers in her hand. "And keeping you on your toes."

I laughed. "That you definitely do."

CLOSED CASKET

I stopped the golf cart and Edie talked to a couple of residents who were walking down the street. It was really just like the president had come into town. I started up the golf cart again after Edie finished her conversation.

"You know you're not Prom queen yet, don't you?" I asked, pushing my sunglasses further up my nose. Driving at this speed meant much less headwind, which meant I felt the heat way worse. At least it was November already, so it was bound to dye down.

"Of course I know I'm not Prom queen yet," Edie said, adjusting her tiara gently in her white curls. "But this is the power of suggestion. I'm acting like I'm Prom queen so the others will see me as such. It's all a matter of how you carry yourself." She gave a royal wave to a few passersby.

"Does that also mean that as future Prom queen you're making sure that nobody else stands a chance?" I asked. "Like playing mind games with your opponents and changing up their campaign buttons?"

"Ugh, that. I already told you I had nothing to do with it. But I wish I had the idea. Sabotaging your enemy is the best defense. And it's not like I was unhappy she got the wrong buttons. I have my utter respect for whoever did it. But wasn't it Dorothy?"

"She said she wasn't it," I said.

"Well, that figures," Edie said. "I can't imagine her admitting that she did. But let me tell you, I sure checked these fliers to make sure nobody meddled with them."

We drove around most of the streets and it was a relief to have my thoughts diverted from Lola and the Falcons. The other residents seemed to take Edie's parade in good humor, even joining in enthusiastically. Some held Edie's hand, treating her like a revered figure.

Our final stop was the hub of the complex, the area around the dining hall, rec hall, administration building, swimming pool and minigolf course. We placed the stack of fliers on the tables nearby and I also took the wireless speakers with me and set them strategically around the table area. I used a music app on my phone to connect to the speakers.

People began to gather, forming clusters, chatting and just enjoying themselves.

I took a seat at a nearby table under an umbrella and let out a breath. I watched the interactions between the residents and how much fun they seemed to have. Maybe Edie was right. It didn't have to be boring when you got to that age.

Gran came out of the rec hall with her poker playing posse. They must have probably heard all the commotion outside and came to see what was going on. I could see Gran rolling her eyes and the others clapping in excitement.

Gran headed over to me and the others joined the group of people around Edie.

"What the hell is going on here?" Gran asked.

"Just the usual," I said and reported to Gran what Edie was up to.

"Maybe you should up your game if you wanna be voted Prom queen," I said to Gran giving her an elbow.

"Sure, I'll wear a princess dress and a crown and have my pumpkin turn into a carriage that I'll be using to drive around here."

"I think you got it all wrong," I said. "That's Cinderella. She wasn't packing."

"Not that we know of," Gran said.

I pondered about whether this was a good time to tell Gran about Lola's tattoo. No, this wasn't the right time. We needed privacy for that. But Gran caught onto my look and frowned. It was hard to keep anything from Gran.

155

"What happened?" she asked.

"Later at the house," I said.

Gran made a move to get up from the chair. "Then let's go."

"You know what? Let's just stick around for a bit and enjoy this gathering. It feels relaxing and I think we need that right now."

"O-kay," Gran said, rolling her eyes and sitting down again.

We watched Edie and the others in silence for a while longer. I saw Sourpuss peeking from behind the corner of the administration building, watching the scenes before her, then with a disapproving scowl, she disappeared. She was probably going home now and conjuring up more grand plans for her campaign.

Whatever. Sourpuss wasn't my main problem right now.

"What is that?" Gran finally asked in a tone of annoyance, so her regular tone. "Is that the soundtrack to Rocky that's running on repeat?"

"That's Edie for ya," I said. "That's the only song she needs."

In that exact moment, Edie came bouncing to us.

"What happened to you?" I asked looking her up and down. It looked like the residents also decorated Edie. She had tinsel swirled from head to toe and a few stickers glued to her arms as well.

"Oh, we're just having fun," Edie said. "Why are you two sitting here? Come and join the fun."

"We are close enough, thank you," Gran said.

"Please, Dorothy, don't rain on the parade," Edie said. "Hey, maybe you'll find a reason to pull out that gun of yours. That would make it fun for you too."

"Don't tempt me," Gran said.

"Anyway," Edie turned to me. "As much as I like that warrior song, because I'm a warrior and all, I think some people are bored. Could you change up the music, please? You know, make it fresh and snappy."

"Make it fresh and snappy?" I asked. Awesome, now I've become the Prom queen's personal DJ too.

"Well, yes," Edie said. "You're the youngest around here. You know how to deal with this technology. We need you here."

A fuzzy feeling crept over me. There was something about that whole being-needed-feeling. Especially after being a zero productive member of society for almost one year and a half now. And by "society" I meant *my* society. I couldn't launder money, I couldn't take in cash and write fake work invoices, I couldn't be my usual self like I was behind the bar at Choppers, I couldn't even threaten someone with a knife, for God's sake. What a sad state of affairs.

So I found being needed by my septuagenarian neighbor at the retirement complex I was currently living in quite fulfilling. Playing her personal chauffeur and DJ. That was the moment it dawned on me that I might end up doing that indefinitely if I somehow managed to get the approval for living here.

That was chilling!

I got up from the chair and pulled out my phone. "Here, I'll do it." I activated the shuffle function in the app, so now the songs were all playing in a random order. Then I gave Edie my phone. "Here, place it in the golf cart so the signal to the speakers doesn't get lost."

Edie's eyes widened. "Whoa, you're giving me your phone? You're voluntarily giving up control of your phone? This is a first."

She was right. I had been extremely careful regarding my phone after we got here in Bitter End. I was paranoid with thoughts of being tracked down by the Falcons. I was still using a prepaid card, making it harder to track me down. There have been, let's just say, a few situations where Edie convinced me to use my phone to snoop around every time we got involved in solving those murders in the last two months. I wasn't very fond of my phone containing evidence that could get me in trouble with the cops.

But more and more, I started loosening "the control", as Edie has put it. In this case, it was about music. I needed to let go of the paranoia when it came to music.

"Take it before I change my mind," I said, laughing.

Edie swiped it off my hand and told us we should mingle and enjoy the music as well, instead of sitting around like two ninety-year-olds with bad hips.

"Yeah, you go ahead, and we'll catch up," Gran said.

Edie rolled her eyes and joined the others, who were suddenly charging up like Energizer bunnies on steroids, all thanks to the fresh tunes.

Gran and I sat there in silence and watched the group of residents having fun, talking to each other, congratulating Edie like she had already won.

"Where's Theodore?" I asked Gran.

"How the heck should I know?" she replied.

I put my hands up in defense. "Whoa, I'm just asking. He usually has a knack for finding you. He just wants to be near you." Then I said in a lower voice, "Poor guy."

"I heard that," Gran said. "Then she shifted in her seat and crossed one boot over the other. "He's running some errands downtown."

I let out a honk of a laugh. I knew it. Gran could act like she didn't like him as much as she wanted. As if I didn't know her.

"Stop laughing, I don't need . . ." Gran said, and I saw her looking over my shoulder. "Well, well, well, speaking of you-know-who, here comes your boo."

"My what?" I said, whipping my head around.

I felt some butterflies in my stomach again as I saw Ryker heading over. The expanse of his broad shoulders, the casual cool of his black T-shirt paired with his jeans and that look in his eyes . . . *okay, Piper. Snap out of it!*

"That's not my boo," I said to Gran.

She repeated my words, "Poor guy."

I narrowed my eyes at her just as Ryker sat down next to us. He let out a long breath and leaned back. "How are you ladies today?"

I frowned. What was with the nice attitude? For a fleeting moment, suspicion crept in and I wondered if he knew about me looking into Lola's death alongside Leonardi. But how would he know? He couldn't.

"We are the same as yesterday and the same as the day before and so on," Gran said in her typical dry tone. "Just trying to survive one more day in this nut house."

Ryker laughed. "I don't believe that for a second. I think you like it here more than you care to admit."

"Whatever you say," Gran said and turned back to the joyful group of people in front of her.

Edie and some others winked at Ryker then he turned to me. "And you, Piper? Why aren't you joining in the fun?"

"I am joining in the fun," I said. "I am sitting here, aren't I?"

"Oh, pardon me, I forgot your definition of fun is a definition on its own," Ryker said, grinning at me.

"Well, they have music thanks to me. I made that happen, so I am a part of it."

Ryker glanced over at the speakers and Edie struggling with my phone, attempting to navigate the screen, a sight that made me wince. "Ah, I see," Ryker said, "You're the DJ."

That made me wince even more. "Yeah, you could say that." I paused then I asked, "So what brings you by again?"

"Nothing much, really," Ryker said. "Just checking in on Grams now and then."

"You're checking up on your grams a lot lately," I said.

"Of course, way more often since you two moved here," Ryker said.

No counterarguments there. This guy was really pushing my buttons.

I was just going to ask him why he wasn't out investigating his own case when there was a loud beep coming from the speakers.

"Edie, what did you do?" I shouted as everyone was covering their ears.

"I didn't do anything," Edie shouted back. The music kept on playing. "I think you got a text message." Edie held the screen in front of her eyes and squinted.

She headed over to our table while I started to regret giving her my phone. A text message? Any text message would pop up on the phone screen and would be visible. Edie was looking at the phone right now. The only person who came to mind who would send me a message was . . . Leonardi.

162

Crap.

I rose to my feet and said, "Let me see."

"Here you go, I just—" she began, then abruptly stopped in her tracks. She stared intently at the screen and blurted out, "'Working on the Lola case'?" as she read aloud from what was displayed.

I could sense Ryker perking up.

"Who's Lola?" Edie asked with a confused look on her face.

Ryker pinched the bridge of his nose. "Lola is the girl they found in Dr. Curtis's casket."

Edie's eyes went wide. "What? You're playing detective without me?"

## Chapter Ten

"UM . . .," I STARTED AND WAS actually out of words. Again.

This was so not me. Not being in control of a situation was something I had to keep on learning here in Bitter End.

Ryker stood and gave me a look. "Really?"

I was doing the ping pong between Edie's and Ryker's stares and at the same time, I saw Gran in the corner of my eye resting her arms on her knees and just shaking her head.

I pulled myself together and lifted my chin up. I didn't have to explain anything to anyone.

"Yes, I am working on the Lola case," I said, although with the newest developments regarding the Falcons I couldn't work the case anymore. Since I haven't talked to Gran yet, trying to find a solution, I wanted to leave a small window of escape in case I continued with the Lola case. "For now. I am not sure if I'm going through with it."

"I don't understand," Ryker said. "You're not a cop and you're not a PI nor anything remotely in that area."

I gave him a piercing look. I kind of understood then why Gran was always carrying a gun. How dared he think so little of me?

"Not that it's any of your business, but Leonardi hired me as his consultant," I said with my hands on my hips.

"As his consultant?" Edie said in a small voice. "Is that even possible?"

Ryker scratched the back of his head and let out a breath. I would say he just realized the gap in the system. "Yeah, he can do that. We could hire freelance consultants without them having a PI license."

"Whoa," Edie said. "That's awesome! But why didn't you tell me that?"

I sighed. "Maybe because you would have wanted to get involved too?"

"Nonsense," Edie said, waving her hand in dismissal. Then she paused. "Yeah, okay, I get your point. But still, you should have told me."

Ryker watched me but didn't say anything. If I had to guess, I'd say he appreciated me trying to protect his grandmother, although I wasn't as successful protecting his grandmother as he was. That was at least one thing we had in common, besides our love for motorcycles, that he had no clue about.

"Like I said, Edie, I'm not sure yet I'm going through with it, so it didn't make sense to tell you until I decided what to do," I lied.

There was a pause and then Ryker asked, "You're not sure if you're going through with it? You already said yes, I assume. Why would you back out? What happened?"

Ryker and his intuition really got on my nerves.

"I'm not sure if this is the path for me," I said, trying to sound as neutral as possible.

Ryker smiled. "What kind of a cheesy line is that? Not the right path for you? No, something happened that made you change your mind. What is it? You probably already started investigating and then found out something that made you want to back out."

Edie's wide eyes were darting from Ryker to me and back. She said, "Oh wow, I didn't even think of that. Yes, that's what I would like to know too. What happened?"

"Hey guys, what are you doing all the way over here?" One of the residents came over, shaking his hips to the music. "Why don't you—"

Edie waved him away without even looking in his direction. "Not now, Cyrus."

Cyrus did an "oops" move, then shook his hips back to the group. I was glad Cyrus wore his hearing device today.

I cleared my throat. "You are way off track, Ryker," I said. "Not only do I not owe you any explanation, but . . . Nope, I'm gonna stick to it. I don't owe you any explanation."

Then I saw Edie's lower lip tremble.

Did Ryker even know his grandmother could have worked as a cross-examiner? She was an expert in getting information out of me. She understood my soft spot and adjusted her behavior accordingly. Ryker did not know how to do that.

"Edie, nothing happened," I said. "This is me here starting a new life, but I really have to think about which way it's going. I already decided I'm not going to do the hairdresser thing but I need to see what other options I can explore and are right for me."

Barf!

That sounded even cheesier than before. But Ryker could ask and prod all he wanted; he would never find out the truth. Edie was not getting anything else out of me either.

I could tell Ryker wasn't thrilled with my response but I made a conscious effort not to care. Actually, I tried hard not to. My concern was more for Edie.

"I thought you would go and work with Ryker," Edie said. "You two are perfect for each other."

Ryker shifted from one leg to another, and I coughed silently. Perfect for each other? A criminal in witness protection and a PI? Right. That sounded more like a corny rom com than reality.

"Piper can't work with me," Ryker said. "Leonardi is more suitable for her, what with him working outside the legal norms as well."

I couldn't correct him there. We all knew that.

"We are both just interested in the end result," I said, and shook my head. Those were exactly Leonardi's words.

"Hey, you guys," a voice from the group shouted over. "Why are you all looking so serious? Come here and party."

"We'll be there in a second," Edie shouted back and readjusted her tiara in her white curls. "Okay, we'll talk about this later at your house," she said. "I need to go and take care of my people."

Ugh. I so did not want to talk about this later at the house. I did not want to talk about this ever. I also knew there was no escaping Edie now.

She turned to leave but then said to me, "I know you're going to do the right thing, Piper. and I trust you. Whatever you decide, I'll be there for you." Then she winked at me. "Especially if you decide to investigate. A Prom queen can always help."

Warmth filled my chest even though this was another typical Edie manipulation. I smiled. "Never does a Prom queen not help."

The others put their hands up in the air as Edie joined them again.

"Are we done here?" Gran rose from her chair. "I'd like to get to the house and turn on the AC."

"Yes, we're done here," Ryker said. "Piper, I hope you know what you're doing. This is not something to take lightly. Especially with Leonardi."

"You see, this is something I just don't get," I said. "Why do you care? Why do you care I'd be working with Leonardi? Because I would be getting in your way professionally? That's it? Seems like a lot of energy just because of that."

Ryker studied me and I could tell he was trying to find the right words. Just as he opened his mouth, Gran said, "Because he cares about you."

169

I saw a blush creeping up Ryker's cheek and I myself felt a bit uneasy.

"That is so not true."

"You've got it all wrong."

Ryker and I spoke at the same time.

Gran laughed and said, "You both are such fools."

Ryker shook his head. "I care about this community here and especially my own grandmother, who's going to get tangled in this now. And if you're involved too, it's only going to cause chaos. I know what you did in the last couple of months, and I appreciate you being there for Grams but you also kind of got her into a lot of those situations. I saw your skills and I know you can take care of yourself, but this is still work that has to be done by a professional."

I tried so hard not to punch him square in the nose. "Maybe that's exactly what this community needs, a nonprofessional," I said.

Ryker shook his head. "I don't know why I bother; you'll do whatever you want anyway."

"That's right," I said. "Why wouldn't I? It's my life, isn't it?"

Ryker pursed his lips. "So that means we're going to clash . . . professionally?"

"I guess we will," I said, putting my hands on my hips. "Can you handle that?"

Ryker cracked a smile. "I can handle you."

I smiled back. "I asked if you could handle it, not me. I don't think you can handle me."

"We'll see about that," Ryker said.

We locked eyes and didn't look away. We were doing one of those staring contests again. Oh my, if our egos weren't this big.

Gran let out an annoyed breath and sat back down again. "Oh, great, this could take a while."

"So what did you find out about the victim?" Ryker asked just as I had expected.

"You're shameless," I said. "Would you tell me what you found out about the dentist?"

"I'm not sure yet," Ryker replied.

"You're not sure yet?" I asked. "I don't believe you. You were very adamant before that you were not going to disclose any information because of confidentiality and our safety and blah blah."

"Yes, but that was before I found out you are working with another PI," Ryker said. "We could see it as a joint venture now. From PI firm to PI firm. Exchanging information could help solve my case too. That would change the whole dynamic of me sharing information with you."

Oh. I did not think of that. I liked what I was hearing.

"So would you care to share what you know about the dentist?" I asked.

"I think I asked you first about the girl," Ryker said.

"Oh, for God's sake," Gran said, throwing her hands up in the air. "I'm getting tired of your conversation. Somebody please do something or I'm going to the house alone."

I wasn't sure if Ryker was bluffing or not. I figured he wouldn't share much information anyway. But I did know that it was getting hot outside and I finally wanted to talk to Gran about Lola's tattoo.

"Ryker, look," I said. "I'm not sure what I can divulge, and I would need to discuss it with Leonardi first." Which was a big fat lie. "So let's just drop it for now and talk soon again."

"Discuss it with Leonardi?" Ryker asked and laughed. "Yeah right, like you need to ask permission."

Of course he knew I was lying. Why did I even bother?

"Okay, listen," Ryker said, "This is a bit of goodwill here. I didn't find out much that you already wouldn't know, like that Dr. Curtis died of natural causes, a heart attack. My next step would be to find out more about Lola Duvall. I assume you know that name by now. Her body is at the medical examiner's office down at the county forensic bureau. They plan on doing her autopsy tomorrow morning."

Wow. It was kind of cute, really. Everything he mentioned was something I could have figured on my own or already knew. But I decided to let him know I appreciated it either way.

"Thank you," I said.

He looked behind him at the group of residents who were now dancing to a salsa song. "I'll leave you two to go to your house now and I'm just going to say goodbye to the others." Then he winked at me. "I'll see you soon. Don't forget about the prom night."

I shook my head. One minute he was scolding me, then he turned all flirty with that prom night thing.

I groaned. The prom night. To be honest, I kind of forgot about that. I was going to the prom with Ryker. How did I end up in this situation?

I watched Ryker walk over to Edie and I was unable to resist admiring his well-defined and muscular back. His confident stride exuded authority and coolness. Yum.

Gran joined me, also watching Ryker. "That's one delicious view."

Shaking my head to clear my thoughts, I refocused. "Let me get my cell phone back, and we'll head to the house."

\*\*\*

As soon as we entered Gran's house, she went straight for the rum. Leonardi took the good bottle but it's not like we didn't have any others. Gran poured two glasses for us. Edie stayed back with the others, who seemed to grow even livelier. She was a bit miffed that I took away their music but at that moment, one of the residents proposed relocating the party to his house where he could play music from his computer, because his grandson showed him how to do that.

Gran settled on the couch, clutching her glass of rum and resting her hand on the headrest, while I sat at the kitchen table. "Do tell," she said.

I updated Gran about Leonardi's and my visit to Ruby and what we found out about Lola. As soon as I mentioned the tattoo on her ankle, all color drained from Gran's face. She downed the rum.

"This is extremely concerning," she said.

I had pulled the picture I snatched of Lola and showed it to Gran. She studied it carefully but I couldn't make out those emotional highs I'd been through. That was to be expected. Gran was just being Gran.

"I feel like this is a dream," I said. "A really bad one. How can it be that we're going into witness protection and then find exactly the people we're hiding from?"

Gran was still looking at the picture, and I could tell she was trying to figure out what kind of tattoo that was. "I don't know what to say," she said. "This looks like our Falcons tattoo but at the same time it doesn't."

"Exactly", I said. "I couldn't have said it better. But that just means we have no idea if she was a Falcon or not."

A silence filled the room.

"So you're thinking if she was a Falcon, then you'd stop investigating her death," Gran said.

"Of course I would," I said. "You know what it would mean if she were a Falcon, and I would butt

175

my nose in. Our lives would be at stake." Gran shot me a look and I added, "More than they are now."

Gran poured some more rum for us. We sat in silence, and I was sure Gran and I shared the same thoughts. How could this be, how did we end up here, was this our life, always on the run, and bumping into Falcons while hiding from them.

"You said she came from Miami?" Gran asked.

I nodded. "That's what her roommate said. I don't have any reason or proof not to believe her."

"Okay, so let's say she was a Falcon," Gran said. "If their headquarters is in Miami and she came to live here, then maybe she wasn't that close to them."

I raised my eyebrow at Gran. "That still doesn't mean we wouldn't be in danger and you know it."

Gran sighed. She knew I was right. She obviously didn't know more about the Falcons network throughout the country than I did.

"What now?" Gran asked.

"I have no idea," I said.

"You could easily walk away from this," Gran said. "From Leonardi and this job he's offering you." She paused. "If you weren't you."

Gran was right. Nobody forced me to continue investigating with Leonardi. There were other job options out there for me—I could even try my hand at being a hairdresser, imagine that! I'd be the one giving shampoos to clients. But the reality was, I didn't pursue any of those alternatives. Instead, I found solace in self-pity, cooping myself up in the house.

I was who I was. I craved the rush, the danger, and the allure of the illicit side of things. That's what made it feel right for me.

We drank some more rum in silence. It was then I realized I haven't replied to Leonardi's text message. I didn't even read it.

I grabbed my cell and saw that he texted, *Re working on the Lola case: meet tomorrow at eleven, my office. Talk about next steps.*

"He really wants me on this case," I said to Gran.

"Of course he does, he's a smart man," Gran said.

I cringed. "You're calling Leonardi a smart man all of a sudden? That's weird."

"I'm not saying he's always smart, I'm just saying he's smart about this."

I smiled at Gran. That was her unique way of complimenting me.

"You know this is going to bug you," she continued. "You need to know if that girl has a Falcon tattoo on her ankle or not."

"Okay, I'm with you on that," I said. "But how do you suggest I find that out?"

Gran put on her evil grin that scared me a bit.

"You'll just have to see it for yourself," she said.

"But how would I—?" Then it dawned on me. "You don't mean . . ."

"Where is the body right now?" Gran asked.

"At the ME's office," I said. "Ryker just told me that."

"Well, there you have it," Gran said.

"So you're saying I should break into the medical examiner's office to look at a dead body's ankle?"

"Not you," Gran said. "Us."

Then we clinked glasses and downed the rum.

## Chapter Eleven

GRAN AND I DECIDED we would sneak into the ME's office tonight. We would have the advantage of darkness and we needed to hurry to find out who we were dealing with. If the ME was set to perform the autopsy tomorrow morning, then that was all the more reason to examine Lola tonight. They would be too focused on her starting tomorrow. Our window of opportunity was today.

I was well aware of the risk we were taking. But I also knew I couldn't keep myself out of it. I needed to know what was up with Lola's tattoo. That held true for Gran as well, so she was coming with me. Together we were stronger.

There was only one medical examiner in this county so I googled the address of his office and studied the surrounding area on Google Maps in satellite view. It was a twenty-minute drive from the retirement complex to the industrial area between a lake and several other administration facilities. According to the website, the office would close at 6 p.m. Gran and I decided to head there around 9 p.m. just to account for the possibility of any employees lingering in the building or the nearby area late into the evening.

I anticipated an easy entry into the building. It wasn't like this was some heavily guarded secret government facility with top-tier security. This town barely had any video surveillance cameras. We decided to bring gloves, flashlights, and our weapons—Gran's gun and my knife. I had a bobby pin on hand for picking the lock. I didn't imagine in my wildest dreams that I'd be needing to break into this many buildings here in Florida. If this kept up, I needed to buy a regular lock picking set.

For missions like this back home, I had my own gun that I had learned how to tuck into my waist so that it wouldn't bulge out. Gran, the master, really taught me everything. As for my knife, I usually carried it in my boot, which provided a surprise effect, but in extreme situations, retrieving the knife from the boot would take too much time. I had learned to carry it in a brown leather scabbard in the back pocket of my pants. That only worked if the pants were tight enough, like the black leather pants I usually wore for these missions. It didn't work with the wider shorts I sported here in Florida on a regular basis.

# CLOSED CASKET

We prepared for this trip as best as we could. Both Gran and I reminisced about our old lives. Needless to say, we had more resources and more manpower back then but there were a couple of times when Gran and I went on a mission by ourselves.

With putting together the plan for tonight I had almost forgotten we were here in witness protection. But here we were again, breaching the rules of WITSEC. Once again, I pushed that thought away and focused on how right these wrongdoings felt.

As we expected, we couldn't find the layout of the ME's building on the Internet, which meant that Gran and I had to blindly search for the morgue section. At the same time, this felt exciting for us, since we've never had a mission like this. Usually, we sent people to the morgue, we didn't look for them there.

Pumped about this outing, we skipped dinner at the dining hall and settled for chips and a can of olives.

I sent a text to Leonardi confirming our meeting at his office the next day, although I was still uncertain about continuing with this investigation. I guessed tonight's events would help me find the answer to this question.

"Are you ready?" Gran asked before we got out of the house. She wore black leather pants and her black biker boots, a black tank top and her fitted black leather jacket. She looked like Batman in his seventies. The only thing missing were the bat ears.

This time around, I didn't frisk her.

I was wearing more or less the exact same thing only I had no jacket on. I still didn't understand how Gran wore this stuff in the Florida climate. I was sure she should be studied in a lab.

Here came the hard part. We turned off the lights in the house and peeked outside through the window. The real danger wasn't breaking into that building, the real danger was not getting caught by our neighbors and especially by Edie.

There was eerie silence outside, and the streetlamps were casting a dim glow over the lewd gnomes on Gran's front lawn. They kind of looked even naughtier at night.

"The coast looks clear," I whispered to Gran.

"You don't have to whisper while we're in the house," Gran said.

I rolled my eyes. "I'm just getting into the mood."

Our car was parked at the curb. The golf cart was in front of the garage door. We looked over at

Edie's house and it seemed to be dark inside, meaning she was still partying with the others.

We tip-toed out of the house and made our way to the car, glancing down the street in both directions and scanning the neighboring houses. Still no movement which was good.

"You do realize how stupid this is, don't you?" Gran whispered to me. "We are hiding from a bunch of old folks. That's the level of danger we're facing at the moment."

I totally got what she was saying. Before, we were hiding from criminals, and now we were hiding from retired seniors.

"I know," I said. "But as it turns out, their nagging and insistence is just as dangerous as a gun."

We were almost at the car, and I already started to let out a breath, relieved that no one had spotted us. Just as I reached for the driver's side door, a voice from behind suddenly said, "Where are you going?"

Both Gran and I nearly leaped out of our skins. In a split second, Gran whipped out her gun, while I instinctively grabbed my knife, quickly turning around. What I saw was a tiara perched atop crooked white curls, a sash around a polka-dotted dress and tinsel draped all over it.

Edie.

"Oh, sweet Mary," she yelped and ducked.

"Edie!" I said. "Why the hell are you sneaking up on us?"

Edie looked up, then patted herself as though to confirm she wasn't injured.

"You're going to give me a heart attack one of these days!" she said, breathing hard.

"We're going to give *you* a heart attack?" Gran said, as she slid her gun back into the small of her back. "Maybe it's the other way around."

I let out a sigh of relief that things didn't take a turn for the worse. "Edie, how many times did I tell you not to do this? You've been warned."

"So if Dorothy takes a shot at me, then it's going to be all my fault?" Edie said, adjusting her tiara, then placing her hands on her hips.

"Yes," Gran deadpanned.

I was not only worried that it could happen one day, but I was also extremely concerned about us not spotting Edie. Where did she just pop out from? Literally nobody was here a couple of seconds ago. Especially with that tiara of hers and the tinsel reflecting the streetlamp's light, we should've spotted her a mile away. How did we miss her? Have we become this rusty since leaving our old life behind? That was deeply troubling and made me doubt our forthcoming mission. If we didn't even manage to evade Edie, how were we supposed to sneak into a building without being seen?

"Edie, how did you just sneak up on us like that?" I asked. "What? Were you hiding behind the bushes just waiting for us to come out?"

"Are you crazy?" Edie asked. "Why would I do that? I was just coming home and headed for my front door when I felt something squishy between my toes. So I bent over to sort it out, and that's when I heard your front door opening. Naturally, I walked over here."

Ugh.

That made sense. She was hidden by her potted plants in her yard when she bent down. And of course something was squishy, she was wearing the leather sandals, trying to be more like Gran. Those straps only gave you an itch.

Even so, Gran and I never experienced this much lousy timing and bad luck before moving to Florida.

"The real question isn't whether I was intentionally stalking you," Edie said. „It's how normal folks manage to have reflexes to shoot and stab someone just because they got startled."

I exchanged looks with Gran. "Because we're big on self-defense classes?"

Edie rolled her eyes. "Yeah, sure, you two always think someone's out to get you. It's like you're living in total paranoia."

I was this close to blurting out, "Yes, we are!"

"It's a weird world out there, okay?" I said. "You never know what bad things are going to happen and this is just the way we cope with it. So can we please just drop it for now?"

Edie adjusted the tinsel around herself. "Fine." Then she gave us the once-over and furrowed her eyebrows. "So, where *are* you going?"

"Um . . . out?" I said.

"Dorothy is dressed like Batman, and you look like the Black Widow," Edie said. "You're going to do something bad, aren't you?"

It was funny how Edie sometimes almost read my mind. I liked the Black Widow reference, though.

After a moment of silence I said, "Define bad."

"Bad, as in, it has something to do with Dr. Curtis and that Lola girl, doesn't it?" Edie said. "You have a lead and you're going to snoop around." Then she didn't even let me answer and said, "Great, let's go."

"No," I said and shook my head vehemently. "That's out of the question. Don't even think about it. You are not taking part in this. Edie, it's too dangerous for you, don't you get that?"

"How can it be too dangerous? Look at you. I'm going there with James Bond and his sidekick. You even said it yourself; your reflex is to pull out your artillery. So, technically, I'm safest when I'm around you."

I so didn't have time for this. I knew exactly what Edie was doing, but I could see right through it. She might have gotten used to our lifestyle in the last few months, but she was still a regular civilian who reacted like one to dead bodies or anything similar. She got a taste of that adrenaline kick.

And wait a minute, was she looking at *me* when she said "sidekick?"

Gran and I could've easily got in the car and ignored Edie completely, but honestly, I was afraid she would follow us and if she did, then she would be doing it in her own car, in that candy-apple-red Chevrolet Impala, just to spite us. That would mean blowing up this whole mission because you could spot that car from the moon.

"Edie, please go home and—"

"Aw, for god's sake," Gran said and threw her hands up in the air. "We don't have time for this. You know she's gonna come with us either way so let's just go. She's a grown woman. If anything happens to her, then she'll take responsibility for it."

Edie put on a wide grin and skipped around the car to the passenger side, pushing Gran aside. "Great, I call shotgun."

I could tell Gran wished she had one right now.

***

We were about two minutes away from the ME's office. Gran reluctantly sat in the back—since this was her mission, not Edie's—but she should have gotten used to it by now. Edie was smiling and looking outside the window, still wearing her party outfit. So there we were. Batman, his sidekick, and the Joker.

I told Edie there was no way I was taking responsibility if Ryker found out she came with us. I did feel a teensy bit responsible, though. That was just the thing. I couldn't say no to her, yet I felt this inner impulse to protect her. I'd never forgive myself if anything went wrong. What was odd was that I usually felt like this for my people back in Oregon. My family members, the Falcons, were the ones I had felt emotional and protective about, not regular civilians who didn't even know who I was. And I suspected I needed to be extra protective of Edie tonight.

The other hurdle was explaining to Edie where we were going and what we planned on doing. I opted to tell her the truth. Well, almost the truth. We explained to her that we needed to see Lola's body to understand the nature of her strangulation wounds and to see what other clues we might find. That is how Edie found out how she died and made the sign of the cross again.

We didn't mention any tattoo.

She gasped when she realized we were going to break into the ME's office to examine a corpse in the morgue. Her expression turned pale.

"I told you not to come with us," I said. "Now you have to deal with what we're up to. If your knees start to buckle, then I'm gonna let you out here and you're going to take a cab back home."

I sensed Edie's nervous gulp, but she quickly recovered. She lifted her chin and adjusted the tiara in her curls and the sash around her body. "No, no, all is good," she said. "This is what I wanted, to feel like I'm living my life."

"Because all of your partying at the retirement complex is not enough?" Gran asked from the back.

"Oh, come on, that's just innocent fun, Dorothy," Edie said. "The only real danger there is if someone is breaking their hip. But that hardly fazes anyone anymore. We have the ambulance on speed dial. But this, *this* is real living."

"With emphasis on living, right?" I asked.

"Of course," Edie said and smiled at me. "You're taking care of me."

"Exactly," I said. "That's what I meant. I have one extra worry now."

We told Edie not to say anything to Leonardi. I scrambled my brain for a reason, and we told her that he just didn't approve of it but I wanted to go through with it anyhow.

Edie frowned and said, "*That* guy didn't approve of this? That's very peculiar. I'd have thought he'd jump at this opportunity right away. He doesn't really come off as a scaredy cat or a rule follower. He comes off more like a slime ball. Piper, tell me again why you're working with him?"

"Edie, we've already been through this," I said. "Let's not do it again. You're going to get the same answers."

"Fine," Edie said. "So if we find out anything, you're just going to keep it from him?" Edie asked.

"No, of course I'm going to tell him then," I said and sought Gran's glance in the rearview mirror. The primary reason behind this mission was to identify Lola's tattoo, something Leonardi knew nothing about. However, we could maintain the façade that our goal was to uncover more about her cause of death or any potential clues on her body.

I parked the car in the neighboring residential area near the outskirts of the industrial zone where the ME's office was. I chose a spot on the second block amidst other parked cars to reduce suspicion.

It was about 9:30 p.m. when we got out of the car.

Gran was sizing up Edie. "You look like a disco ball," she said.

Edie threw her hands up in the air. "Well, we needed to go right away, so what do you want from me?"

"You didn't exactly have to come with us, did you?" Gran shot back.

I got in between them and said, "Guys, we don't have time for this. What's done is done, Edie is here with us, so we're just going to have to roll with it."

"You know, the way I'm dressed isn't too bad," Edie said. "If something goes wrong and we get caught, I can always play the innocent, confused old lady card."

I blinked twice.

Goddammit, I hadn't thought of that.

It was brilliant!

"She's right," I said to Gran. "What would the cops do if they found a senior wearing a tiara and tinsel over a Prom queen sash late at night out here?"

Gran shifted from one leg to another and seemed to think about it. "Well, for starters, they would call to see which mental hospital Edie escaped from. But yeah . . . I guess that could work. I'd buy the confused old lady number. Maybe we could add some more stuff to her."

"Now let's not get carried away, okay?" Edie said, putting her hand up.

"But if you're the confused old lady, then who are we?" Gran asked.

Edie stepped back and studied us. Then she shrugged and said, "You're the two orderlies who were after me."

Gran and I looked at each other. Yep. The only thing missing was the tranquilizer gun.

"Alright, listen up," I said. "We have about a six-minute trek to the building. Here's what we're gonna do when we get there."

I assigned Edie to be our lookout right outside the building entrance. That was after we'd decide our best point of entry. I preferred avoiding the front entrance, opting instead to check for any accessible back doors or open windows. Edie put up resistance since she wanted to get inside with us, however, I explained that joining us would mean she'd come face to face with a frozen, naked dead body. Edie then said, "Okay, I didn't think this through." And agreed to be the lookout.

Surveying the surroundings to avoid being seen, we made our way to the building. We passed the small lake and we crossed a huge almost vacant parking space and reached the building of the ME's office. Further in the distance, other administrative building structures were visible, and I could see light in some of the windows. Luckily, we were far enough to remain inconspicuous.

"This is it," I said, looking at the map on my phone screen. "Lola is somewhere in there."

Edie shivered. "That sounds morbid." She readjusted the tinsel around her body for the umpteenth time, along with the tiara nestled in her curls. "I'm ready."

We glued ourselves against the side wall of the building put on the gloves. Luckily, we always brought extras, so we had a pair for Edie too. I went ahead and circled around to scout the area and identify the optimal entry points. After a few minutes, I returned and was relieved to see that Gran and Edie didn't get in each other's hair. I didn't hear any gunshots and didn't see any bloodshed. So far, so good.

I reported that all the windows were closed, given the building's flat structure, there was no need to concern ourselves with upper levels. I saw no light inside, indicating no one was there. I suggested that the metal back door was our best shot to get in. The lock seemed easy enough to crack and there were obviously no video cameras around it. Or anywhere, for that matter.

We all tiptoed to the back door and listened carefully for any movement. We heard nothing so I did my thing and started working on the lock.

194

"I know you've done this before but it's fascinating," Edie said, staring at my lock-picking art. "I still don't know where you learn to do this."

"You know there are classes where they teach you this, don't you?" I said, still focused on the lock.

"Just like those self-defense classes you're talking about?" Edie said.

"Edie, you're distracting us," Gran said.

Edie nodded then mimed the move of locking her lips and tossing the key away.

Gran rolled her eyes. "As if that's going to work," she said.

I did quick work of the lock then opened the metal door. I pushed it wider and was trying to hear any movement coming from inside. But nothing came. It was total darkness.

"Okay, Edie, you stay here pressed to this wall next to this door and watch out for any movement outside. If anybody comes, you send that text message right away. Got it?"

We gave Edie Gran's phone, since Edie never used hers. We pre-texted a message that read "Danger!" that Edie only had to send out.

Edie nodded, fumbling with the sash around her polka-dotted dress. I shook my head. If this was our lookout, then we were in big trouble. I just hoped I'd given her clear enough instructions and that she could discern when a real dangerous situation arose.

"So you got it, right?" I asked again. "You don't send that message if there's a rat scurrying around or a raccoon or an alligator pass by. Just when you see a person."

"You mean you're more afraid of a human being than you are of an alligator?" Edie asked.

I thought about it. An alligator wouldn't have me kicked out of witness protection. "Yes, that is what I mean. For an alligator we have Gran's gun."

"You have that for people too," Edie said and glued herself to the wall.

"And with good reason," Gran said. "Now let's stop yapping and do this."

We left Edie at the door, and I flicked on my flashlight as Gran and I entered and maneuvered through the dark corridor. We refrained from using both flashlights simultaneously to minimize the risk of drawing attention. As long as Gran stayed near me, we found that only one flashlight was necessary.

We moved down the hallway, my flashlight sweeping from side to side. I was completely absorbed in the moment, my attention fully engaged.

To our left and right stood offices, while some rooms seemed designated for janitorial purposes.

We continued moving forward and a spacious area opened in front of us. As I directed the flashlight around, I realized this was the reception area. Desks were strewn about, and file cabinets were placed against the back walls. On the opposite side from us I could see the entry to another hallway and Gran and I made our way toward it, traversing the waiting area and passing by what appeared to be the main entrance. A dim, neon light flicked from the ceiling in this hallway. Here, there were other rooms, but these ones were closed.

While shining the flashlight beam on the doors to our left and right, I accidentally tripped over a low cart on wheels, creating a loud clang of metal. Gran collided into me from behind.

Both Gran and I let out a groan.

"Ugh, my foot," I said in a whisper.

"What are you doing?" Gran asked, de-glueing herself from me.

I pushed the metal cart away. "I thought this would be a good time to smash my foot, what do you think?"

Even in the dark, I could feel Gran rolling her eyes.

We slowly opened every room only to find they were more offices, laboratories and meeting rooms. We moved even further down the hallway, and I checked my phone just to see if everything was okay. Edie had not sent the message and I hoped she didn't need to.

At last, we came across a large glass window and a door next to it. We entered and I shone my flashlight around. This was the morgue, enveloped in an eerie chill. Rows of metal tables lined the area, alongside various instruments, resembling a sterile hospital setting. Along the walls there were slender neon blue lights that cast a somber ambience. Not a single window was present within the room, there was only the glass pane facing the hallway. That reminded me of observation windows during medical procedures.

It was only now that Gran switched on her own flashlight. We scanned the back walls, looking for the body storage refrigerators. I felt a ping of excitement and sensed a reminiscent aura of my former life while on this mission with Gran. There was this unspoken understanding between us. We moved seamlessly, knowing our roles instinctively. In those moments, I felt in control of my life again. I felt like myself. I felt alive again.

# CLOSED CASKET

We closed the door behind us and approached the refrigerators.

Gran wiped her forehead with her brows drawn in concentration. At least it was cooler in here, but we were still warm coming from the outside.

"Why did you even wear the jacket?" I asked. "You have to make peace with the fact that you're in Florida now."

Gran let out a low snort. "Pot calling the kettle black much?"

I sighed. That was always her retort, and I couldn't argue with it.

"Here it is," Gran said and directed the flashlight towards four closed solid-looking metal doors, two on top and two beneath.

Behind one of those doors lay Lola. We didn't know if the other ones were empty or potentially housed another frozen corpse. Good thing Edie wasn't here, she would instantly faint. Thankfully, she would have all that tinsel and the sash to cushion her fall.

"I'm opening the lower ones first," Gran said while I moved closer to her. I shone the light as she opened the first door and icy air greeted us. We peeked inside. The chamber was connected to the one next to it.

No corpses on the trays.

Then Gran moved to the upper ones. She opened the one in the upper left corner. I shone the light inside and we saw two feet. Regular civilians would freak out right about now. Gran and I were totally unfazed. We were all going to end up like this, so why the drama?

Gran pulled out the tray and the whole body came out. It was covered with a morgue sheet. Although the feet looked like they belonged to a man, Gran uncovered the dead body's face and we leaned in closer. Nope. This was not Lola. This was indeed a guy. We didn't know the guy so we didn't care about the guy. Gran pulled the sheet over his face again and shoved the tray back in and closed the door.

We moved to the door next to it and I felt my heart rate going up. This was the last one. Lola had to be in there.

Gran hesitated for a second. I was sure she was just as nervous about it as I was. She then opened the door and I directed the light inside. Again, we saw two feet, but they looked more feminine.

Gran and I shared a glance before she pulled out the tray. With a swift motion, she revealed the face.

There she was.

Lola.

Her reddish hair was almost sparkling in the beam of the flashlight. It matched the same reddish strangulation marks around her neck. I looked closer. There was a slightly larger circle mark on the left side of her neck. I deducted the killer must have had a ring on his finger. That was not enough of a clue to her killer, a lot of people were wearing rings.

Gran gestured towards her feet. "Lift the cover and let's check out that tattoo," she said.

I moved at the end of the tray and just as I was about to pull up the cover, a loud clank echoed from somewhere outside the room.

I froze and cut my eyes at Gran.

"What was that?" she asked.

"That was the metal cart from outside," I said, gulping hard. "Someone's in here."

# Chapter Twelve

GRAN AND I INSTANTLY turned off our flashlights and stiffened. The metal cart was around the reception area and I recounted how much time it took us from the reception to this room.

Crap.

We needed to hide fast if the person was on their way here too. Even with our flashlights off, the neon blue lights were still casting enough light so anyone passing by the glass pane could easily spot us.

"Wait," Gran whispered, as I just started to move. "What if it's Edie?"

I had thought about that too.

"But why would she be coming in?" I whispered back.

"Uhm, because it's Edie?" Gran said.

Okay, she had a point. But still. We couldn't risk it not being Edie and Gran knew that. I gave her a look and she understood.

We frantically looked around and our eyes zeroed in on the two empty refrigerators. Then we looked at each other and we both sighed. We needed to do what we needed to do.

But also, we came here to do one thing, the most important thing, and some idiot was keeping us from it. I quickly uncovered Lola's feet, but I couldn't see the exact shape of the tattoo in the dim light. I snapped a picture with my phone, without using a flash so I had no idea if I did it right. Using a flash would have been a dead giveaway.

We sprang into action and in one jump, we were opening the lower doors. Just as we turned to get in there feet first, Gran's jacket snagged on the door handle.

"What are you doing?" I whispered hastily. "Get in here."

"My jacket's stuck!" she whispered back, and I could see she was struggling to get free.

"Well, then take it off!" I said.

Gran cursed under her breath but in one fell swoop, she ripped the jacket off and left it hanging from the door handle. Then we quickly moved inside and slid ourselves onto the tray.

God, it was freezing in here. How ironic was that? *Now* I was too cold. On the verge of, if we stayed in there long enough, becoming corpses ourselves.

Because the two chambers were connected, I could see Gran laying on the tray beside me. I felt

kind of sorry for her now that she was jacket-less.
Funny how she was wearing that jacket out in the
hot temperatures but was here in the freezing cold
only in her top.

We didn't fully shut the doors to the chambers.
We left them slightly ajar to maintain somewhat of a
view of the room outside.

My heart rate was through the roof as I heard
the door to the morgue slowly opening. So many
thoughts ran through my mind. Was this Edie? This
couldn't have been her. She had clear instructions
what to do. Why would she come in sneaking? But if
she was still outside at the back door, where did this
intruder come in? Through the main entrance?
Through a window? I had already established that
the back door was the most efficient way to get in.
So why use other entrances? Then again, I had no
idea who this person was and what their expertise
was. Often times, I have dealt with complete idiots.
You would think I'd rather deal with idiots rather
than with geniuses, but I didn't. Idiots were more
unpredictable, making them more dangerous.

But what if this person was a Falcon? Then
we'd be royally screwed.

The way I was wedged into that frozen
chamber, I couldn't reach my back pocket to confirm

Edie didn't send that text message, but I was sure she didn't, since I had the phone on vibrate and I also didn't see any messages displayed when I pulled out the phone to snap a picture of the tattoo. So that meant the intruder used another entry point. Or even worse. He used the same back door only he put Edie out of order before she could send the message. Shivers ran down my spine. If anything happened to Edie, I would make them pay so bad, they'd regret ever coming here.

I heard the door opening wide and footsteps coming in. From our vantage point, neither Gran, nor I could see the person coming in. I suspected we couldn't have seen much either way, since the fluorescent blue glow didn't provide much light. We would probably see more of an outline rather than distinct lines.

Gran's jacket hanging from the door handle stressed me out. Wouldn't anybody who came in think: what is a black leather jacket doing hanging from the door of a body storage refrigerator in a morgue? Hopefully they'd think a staff member just left it here, even if that was far-fetched.

The footsteps were nearing just as I felt my phone vibrate. Damn it. I couldn't even pull it out to read the message. Was it Edie sending the message?

Was there another person outside and Edie deemed it dangerous or risky?

And the most important question of all was: what was the intruder doing here? Clearly it was someone who was not supposed to be here, or else they would have come in a different way. This person here was sneaking around. It was not the ME nor a staffer. No, this was someone else. With their own agenda.

I glanced over at Gran and she seemed just as focused looking through the door crack and try to distinguish what was going on in the outside.

I peeked again and the footsteps had gotten so near, the intruder was literally on the other side of the refrigerator doors. I gulped hard. I felt torn between the distress of getting caught and the rush of adrenaline from my past life that I longed for.

The intruder stopped in front of the chambers, and I could almost feel him trying to decide which ones to open.

Crap!

If they decided to open the ones we were hiding in first, our only option would be to jump out with guns and knives blazing. They would have a heart attack! But we didn't know if they were armed, and our training was different, so we would do what we had to do.

Unfortunately, I still couldn't get a glimpse of the intruder.

I could feel Gran tensing up beside me. She too was ready for the battle if it came to it.

Then I heard a soft groan. Definitely male. By the sounds of it, he saw Gran's leather jacket hanging on the door handle.

Double crap.

I heard some more grunting, then I could hear him take the jacket and move it on an empty tray a couple of feet away. Gran tensed a bit more. That's when I saw a glimpse of dark-blue jeans. Okay, it wasn't much, but it was something.

He moved back in front of the refrigerator, and I heard a handle and a door clicking.

I let out a breath. He was opening the upper chambers.

So he also came here for Lola. It couldn't have been for the other dead guy. But why? Why risk it? The only explanation would have been that he was Lola's murderer, and he came back . . . for her? Okay, we also came here for Lola, but I knew we were not her murderer. The only reason her murderer would come for her was to hide clues that would make him a suspect.

I heard a disgusted grunt as he opened one of the chamber doors and pulled out the tray. By the sound of it, it was the other dead guy that he spotted. He quickly shoved the tray back in.

He then slid the other door open, and I couldn't believe our bad luck that he was standing so close to us on the other side of the door, and we still couldn't see him through the open door slip. I could almost hear him breathing, though.

With a creak, he pulled out Lola's tray. My pulse surged. I was anxious to find out what he intended to do now.

Just as I held in my breath, a voice echoed down the hallway, a cheery "hello" accompanied by the unmistakable clatter of someone stumbling into that damn metal cart.

It was Edie!

Right on cue. The timing couldn't have been better if it was rehearsed by a Broadway director on a caffeine high.

The intruder grumbled and shoved the tray back in. He turned and I could hear him making a run for it. But he would be bumping into Edie outside and who knew what he would do. Gran must have figured the same and we both burst out of our icy hideouts at the same time like two ninjas dressed in identical black attire.

I was hoping to get a somewhat visible glimpse at our intruder, but he was already out the door of the morgue. Just as Gran and I pulled out our weapons, we heard a loud thud outside in the hallway. We flew through the door and saw Edie on her back, wiggling her arms and legs in the air like a stranded turtle. She held a mop in one hand. The intruder kept running, presumably to the main entrance.

"Don't shoot!" I shouted to Gran, just as she was taking aim. "See if she's okay!" I pointed at Edie as I started running after him.

We needed this guy alive, and we needed to know why he was here and if he was a Falcon, although coming here alone was not exactly typical of a Falcon.

I raced through the dimly lit hallway. The intruder had a head start but I knew what I was capable of and how good I was at this. Another thing I couldn't exactly put on a resume.

Just before reaching the reception area, I gained in on him and pulling my knife out, I pounced. We both landed on the ground, and I had his legs locked together. In the weak beam of the hallway light, I saw the guy was wearing a checkered blue shirt and some kind of golden trim along the edges. Weird.

He instantly started kicking and I tightened my grip on his legs. I extended my knife-holding arm, and I could feel the blade scratching his flesh. It was most likely his arm or his hand. But it wasn't too deep, I didn't want the guy to bleed to death.

Just as I was about to threaten him with his life, he pushed hard into my shoulder, and I let out a grunt. He used that moment to reach for that stupid metal cart and pushed it right into me. Instinctively, I let go of his legs and he sprang up and ran for the entrance door. The pain in my shoulder and in my upper body paralyzed me for a few seconds. Those seconds were vital and by the time I thrust away the cart and got up, half running, half wobbling to the door, he was already gone.

Cursing, I glimpsed some movement in the distance, but I knew I wouldn't be able to catch up with him. I shook my head. Then I saw the front door was forcibly opened. Probably used a crowbar. Who was this guy? Who breaks into a building like that? It couldn't have been more obvious. Like I had already thought, this guy was an idiot. A desperate one but a lucky one that got away. One that had no idea how to do this smoothly. This was not a professional intruder. This was not a Falcon member, nor someone hired by them. This was too amateurish.

A few windows opened in the buildings farther away. The few people who were still working probably heard some commotion and were now in alert mode. Great. Just what we needed.

I quickly shut the door and trudged back to the others, just as Gran was running towards me in the hallway.

"Where is he?" she asked out of breath. "What happened?"

"He got away," I said, and almost put my fist through the wall.

"See?" Gran said and shoved her gun back in her waist. "I should have shot him."

Back to Edie, she was already standing and still clutching that mop. She didn't even wait for me to talk and said sheepishly, "I found this in one of the rooms. Thought it might come in handy."

"Of course you did," I muttered. "Are you okay? Are you hurt?"

She nodded. "I'm fine. Really. Just hurt my elbow a bit."

"What were you thinking?" I threw my hands in the air.

"I'm sorry," she whined, "but I didn't get a reply to my message, so I got worried, because you were taking so long. So I decided to check if everything was okay." She explained she had sent a message asking us if everything was okay.

"Oh, for the love of Pete," Gran rolled her eyes.

I shook my head. "Edie, you had specific instructions. These were not it. What if the intruder had a weapon?"

Edie scratched the back of her head then pointed to the mop. "I had this."

I pinched the bridge of my nose. "I don't even know what to say. We don't have time to argue right now. We need to get out of here."

"But did you find out what you needed to find out?" Edie asked.

I exchanged glances with Gran.

"We heard the guy come in just as we were about to find that out," I said.

"Well then go ahead and look again," Edie said. "The guy is gone."

"We can't," I said. "We have to leave like right now. The cops will be here any minute."

I explained seeing windows being opened in the other buildings. Someone had to have called the police.

We needed to scramble.

Gran quickly ran inside the morgue again, grabbed her jacket which made Edie frown and I turned on the flashlight that guided us to the back door where we came in. I peeked outside and the coast was clear.

We trudged in a beeline back to where I parked and just as I was starting up the car, we heard sirens in the distance. Luckily, we weren't even near the building compound, and I patted myself on the shoulder that I parked the car in this residential area.

We drove off and we collectively exhaled loudly when the siren noises were swallowed by the night. There was complete silence in the car for a couple of minutes longer and my body starting aching, as the adrenaline rush wore off.

Edie finally broke the silence. "What the heck happened in there?"

"You butted your nose in and ruined it, that's what happened," Gran said.

Edie huffed. "I thought you were in trouble. Which you were."

"We had it under control," Gran said from the back seat. She dusted off her leather jacket, as if it had morgue cooties all over it. "Piper, did we leave any evidence behind?"

"I don't think so," I said. Sure, there would be evidence that someone broke in and we also left the broom in the middle of the hallway, but we all had gloves on, so we didn't leave any fingerprints. When I made my way from the main entrance back to Edie and Gran, I saw no blood splatters on the floor where I cut the guy with my knife. At least, nowhere I pointed my flashlight at. And as for Edie . . . somehow, she was still intact in her party outfit. I just hoped she didn't leave any tinsel bits behind or else she would really have to play the confused old lady card.

"Who do you think that was and what was he doing there?" Edie asked.

That was the burning question, indeed.

"Do you think that was Lola's killer?" Edie continued.

"Well, who else would be lurking around at night in a morgue?" Gran asked.

"Um . . . us?" Edie deadpanned.

I let out a laugh although I really didn't feel like it. We were so close to getting caught but we were also very close to catching a potential killer. I also felt a bit relieved. I was pretty sure that couldn't have been one of the Falcons or a hitman they hired. The behavior just didn't scream professional.

"We don't know who that man was, Edie," I said. "It's safe to say that could have been Lola's killer coming back to find evidence of his murder and make it disappear. A.k.a. make Lola disappear. He tried it once, but it didn't work."

"Well, I'll tell you one thing," Edie said as she looked down at her elbow. "I regret so much letting him get away. I should have swung that broom harder. This is going to leave a huge bruise. How am I going look in my prom dress with a purple bruise on my arm?"

"Is that what you're thinking of right now?" Gran asked. "Prom night?"

I laughed. "She's been spending too much time around us."

"Which is a good thing," Edie said. "You two are bringing fun to a whole other level."

Oh, good god. If even Edie thought this was fun, then we were in big trouble. Our future looked very grim. If I continued to work with Leonardi, I might have to bring Edie in as well or else she would force herself in. Without pay.

"You already have your dresses picked out?" Edie asked us.

Another long moment of silence fell over us. Dresses? I didn't even think of that up until now. Prom nights required dresses for the women. For normal people. We were not normal.

Understanding what the silence was all about, Edie sighed and said, "Do you even wear dresses? Like ever? I've never seen you in one, Piper. And I've only seen Dorothy in a dress once."

"Yeah, she burned the dress on that same day," I said.

That was the I'm-trying-to-fit-in-here-in-Florida-dress.

What a surprise, it didn't work.

"You wouldn't catch me dead in a dress again," Gran said. "Where would I hide my gun?"

"I'm sure you could use a garter for that," Edie said. "If it would make you feel any better, we could shop for a black leather dress for you."

Garter? Black leather dress? I cringed. I did not want to have images of my grandmother wearing a black leather dress and a garter underneath. Although I was sure Theodore would have a heart attack seeing Gran in an outfit like that. The good sort.

"It makes me nauseous even when you talk about it," Gran said to Edie.

But Edie completely ignored her. "Well, there's still a couple of days until the party on Saturday," she said. "We have some time to jazz you up and make you presentable for it."

Gran and I knew better not to argue with Edie. We both knew we wouldn't let anyone jazz us up but we decided to let Edie believe that.

"Edie, we have more important things to deal with right now," I said.

"You're right," Edie said. "We have to catch Lola's killer."

"Excuse me?" I asked.

"We're still on the case, aren't we?" she asked as I passed the welcome sign to the retirement complex. "We won't let that guy get away, will we?"

"*We*?" I asked.

"Of course we," Edie said. "That guy pushed me to the floor and almost broke my elbow. I'm in on this too now. Are you telling me you're letting him get away after he hurt me?"

She was doing it again. Emotional blackmail as one of the traits of her complex personality. She was a master at it and exploited that for her own personal gain and entertainment.

I was growing to have respect for that even if I was on the losing end.

"No Edie, nobody is letting him get away," I said. "If he's indeed Lola's killer, then he'll get caught eventually."

"Exactly, and we are the ones who should get him."

Neither Gran nor I answered to that. I was sure Gran was thinking the same thing I was. Which was we had no idea what to do. The intruder may not have been a Falcon and may not have had any affiliations to them, but we still needed to find out about Lola's tattoo. When we got to Gran's house, we would have to look at the picture I snapped. I still couldn't believe our bad timing and the intruder appearing at the exact worst possible time. With the cops on their way to the ME's office, I also knew there wasn't any time to pull out Lola's tray again, take the picture, and shove the tray back in. There was only time for Gran to quickly grab her jacket.

It was almost eleven p.m. when I steered the car onto our street. As I was pulling up to the curb in front of Gran's house, an unexpected loud rumble startled me.

Man, I was really on edge. The old Piper would've been way more serene and composed on a mission like this.

A sexy looking Harley rolled with a thrilling purr from around the corner, its black chrome gleaming under the streetlights.

There was only one sexy bike around here and I knew whom it belonged to.

Ryker.

# Chapter Thirteen

"UH-OH," EDIE SAID and adjusted her tiara. "We're in trouble."

I cut the engine and rested my head back. "How? Like how? How does he do that?"

"Because he's good," Edie said.

"We have to be better then," Gran said.

None of us got out of the car. We all waited for Ryker to come to us. Which he did. He parked his Harley right in front of Edie's house and I tried not to drool at the sight of him. I mean, *it*! At the sight of *it*. The bike.

I was trying hard to focus on that beauty of a bike and ignore Ryker's body that looked good even under the beam of the streetlamps. He took his helmet off and walked to us in long, determined strides. I could already see on his face he was not amused.

"Deny everything," was all I was able to say to the others before Ryker made a sign that I should lower my window.

This guy had like a sixth sense for the trouble we kept getting ourselves in and it was like trying to hide a lit firework in a dark room when he was around.

He leaned down and rested his elbows on the window frame. He glanced at every one of us, his brows furrowing at the sight of Edie, the tinsel-wrapped, tiara-wearing future Prom queen, who giggled nervously.

"Hey Ryker, what's up?" I asked, feigning innocence.

He didn't return the greeting, instead still looking at us with the scrutiny of a hawk eyeing its prey. "What the hell were you three doing at the medical examiner's office?"

I gulped hard. He went right in, didn't even soften the blow of the question.

Then he added, looking at Edie, "Dressed like that?"

"Where? What office?" Edie's eyes widened in surprise.

"What makes you think that?" I asked.

"We were . . . um . . . dress shopping, not that it's any of your business," Gran added from the back. I gave her a look out of the corner of my eye. Awesome. That was what stuck with her.

Ryker raised an eyebrow. "Dress shopping? At this hour?"

"Late-night shopping," Gran said, shifting in her seat. "You know, for the prom."

I got in there. "It's a special, um, night shop." I was trying hard to keep a straight face.

Edie leaned over my lap, her tiara sparking in the streetlight. "Ryker, we had to get the perfect dresses for the prom. You know how these things go."

Ryker glanced inside the car. "And where are those dresses?"

There was silence.

"We placed the dresses on hold," Edie finally chirped out. "We're still not sure about them yet."

Ryker didn't sketch one move of his face. "I got a call from one of my contacts in the PD. Something went down at the ME's office and witnesses reported a couple of people emerging from the building, one of them looking like the lovechild of Mardi Gras and Fourth of July."

Gran and I burst out laughing. Tears streamed from our faces. I couldn't have described it better.

Edie scrunched up her nose. "Hmph," she said, and I could tell she was swallowing down her pride. "Those people clearly saw someone else."

"So you're sticking with your dress shopping story?" Ryker asked.

I wiped away the tears of laughter and got serious again. "We're not sticking to anything. That is what happened."

"Sure, 'cause when I look at you, the word 'dress' immediately comes to mind," he said, casting a glance at Gran.

She leaned forward. "What I wear and when I wear it is not your problem."

Ryker ignored her. Then he asked, "Where was Leonardi? Wasn't he with you?"

There was silence again.

"Like I've already told you, we were not at the whoever's office and neither was Leonardi," I said.

Ryker grinned. "So you did this without him? Interesting. Trouble in paradise?"

This guy really exasperated me. He was too good for comfort.

"I can't keep repeating what we've just told you," I said.

Great. This was supposed to be a mission for Gran and myself. Now, not only there were two additional people who got involved, but they could also inform Leonardi about the outing tonight. I didn't have an explanation ready for him regarding our decision to leave him out of it. Especially since I told him I was not sure of continuing working on this case. Ugh.

"Look, Ryker," I said, ready to end this evening. "We don't have to justify anything to you. Gran and I are heading inside now."

"Yeah," Gran said. "We're tired from . . . a long night of shopping."

We stepped out of the car and Ryker must have sensed he wouldn't be getting anything else out of us. Did he really expect that, though? He was dealing with pros here. His own grandmother was the best one.

"I wish you wouldn't keep putting yourselves into danger," Ryker said, as Gran and I turned to head inside.

I saw Edie giving us a subtle wink and I took it to mean that she would be over at Gran's house first thing in the morning. What did we get ourselves into?

***

As soon as we got inside, I shut the door behind me, and Gran said, "Show it to me."

As I pulled out my cell, she added with a shake of her head, "This is exhausting, having to hold back every time. I want to go back!"

224

Wow. It was not so often that Gran really expressed her deepest emotions about our current situation. This one really struck a chord with her, or maybe it was a buildup of stressors.

"I know, Gran" I said. "I miss our home too."

Tears welled up in my eyes. That was how fast this could go. That longing in my heart was so deep, and I always tried to push it down. And then it took one mention of it, and it all came out.

Then I shook out of it.

I pulled up the picture of Lola's tattoo and we were both staring at it.

It was blurry and almost black.

Gran looked up at me. "This is it?"

I sighed. "This is it."

"We went through all that trouble and almost got caught for basically nothing?" Gran asked.

"Well, not nothing," I said, squinting. "It is something. You can somehow see the shape of a bird."

"Yeah, but we already knew that," Gran said. "We didn't find out anything else about that tattoo."

"Don't you think I hate this as much as you do?" I asked, throwing my hands up. "Especially since now, no way can we go back there. The cops would have it covered by now. They'd probably set up

security now, knowing that Lola is of that much
interest."

"You know what we could do if we weren't here,
in this dump?" Gran asked. "We could hit up Petal
Petey. He'd scrape that picture clean in a jiffy. Then
we would see a clear image."

I felt my eyes watering again. I remembered
Petal Petey. He got that nickname on account of him
running a flower shop. Another great venue for
laundering money. I sometimes used to watch over
his shoulder as he hacked into the city surveillance
cameras—just for kicks—swapping the regular
traffic footage with videos of dancing clowns. God, I
missed him so much.

But obviously we couldn't turn to Petey now.
We didn't have him at our disposal anymore nor as a
friend. And since Petal Petey was one of the Falcons,
he probably wanted us dead now too.

"What do we do now?" Gran asked.

I breathed out deeply. "I have no idea."

\*\*\*

My heart nearly leaped out of my chest as I
heard a loud bang.

Ugh.

It was like Groundhog Day ever since we got to Florida. We didn't need an alarm clock. We had Edie.

I threw the blanket away from the couch in a rather aggressive move. I felt cranky.

I trudged to the door and swung it wide open just as Edie was about to knock again. She yelped and immediately ducked, holding a tray of strawberry pie in her hands. The tray trembled, almost toppling to the ground, but Edie managed to steady it with a series of wobbles.

I rolled my eyes. "Relax, I don't have my knife on me."

"Well, who the heck can tell when you don't?" Edie asked, standing back up. "I've developed the most curious reflexes since you and Dorothy got here."

*Tell me about it.*

"Fair enough," I said. "Come on, Gran is not up yet."

"I can see you're in a bad mood," Edie said, closing the door behind her.

I headed over to the coffee machine. "You would be right. I am."

"Is it about your new job?" Edie asked and took her seat at the kitchen table. She put the pie on the table and started cutting pieces.

227

"I don't know if I *am* doing this new job," I said.

"Well, we broke into a morgue last night and you poked around a dead body," Edie said matter-of-factly. "I'd say you're definitely doing this job."

I put on coffee then turned around and faced Edie. It was then that I saw something sparkling in her white curls.

"Why are you still wearing the tiara?" I asked.

"Why wouldn't I?" Edie said, like my inquiry was the one that raised questions.

I waved my hand in dismissal. "You know what? Never mind. I'm surprised you didn't wear it even before the prom contest."

"Me too, actually," Edie said, grinning.

I eyed the divine smelling pie on the table. "Is that fresh?" I asked.

Edie nodded vehemently. "Of course. Baked it this morning. Let it sit out for an hour or so. That gives it the best texture and taste."

I looked at my cell. 8:07 a.m. I looked back up at Edie and raised an eyebrow.

"You're sleeping your life away," she said.

Little did she know about my sleeping rhythm when I was working behind the bar at Choppers. I would often get in bed at around 5 a.m. and sleep until noon. Another memory that I pushed out of my mind.

"How's your elbow?" I asked.

Edie contorted and looked at her arm. "Bruised like a peach. You know, you get to this age and all it takes is a peck and you're all blue-d up. How's your shoulder?"

"Better," I said. My whole upper body ached a bit, but I had felt worse pain in my life, so I really didn't care about that right now.

Ten minutes later, we were sipping our coffee over pie as Gran trudged out of her bedroom. She peeked inside the living room, stared at us, let out a soft grunt, then trudged into the bathroom.

"*She* could use a tiara," Edie said.

I smiled. When Edie was right, she was right.

Another thirty minutes later, Gran was sitting at the table next to us with her own mug of coffee. We were debating our case at hand. Well, at least the part we could debate with Edie around.

Last night, Gran and I were discussing the other parts that concerned us and only us but were somehow interlocked with finding Lola's murderer. The picture of Lola's tattoo was not really useful to us. But what we decided on was that whoever broke into the morgue after us had no affiliations to the

Falcons. No way, no how. Furthermore, if we were to assume that the intruder was Lola's killer, then she wasn't murdered by a Falcon. Of course, we didn't know for sure. It was just the evidence that was pointing to it.

I still hadn't decided if I could go on investigating this case, though. I needed to be extremely careful when it came to the Falcons. Our lives depended on it. So on the off chance they were still involved, I should keep out of it.

Edie had reported about the rest of her night with Ryker. As usual, and by that I meant since we started our shenanigans that we were always trying to hide from Ryker, Edie has become a master at lying to her grandson. I was sure she didn't even feel any remorse about that by now. She knew Ryker was looking out after her and they had a very loving relationship. But Edie was spicy too, spicier than Ryker would have had it.

We were curious about Ryker's own investigation, and Edie mentioned she had a feeling that the dentist's wife, Eleanor, hired Ryker's firm to make sure the dentist's reputation wasn't being dragged through the mud, particularly in connection with Lola. It wasn't that Eleanor was concerned about Lola herself, she was focused on the family's name more.

What I gathered from Edie's story was that Ryker was hired to help this Eleanor Curtis save face, whether she knew about her husband having a potential affair with Lola or not. Ryker basically didn't have to do much.

Which led us to Eleanor. Gran, Edie and I talked about the possibility of her being Lola's murderer. But the intruder was male.

"Maybe she had an accomplice," Gran said.

"Could be," I said, taking another sip of my coffee. "Or maybe she wasn't involved at all."

"You went after the guy yesterday," Gran said. "You had him in your grip. Didn't you pick up on something?"

I thought about it. The guy must have gotten a visible gash on his hand or arm after I cut him with the knife. Then I told them about the checkered blue shirt with the golden trim along the edges.

"I may be mistaken," I said. "It was half-dark in there."

Edie perked up. "Did you say checkered shirt with golden trim?"

I nodded.

"I've seen that before," Edie said and seemed to think about it. "At Eleanor's boutique."

Gran and I blinked twice.

"What did you just say?" I asked.

"I saw a shirt like that before. At Eleanor Curtis's clothing store. The Couture Corner."

We all exchanged glances.

"Well, butter my butt and call me a biscuit!" Gran said.

"Edie, I could kiss you square on the mouth right now," I said, beaming. "You just provided us with a huge clue."

Edie blushed then moved her eyebrows up and down. "It's what I do."

"Are you sure it was a shirt like that?" I asked. "It was a man's shirt."

"I was there about a week and a half ago, right after my visit with the late Dr. Curtis," Edie said. "I saw a shirt just like that in the men's section of the store. Blue ones and black ones. Wide checkered pattern. Golden trim at the edge of the collar, cuffs, and the hem. I remember specifically, because they had just unloaded another shipment or something and hung them in the store."

I was amazed.

Edie's involvement gave our investigation a significant push.

"Now you're glad I came with you?" Edie asked with a grin.

Gran did her eye-rolling gesture in response.

So the intruder shopped at Eleanor Curtis's boutique. But that was only speculation. Probably that was not the only store where you could get that shirt. Or the guy got a gift from someone who may have gotten the shirt at that boutique. Still, the coincidence was too big.

Getting this clue now made it even harder to step away from this investigation. I still didn't know what to do.

"Okay, let's eat some more pie and get going," Edie said.

Gran and I looked at each other, then at Edie questioningly.

Edie sighed. "We're going to the Couture Corner, duh."

Okay, guess Edie has decided for me.

"Why are we going there?" Gran asked.

"Do I have to spell it out for you?" Edie asked. "We need to talk to Eleanor. She runs the boutique. And assuming the intruder bought his shirt from there, that's the connection. Besides, we can combine work with pleasure. We can see about those dresses for you for prom night."

Gran nodded and said, "Great, you two have fun."

I turned to Gran in disbelief. "Us two? Nuh-uh, if I'm going dress shopping, so are you."

"I don't need a dress," Gran said. "I don't even want to go to that stupid prom. You're the one investigating the case, so you go."

"Don't be silly, Dorothy," Edie said, totally unfazed. "You're one of the nominees. Of course you're going to the prom. Besides, you're Theodore's date, you have to go." Edie was smiling broadly and I laughed under my breath.

Gran narrowed her eyes at Edie. "Maybe he's my date, not the other way around."

I rolled my eyes. Only Gran could make a feminist statement out of it. I thought about it. Well, okay, so would have I.

"So you admit you have a date with Theodore?" Edie said, but that came out more as a statement than as a question.

"I . . . I don't . . ." Gran started, and my eyes went wide. Whoa. Gran didn't have a retort. Edie was check-mate-ing her.

"Cool, it's a plan then," Edie said, digging into her piece of pie.

***

We opened the shiny glass door to Couture Corner and entered.

The boutique radiated an ambiance of sophistication and intimate charm. Eclectic artwork hung on the walls, and muted lighting illuminated the space, casting a warm glow upon racks with expensive looking clothing. There was a plush seating area with velvety cushions that looked like a cozy spot for clients to drink a glass of champagne while they listened to the sound of soft jazz music wafting through the air.

Edie explained we would mostly find haute couture clothing mixed in with eccentric pieces. The checkered shirt with the golden trim made more sense now.

I was in part amazed that I was still on the case and in part amazed that it didn't occur to me before that we could leverage Edie as a connection between us and Eleanor Curtis. We didn't come here as private investigators, we came here as regular shoppers, and Edie acted as a sympathetic member of the community, offering condolences to Eleanor. Since they had already interacted and developed a rapport, it was much simpler to engage in conversation with her this way.

Edie didn't even need specific instructions. She had already devised a plan to portray herself as a concerned but thoughtful patient of Stephen Curtis and a customer of Eleanor Curtis to gather information from her.

I was impressed with Edie's way of thinking. Soon, she would overshadow us, and Leonardi would want to work with her. Ugh. Now I couldn't get that image out of my head. Edie, wearing her polka-dotted dress and her chunky sandals, her curls perfectly styled, a tiara nestled in it, staring up at Leonardi's salami chunk stuck in his front tooth gap. They'd be an unexpected duo, for sure. Nobody would see them coming, thus giving them the upper hand. Sometimes, it was good to be underestimated.

Speaking of Leonardi, I had to tell him something. I couldn't reveal our morgue trip to him. He would freak that he wasn't a part of it and he would never buy my lies as to why I went there without him.

Before leaving Gran's house, I had called him and told him half of the truth. That Edie knew the wife and her boutique, and we were going there under the guise of potential shoppers to talk to her. Just as expected, Leonardi protested at first, being left out of the loop and everything, but I knew he would concur. He knew his presence there would absolutely not help matters and Eleanor Curtis would definitely not talk to us as freely. I promised to keep him informed about what we would find out and we disconnected.

"Look at all these pretty colors," Edie said and moved over to the rack on the right side of the boutique, her fingers gently caressing the fabrics. "Dorothy, look. This one has your name written on it. This one is couture elegance."

Gran and I got closer and saw a black cocktail dress. The bodice was strapless, crafted from supple black leather. The dress gracefully transitioned into layers of delicate black tulle with other small details encrusted in leather.

"What am I, a stripper?" Gran asked. "I'm only missing a whip."

"You could wear that garter we talked about," Edie said.

Cringe, cringe, cringe.

"Stop it, please," I said, covering my ears.

"I don't know why you react like this," Edie said. "You're throwing knives like you're at an Olympiad but you're a wuss when it comes to real, human interactions."

Another checkmate from Edie. How did she do that? One moment come off as aloof, and the next, dropping one of these unexpectedly deep and profound statements.

"Okay, let's just keep this professional," Gran said. "We're here to talk to the wife. Where is she?"

Edie had assured us she would be here. She was told that Eleanor Curtis would be in today. Occasionally, she engaged with her customers, but often she worked in her office in the back. Edie found out through the grapevine that Eleanor didn't really slow down with work and supposedly, this was her way of coping with her husband's death.

A shopping assistant approached and asked how she could help and just as Edie was gesturing towards the dress rack, I saw Eleanor Curtis emerging from the back, carrying a stack of garments over her shoulder. She began arranging the clothes on their respective racks. Her demeanor didn't quite match with the picture of a grieving widow; instead, she seemed composed, her movements deliberate, almost unaffected by the loss of her husband.

She did a double take when she spotted Edie.

"Edie!" she said. "So glad to see you. Wait a second, let me hang these things here and I'll be with you in a minute."

Edie nodded then whispered to me and Gran, "Just follow my lead."

Gran let out a subtle scoff, and I stifled a laugh. I was glad we managed to convince Edie to leave her tiara back at the house.

## Chapter Fourteen

ELEANOR CURTIS FORCED A SMILE as she approached us then her smile turned into furrowed brows as she saw me and Gran.

"Eleanor!" Edie said a bit too loudly for my taste, then they both hugged.

Oh wow. We should have sooo used Edie earlier for this.

"Eleanor, I want you to meet Piper and Dorothy," Edie said nodding to us.

"Oh yes, I have seen you at the funeral yesterday," Eleanor said to me.

We explained that Gran had moved to the retirement complex in Florida, and I came with her. We gave her our usual story, that Gran retired, I was a hairdresser, and our hometown was in Idaho. We knew our back story by heart by now.

Eleanor bought it, obviously.

Then she shook hands with Gran and looked her up and down. Eleanor had the same face expression a lot of people had when they met Gran for the first time and took in her usual biker's outfit. Which was a look of dismay combined with embarrassment and shock.

Eleanor herself was wearing a tailored black pantsuit with a cream blouse and her dark blond hair was pulled back.

"Eleanor, I didn't really have a chance to express my condolences yesterday at the funeral," Edie said, taking Eleanor's hand in hers. "I am so sorry for the loss of your husband. We all loved Dr. Curtis. He helped out so many people and you know how he was our favorite dentist at the retirement complex."

Eleanor 's eyes started watering. "Oh Edie, that is so nice of you to say. Yes, that was Stephen, he was so beloved by everybody. And I know he had a soft spot for you and all the other residents at the complex."

I inwardly rolled my eyes. I could puke at this much exaggerated kissing in the butt small talk. Gran and I were different. When somebody died, especially someone who wasn't really close to us, then we were more like "Oh, that's a shame," and go on with our lives.

Eleanor nodded at Edie then looked over to Gran and me expectantly. Oh great. We had to do the dance as well.

I elbowed Gran who also seemed to have checked out.

"What? Huh?" she said, looking confused.

I took the lead and took the bullet for us. "Mrs. Curtis, we too would like to express our deepest condolences for the death of your husband. We haven't met him personally, but we know how much he meant to the community here in Bitter End."

I could feel Gran trying to stifle a laugh beside me. I elbowed her again. She cleared her throat. "Yes, me too," she said.

We all waited for more, but nothing else came. After a few moments of awkwardness, Eleanor turned her attention back to Edie.

"Eleanor, I can't imagine what you're going through what with all the commotion at the funeral," Edie said, and Gran and I perked up. "We were all so shocked about what happened. I mean, who would have expected a second body just popping out of the casket? Who would have such a sick mind to do something like that? Poor Dr. Curtis."

Eleanor tensed a bit and quickly looked around her. There were only a few other shoppers that were busy browsing the clothes. "You know what?" she said quietly. "Let's move to the side."

It was obvious she tried avoiding airing dirty laundry in public. She also probably knew Edie wasn't having it and there was no way to get rid of her now.

We went to the seating area and made ourselves comfortable on the couch and the two armchairs. I could tell the plush rug underneath was high quality and so was the coffee table in the middle of this area.

As soon as I sat down, I scanned the store rigorously. I was looking for the men's clothes when . . . I spotted a rack section that had checkered shirts hanging from them. They all had a golden trim, sparkling in the glow of the light fixture.

Bingo!

Those were it.

Our intruder in the morgue last night wore a shirt exactly like that. Edie was right. She had seen them here before.

I wondered how unique Eleanor's stuff was. Could the intruder have bought the shirt somewhere else? It would have been a huge coincidence, and I wasn't a fan of those. For now, I was assuming the intruder got his shirt from this store.

"I can't even begin to tell you how heartbroken I am, Edie," Eleanor spoke softly as she crossed one leg over the other. "I agree with you. I don't know who could have such a sick mind to do a thing like that. And to involve my Stephen." Her voice started to tremble. "I hope they catch whoever is responsible for this."

I watched her intently and tried to figure out if is she was telling the truth or lying. If she was lying, then she was a really good actress. Still, there was something that I just didn't like about her. Something was just a little bit off.

Edie patted Eleanor's hand. "I hear you. It was an absolute disgrace. And to think that whoever did it almost got away with it, right?"

Oh my, Edie was good.

We all leaned forward and watched Eleanor. I could tell she tried to stay composed. She said, "Get away? I . . . What do you mean they almost got away?"

I wasn't sure if Eleanor just didn't get it or if she was plain dense.

"I mean, if they wouldn't have let the casket slip, then we'd never have found out about that girl inside," Edie said, and I saw Eleanor shivering a bit. Edie must have sensed it too because she added, "I'm so sorry, Eleanor, I didn't mean to bring this up, it's just, you know, it's the talk of the town right now. But people should be thinking of you as well and what *you're* going through."

Excellent.

Edie was really good.

I was convinced now; Leonardi should definitely work with Edie. She may not know how to handle weapons, but she was a pro at this other stuff that him and me were too harsh for.

"Oh, please," Eleanor said, waving it away. I could tell she was trying to remain collected, even though she clearly didn't want to discuss it. But proper etiquette stopped her from just standing up and leaving. "I'm fine. Sort of. And I understand what you're saying. It's just that, the thought alone that my Stephen could have been buried with that stranger ... her being ... unclothed ... it just makes me sick to my stomach."

"Oh, so she was a stranger?" Edie said, feigning surprise. I glanced over at Gran and noticed a great deal of admiration reflected in her expression as she looked at Edie.

"Of course she was a stranger," Eleanor said a bit annoyed. "I don't know who that girl was, I haven't ever met her. And I have no idea how she got there."

"I'm sorry, I didn't mean to put you on the spot," Edie said to Eleanor.

Hell yeah, she did, that's why we were here.

Edie continued. "I just assumed that because the girl was in Dr. Curtis's casket, that there would be some connection to him."

I felt that Edie was pushing it a bit, but Eleanor hasn't kicked us out yet, so we were still good. Edie was sneaky and smart. She subtly put Eleanor in a challenging position without directly confronting her. It was all in the way she framed her words. In the end, it was a good call to tell Edie that Leonardi and I had visited Lola's roommate and that we found stationery in the trash bin that came from Dr. Curtis's office. Edie knew exactly what to ask Eleanor having this information.

"No, there is no connection," Eleanor said, and I could tell she felt a bit offended. I couldn't decide if it was because in no way would her husband be connected to Lola or because she didn't want people thinking that.

Also, the fact that her answers were very short didn't sit well with me. That was a sign she was lying. We were pretty sure Dr. Curtis was having some sort of affair with Lola. It wouldn't have been too far-fetched for the spouse to have figured that out and to plan some sort of revenge.

"Again, Eleanor, I am so sorry for just assuming," Edie backtracked. "I really hope the police can sort it out and quickly too. Especially since we don't want Dr. Curtis's reputation to get tainted. What with that girl working in the sex industry—" Edie's hand quickly flew to her mouth and I almost fainted. Gran was grinning wide. "Oh, I'm so sorry, Eleanor, there are rumors that the girl's job was . . . you know . . . a call girl." Edie said that last word in a whisper.

I was almost certain Eleanor would kick us out now.

But she didn't. She tensed up even more and pressed her lips.

Bullseye. She did know Lola was a call girl. And probably not from the cops.

"Yes, well, I too have heard about that poor girl's choice of living," Eleanor said, and I could tell she was trying hard to find the proper words. "That is why it's so disgraceful to my poor Stephen. Couldn't have somebody just put her in her own casket or something and not get us involved?"

"Well, the girl *was* murdered, so that was the whole point of it, to hide her in your husband's casket," I said. Oops. That just slipped out. Edie turned to me in disbelief and subtly shook her head as if trying to say I should butt out.

247

I cleared my throat. "At least, that's what I heard, that she was murdered." I mean, wasn't that obvious either way? Who would put a dead body in another casket if something fishy didn't occur?

Eleanor eyed me suspiciously. "Yes, that is what the police had told me as well. That she didn't die of natural causes. But like I've said, I don't know what happened there." She turned back to Edie and frowned. "I guess it's no secret to you that I hired Ryker to do some research as well."

Well, it wasn't a secret with neither one of us. Ryker had told us about this at the dining hall with Beatrice and Theodore around as well. So that part wasn't confidential at all. Which made me think Eleanor *wanted* people to know she hired Ryker. How that was going to help her save face, I had no idea.

The mention of Ryker to Edie came off a bit as a jibe, though. But Edie wasn't fazed at all.

"Eleanor, don't you worry," Edie said. "You know Ryker is a professional and wouldn't telltale. This is just me being concerned about you and the reputation of Dr. Curtis. He was such a fine gentleman and a very good doctor in the community. And you are a vital part of our community as well, what with your store thriving and the great selection of clothing you're carrying."

I could see the corners of Eleanor's mouth twitching upward. She bathed in Edie's compliments, which were actually so thin, I could see right through them. Edie successfully shifted the conversation from the topic of Ryker back to what we needed to find out.

"Thank you, Edie, that is more than nice of you to say," Eleanor said. "And yes, I know Ryker is an absolute professional. Actually, I thought he'd be here with you when I saw you come in. He said he would come by today."

Aw, great. Of course he would. Why was I not surprised? If we did end up running into each other here too, Ryker would instantly know we were butting our noses in the Curtis-Lola case. Luckily, we could camouflage it under the guise of social protocol. The key was not giving him any concrete evidence of our meddling.

"Oh," Edie said, dawning it on her that Ryker could show up at any second now. "I didn't know about his visit to you today. See? What did I just say? Ryker is a professional."

Eleanor nodded and seemed pleased with Ryker's mode of conduct. To be honest, so was I. The man was getting on my nerves, but he was a professional and I had respect for that.

"Again, such a shame for the poor girl and also such a disgrace for Dr. Curtis," Edie pressed on.

My respect for her grew as well.

Eleanor nodded. "It seems like a bad dream. It's bad enough that my husband died but to have this happen at the funeral . . . I just don't know how I'll get over it. I'm here at the store trying to distract myself but it's always in the back of my mind."

"Of course, of course," Edie nodded, and her curls were bouncing up and down. "You're managing wonderfully. Sitting alone at home would only make you think about it and that would probably make you crazy. It's best to be out and around people." Then Edie perked up as if she had an idea. "You know what? You should come to our prom night on Saturday."

Oh, good Lord. What just happened? I exchanged glances with Gran who was also frowning.

Eleanor seemed surprised as well. "To your prom night? What do you mean?"

Edie told her about the party organized at the retirement complex and that visitors were always welcome, and she would like to extend the invitation to her as well.

"Edie, that's very nice of you but being out partying is not really appropriate after my husband's dying," Eleanor said.

"But you wouldn't be partying, you would be starting to heal," Edie said. "What would you do otherwise?"

Eleanor thought about it. "I would stay at home?"

"See?" Edie said. "You would stay at home and think about the horrific thing that happened and I know that grief is something that everybody needs to get through to heal but this is an opportunity to move ahead. Besides, you could kind of come to the party as our stylist and make sure that everything sits right."

Our stylist? What was Edie up to now? I felt Gran starting to move up, but I instantly placed my hand on her thigh, signaling her to stay put.

"What do you mean?" Eleanor asked just as surprised.

"Well, isn't it obvious?" Edie said nodding toward us. "We're all here to shop for new dresses for the party."

I had to firmly press my hand into Gran's thigh to keep her seated. I too wanted to bolt but I sensed this approach might soften Eleanor, potentially leading to more information from her.

Eleanor's eyes sparkled as she looked over at Gran and me and I could tell she finally understood what the heck we were doing there all this time.

"I . . . guess . . . that would be fine," she said. "I can help you look for new outfits for the party. And then we'll see about me joining you there. It might be too tacky."

I noticed she was more focused on it not being socially appropriate rather than her saying she was grieving her husband and wanted to be left in peace. Something was up with this broad and if I had to guess, I'd say she didn't care much about her husband and she knew about him and Lola.

Edie nodded vehemently. "Yes, please think about it, we would be really happy to have you there," she said. "And as for us now, what would you recommend?"

Eleanor glanced at Gran and me, a slight grimace crossing her face. She seemed to struggle with the mental image of us in dresses. Well, probably more Gran than me.

But before Eleanor could speak, Edie jumped in and grinned wildly at Gran. "I'm thinking Dorothy would look really good in that black leather dress you have out there."

Gran narrowed her eyes at her. "No, that dress wouldn't look good on me. I'm actually good not wearing a dress."

Eleanor was taken aback. "But what would you be wearing then?"

Gran looked at herself then looked back up at Eleanor. "This."

I swear, Eleanor almost slipped off her seat. "You can't be wearing . . . that . . . to your prom party. You need a proper dress and a nice one too." Without waiting on Gran's reply, Eleanor got up and walked to the rack with the leather dress.

"Why is nobody listening to me" Gran asked as we all moved to the front too.

"We are listening, we're just ignoring you," I said smiling. "We all want to see you in that dress."

"Well, if I'm wearing a dress, then so are you," Gran said to me.

"I don't have to wear a dress," I said, expecting Gran's response. "I'm not nominated for Prom queen. You are."

"You are what?" Eleanor asked with eyes wide. "You are nominated for Prom queen?" She said that as if it were more possible for an asteroid to fall on earth.

Surprisingly, I could tell Gran felt slightly insulted by Eleanor's presumption. She put one hand on her hip. "Yeah, I am, you got a problem with that?"

Edie stepped in front of Gran and waved her hand in dismissal as Eleanor backed away, looking frightened. "Yes, yes, Dorothy is nominated for Prom queen, it's because of all this fire she has in her, you know? The residents all love that." Edie tried to deescalate because Gran was escalating yet again.

Eleanor seemed to calm down and cleared her throat. "Yes, sure, I can see that. That's why I think this dress would be perfect for her. Let me bring it to the fitting room for you."

Eleanor marched to the back and Gran immediately said, "What the heck is going on here? Why am I trying on dresses now? I thought we were here so that you could find out some useful information. I don't understand how I got involved in this again."

"We're trying to find out information and this is a part of it," Edie said. "You think if you came here and said you were a private investigator, she would talk to you?"

As sorry as I was, Edie was right. She turned to me. "You too. You have to get in on it and try on a dress."

I cringed as Gran smiled at me. "Are you happy now?" I asked her.

She nodded. "If I'm going down, you're going down with me."

I groaned softly as I shifted to other dresses on the rack and started browsing through them.

"Piper, wait," Edie said. "I just saw a dress here that's just perfect for you. Ryker would love it."

Gran burst out laughing and I felt a headache coming on.

Twenty minutes later, Gran and I were standing in front of the mirror, and I've never felt sadder in my life. Gran had the black leather stripper dress on, paired with her black biker boots, and she was fussing at her chest, worried something might pop out.

I, on the other hand, was wearing a floor-length, red, silk dress with barely-there straps and a pouch around my chest, along with my white tennis shoes. Needless to say, neither Gran nor I wore bras with our outfits.

I've never felt more out of place.

"Aww, you look so pretty," Edie said, beaming. "Both of you."

Was Edie seeing the same people in the mirror?

"I feel like a ripe cherry ready to burst," I said.

"I feel like a deluxe dominatrix," Gran said, still plucking at her dress.

"Nonsense," Edie said. "You look great. Now we need heels."

"Heels?" Gran said. "No. Nuh-uh. I draw the line at heels."

"Well, what are you going to wear then?" Eleanor asked.

"My boots and my gun," Gran said.

Eleanor almost made the sign of the cross.

If we kept this longer, we would be driving back to the house with wedding dresses, jury duty dresses and award show gowns.

I needed to bring back our conversation to what really mattered to us.

"You know," I said to Eleanor, "my date may need some newer outfits as well."

Edie frowned. "Really? You want to buy him an outfit?"

Gran frowned too. "Your date? Really?

I rolled my eyes. Didn't anyone get where I was heading with this?

"I can see you are carrying men's clothing as well," I said to Eleanor.

She nodded. "Yes, yes, these are exquisite fabrics, soft but also resilient."

"Yes, I really like your stuff," I said to her. Compliments were usually the way to go.

Eleanor scrunched her nose. "Stuff?"

Okay, maybe not always.

"I mean, your gorgeous garments," I corrected myself. "Are you working with specific designers?"

Eleanor looked very pleased with herself. "Why of course. The designers are handpicked by me."

I lifted the hem of the dress to be able to walk and moved to the men's clothes and brushed my hand against the fabric. "You're right, this really feels soft." I strategically positioned myself in front of the checkered shirts. "These look fantastic. These must be your bestsellers, right?"

Gran and Edie were now behind Eleanor, and I could see Edie frowning and Gran trying to keep a straight face. One was getting it, and one was not getting it yet.

Eleanor was beaming with pride. "These shirts right here are the newest on the market. I've only gotten them like two weeks ago."

I tried not to look surprised at this new piece of information. Two weeks ago? She only got them two weeks ago? So if we were still assuming that the intruder bought his shirt from here, then it had to be in the last two weeks. That definitely narrowed things down. The only problem was finding out who that was.

"Only two weeks ago?" I asked.

"Yes, I've just started selling them," Eleanor said. "Usually, it takes a while for sales to pick up."

"I see," I said. "So there were only a few men who bought this shirt?"

"Yes, there were a few," Eleanor said, and I wasn't sure how much I could push it. But I did.

"How many would you say?"

Eleanor eyed me suspiciously. I could see Edie and Gran behind her, scrunching up their faces like, was this maybe too much?

"I don't know why that's important," Eleanor said.

"Well . . . because . . .you see, I would like my date to wear something really special, you know? Not something that everybody wears. That's why I'm wondering how many men have bought this."

Eleanor's face lit up again. Edie and Gran did a thumbs-up from behind her.

"Oh, I see," Eleanor said. "I can respect a woman who wants her man to be one-of-a-kind. So don't you worry, I've sold this shirt to maybe a handful of customers."

Interesting. This really narrowed things down a lot. But we still needed to know who the men were. Eleanor yapped about something about the fabric of the shirt and so on, but my mind was somewhere else. How to find out who bought that shirt?

I looked around. It was shortly before noon and the store was moderately full. There was Eleanor and two other shopping assistants, who were now minding their own business talking to customers. I had seen Eleanor coming from the back before, where presumably her office was. She most probably had a computer there or any other form of accounting. I could browse around and find out who bought that shirt.

Great.

I was contemplating breaking and entering again.

Or maybe not. We were already inside the store. Actually . . . this was way better than breaking and entering at night. Oftentimes doing it under everyone's nose was the better option with a reduced risk of getting caught. But even so, I would have to get into Eleanor's office undetected. I couldn't just waltz in there.

What we needed was a diversion so I could get into that office. I glanced at Gran and Edie. I had just the right people for that.

## Chapter Fifteen

"So how about those dresses?" Eleanor asked, clearly wanting to make a sale. "Should I wrap them up?"

"Um . . . you know what?" I said. "I think we need a couple of more minutes to decide."

"Of course," Eleanor said, and I sensed she tried to hide her annoyance. "I'll leave you ladies to it. Browse around some more, if you want to." Then she moved over to one of the assistants and pointed to some rack of clothes.

Gran, Edie and I regrouped at the seating area.

"Can I take this off now?" Gran asked, as she stomped around in her boots, still wearing the dominatrix dress.

"Not yet," I said, pulling up the dress hem again to avoid stumbling. Then I pulled at the front, since that damn chest pouch made it feel as if I was totally exposing myself.

"Stop it, it won't fall off," Edie said. "It fits you like a glove. Are you even aware that you are an extremely attractive woman? Please tell me you're going to buy these!"

I felt a blush creeping up. But still felt like an alien in that dress.

"I don't know, whatever," I said, scanning to see nobody was near us. "We don't have time to think about that now. I need a diversion."

Gran and Edie both raised their eyebrows, and I explained the situation.

Edie put her hand over her mouth then said, "That is genius, Piper. But what do you want us to do?"

"Not sure exactly," I said. "But you're both . . . um . . . you know, seniors. There has to be something there."

Now they both narrowed their eyes at me.

"Who you calling a senior?" Gran asked.

I rolled my eyes. "Gran, please. I really need your help right now."

"She's right," Edie said to Gran. "We need to use what we have at our disposal." Then she turned to me. "So what's our poison? Faking chest pains? A hip break? Hot flashes?"

Gran cringed. "Good Lord," she mumbled under her breath.

Edie said, "Well, do you have any better ideas?"

"I could hold them all at gunpoint," Gran said and patted her thigh.

Edie smiled wide. "Oh, so you did go with the garter, didn't you?"

I put my hands up. "Edie, please, let's not get into that now. Or ever, for that matter. We need to focus. There will be no gun shooting here."

"Fine," Edie said. "Then let's do the chest pains. That's always a crowd pleaser."

"You say that like you've done it before," I said, eyeing Edie.

"Who, me?" she said, batting her eyelashes. "Please, I would never." Then she winked at me.

I smiled. Edie was like peeling an onion. Layer upon layer beneath the surface.

Never in my previous life would I have even conceived hanging around or being on a spontaneous mission with a septuagenarian making a statement like that.

"Good," Gran said. "I'll wait here on the side until you're done."

"Wait?" Edie frowned. "Nuh-uh, why do you get to wait? You could be faking the chest pains too."

I looked the other way trying not to laugh. Gran was absolutely the worst person for this, although she did it once when we had to. It was at Edie's house shortly after we got to Bitter End. We needed a diversion then also and Gran totally pulled it off, although she stomped down on her pride to do it.

"You're joking," Gran said. "Why do you keep involving me in your world? This is not my world."

"But it is now," Edie said. "You're here, aren't you?"

Gran pursed her lips.

"Guys, someone has to do it," I said.

"Okay, let's do rock, paper, scissors," Edie said, holding out her fist in the palm of her other hand.

"You wanna do rock, paper, scissors for who gets to do the fake chest pains?" Gran said and I was one hundred percent convinced, she didn't ever think of making that statement ever in her life.

"That sounds good to me," I said with a grin and tried to avoid Gran's death stare.

Gran mumbled something as she held out her hand, but Edie and I ignored it.

"Okay, here we go," Edie said. "On three."

"On three or after three?" Gran asked.

"On three," Edie said matter-of-factly. "Or I would have said *after* three."

"Jesus," Gran mumbled.

"And it's three out of three," Edie added.

"Fine," Gran said.

It was funny to see Gran in such novelty situations. I had the feeling she herself had no idea how to act and how to handle it. Knowing she wouldn't be able to get back to her normal life, she often resisted verbally, but then eventually gave in and went along with whatever mischief we ended up in.

"Okay, give me your best shot," Edie said.

I watched amused how they both swung their hands and threw out their fists. Luckily, no one was near us in the store.

"One, two, three," Edie said, and they both got rock.

"One, two, three," Edie said, and she got paper and Gran got rock again.

Gran did not look amused.

"One, two, three," Edie said, and she got rock and Gran got scissors.

"Woohoo, I win!" Edie said and clapped her hands like a little girl.

"Congratulations," Gran said. "You win. You get to do the diversion."

Edie laughed. "Nice try, Dorothy. You lost, you're up for the fake chest pains."

I shrugged. "Gran, you know the rules of the game."

Gran cursed under her breath but she got in position. She looked around and chose the spot in the store farthest away from the back door where we presumed the office was. I stood back, prepared to dash to the back.

"Aaaand, we're rolling," Edie giggled and pretended to look at a rack of clothes nearby.

Gran started pulling at the bodice of her dress and breathed in heavier. She moved closer to one of the shopping assistants and then said in a weak voice, "This dress is too tight. I can't breathe." She clutched on her chest and started moving around as if she were dizzy. The shopping assistant immediately went white as a ghost and jumped over to Gran.

"Oh my god, are you okay?" she asked.

Gran flushed herself and still pretended to have a hard time breathing.

Edie jumped to where Gran was standing, looking worried. "Dorothy, what's wrong? You can't breathe? I told you this dress was too tight for you."

I swear Gran almost jumped at Edie's throat. But she had to keep up the act. So she just shot Edie a fierce glare while still pretending to be in pain. I had to play along too, but with Edie's antics, it was a real struggle not to burst into laughter.

"What's going on here?" Eleanor asked, as she made her way towards the commotion.

She gasped as she saw Gran clutching her chest. "Oh my god, somebody call nine-one-one," she said.

So that was the thing with the fake chest pains. We needed it to be a commotion, but not that much.

"No, no," Gran said putting her hands up in the air. "I'm fine, I'm just feeling dizzy in this dress."

"She just needs some water and to sit down," Edie said, taking command. Then she shouted, "Somebody please get a chair and some water." She winked at me and that was my cue.

I was standing a couple of feet around the group of people that now surrounded Gran. I dashed into the fitting room first and grabbed my cell from my pants pocket and slipped it into my cleavage. Brr, cold. For a couple of seconds, I felt like the female character in a James Bond movie, one of those femme fatales who are wearing revealing and sexy dresses and still manage to hide their weapons somewhere. Only this biker chick right here was a far cry from a femme fatale. I was the one in the black biker boots, hopping on a Harley, revving up the engine. However, as I've gathered from the previous men in my life, that had its own unique appeal.

With the cold metal of the cell phone in between my boobs, I slipped to the back and landed in a small hallway. Unfortunately, I was still wearing the damn dress and felt zero comfort hurrying up in such an outfit. I felt like any time the dress would fall right off and I would provide everyone with a peep show.

From the hallway I saw a restroom to one side and a door ajar to the other side. I peeked in. That was the office. I ran inside and closed the door behind me a bit.

My eyes landed on the computer on a desk and in two seconds I was standing behind it. Luckily, when I moved the mouse, the screen lit up and I didn't have to put in a password. Just as I had expected. Probably Eleanor typed in a password every morning and that was it for the rest of the day.

Now how to find which customers bought that kind of shirt? Eleanor must have had article codes for each item that she kept in some kind of database. I looked on the screen but I didn't need to search any further since the program was open already. Probably Eleanor was working on it before she came into the store.

I scanned the interface as fast as I could. I saw a lot of doodahs that were not what I was looking for. I

saw a search field and just typed in shirt. A list of
clothing items came up. Luckily, they all had pictures
beside them. I scrolled and scrolled until I saw the
picture of the checkered shirt with the golden trim. I
clicked on it and a whole lot of other details came up.
Fabric type, distributor, list of sales. I clicked on that
last one and another list came up. It was the date
and the number of shirts sold. Under each sale, there
was the sale transaction, including credit card
number and cardholder.

Bingo.

I pulled my cell out of my cleavage and snapped
pictures of that list without really looking it through.
We would do that undisturbed after we got back to
the house.

I slipped the cell phone back between my ladies
and let out a "aaah", although the metal part had
already gotten warmer, and closed the program on
the computer.

I needed to get out of here lest they wondered
where I was.

I peeked outside into the hallway. The coast
was clear, and I could still hear the commotion
coming from the front. Gran and Edie were a good
team. Even if one of them didn't think so. I heard

someone say, "She's fine, she's fine, now that she's sitting in a chair."

I walked out of the office, down the hallway and just as I was about to turn the corner back into the store, I bumped into a hard chest.

"Umph," came out of my mouth as I unglued myself from the hard surface.

I looked up and immediately rolled my eyes.

Ryker. Who else?

"That's a nice greeting," Ryker said, looking me up and down.

"Sorry, it's just . . . I didn't expect you here," I lied, and started fumbling with my dress and adjusting the straps that were so thin, I wondered if they ran out of fabric. Okay, what happened here? I suddenly felt totally self-conscious wearing that dress in front of Ryker.

He grinned as he took me in. "I like it. It brings out your—"

We both locked eyes.

"Your . . . um . . . slender figure," Ryker finished, scratching the back of his head.

I felt a blush creeping up my cheeks and I hated it.

"Um . . . thanks," I said, patting down the dress and pulling at the chest pouch. I hoped he didn't notice my cell phone tucked in there.

Then he got all serious like he tended to get when he caught me in places I shouldn't have been.

"What are you doing here?" he asked, his eyes darting behind me.

"What's it to you?" I replied, crossing my arms over my chest.

"Well, your grandmother is having some sort of problems outside and you're in here," he said. "That doesn't add up."

"Not that it's any of your business, but I ran to the restroom to get her some water for her," I said confidently.

"From the restroom?" Ryker asked, raising an eyebrow.

"Yes, from the restroom," I replied. "They usually have a water dispenser kind of thing right outside of the restroom."

Ryker stared at me.

"They don't have that in here," I said.

His stare bore right into my eyes, but I didn't look away. I didn't even blink. I could win at this staring contest easily.

"You don't seem so worried about your grandmother," Ryker continued.

"How do you know if I'm worried or not?" I asked. "By what standard are you measuring my worry?"

Ryker shifted from one leg to another.

Ha. Got him.

"What are you doing here?" I asked. "It seems that you're following me, making sure I worry enough for your taste."

Ryker frowned. "I came to see Eleanor and was just in time here for Dorothy's show. And since you were missing from that scene, I came looking for you."

It was just our luck that Ryker had to come here just as Gran was putting on the drama show. Ryker once again proved he was not stupid. He sensed the show. He just couldn't prove it.

"Well, then, you found me," I said. "Now let me see how my grandmother is feeling." I softly pushed him aside, trying to ignore his pecs that were nothing but solid rock, and walked past him, taking in his great smelling cologne. But just a second later, when I leaned forward to pull up the hem of the dress again, I knew I had made a mistake. I sensed my cell phone sliding further down beneath the fabric, skimming my stomach, and landing with a dull thud on the floor. At least, the plush rug cushioned its fall.

I stopped and froze.

Ryker heard the thud as he looked down on the floor.

"What was that?" he asked.

I didn't move. The cell was on the floor, in between my feet, but my dress was covering it up.

Unfortunately, I couldn't hide this one out.

I moved to the side and picked up the phone. "Oh, it's just my cell. Fell on the floor," I said and tried a nonchalant tone.

Ryker scanned my whole body again. Then he was the one to blush a bit. Which I thoroughly enjoyed.

He cleared his throat. "Where did you . . . um, have that phone stashed?"

"Oh, it was . . . just in here," I said and pointed to my chest.

Ryker's eyes flew to that spot, and he grinned.

After three seconds, his gaze hasn't moved. He didn't even blink.

"Okay, buddy, that's enough, eyes up here," I said and pointed two V-sign fingers at my own eyes.

Ryker looked up. "Interesting spot to stash a phone. Why did you need to hide your phone to go to the restroom?"

He glanced in the direction of the office in a very obvious way. He must have already decided it didn't make sense to ask me if I was in there because I would only deny it.

"I didn't hide it," I said with my chin high. "As you can see, I don't have any pockets, Sherlock."

"But why did you need to take your phone with you in the first place?" he pressed.

"Well, that's really none of your—"

"Business, is it?" Ryker finished my sentence.

I paused for a second before I said, "Exactly."

Then we both smiled at each other.

I snapped out of it. "Okay, gotta go," I said. "Grandmother not breathing well and all."

Ryker nodded then glanced at me one more time. "By the way, I wouldn't mind you wearing that dress for our date at the prom."

I rolled my eyes but also got all warm inside, for some reason. "It's not a date—." I sighed. There was no point. This guy was just trying to push my buttons.

"Whatever," I said and headed back to the store.

Where I found six people hovering over Gran, who sat on a chair and sipped water from a paper cup. She locked eyes with me as soon as she spotted me, and I could tell she was one second away from pulling out her gun. From her garter. Cringe!

"Oh, there she is," Gran said, when I made my way to her. "No need to call an ambulance, really."

"Gran, are you okay?" I asked in an exaggerated tone, taking her hand in mine. I guessed nobody wanted to tear that expensive dress off her, but I saw the zipper in the back was letting loose. "I tried to find some water for you."

"They already gave me some," Gran said, lifting her paper cup, still pretending to breathe hard. "Too bad it's not Vodka." She downed the water.

Everybody frowned and looked slightly embarrassed. They were probably wondering if she really meant it.

Edie laughed embarrassed. "Oh, she's just joking. She's always confused when she's having one of her episodes." Then she whispered as if Gran was a patient who didn't hear her, "It's the age, you know?"

Everybody nodded in understanding and there was a collective sound of "aah".

Uh-oh. That was a mistake.

I saw Gran's hand immediately going for her garter. We didn't need a blood bath right now, so I pushed Edie aside and took Gran's hand in mine as if to comfort her but what I actually did was keep it away from her gun. "There, there, Gran, we'll take you home now."

Gran stood and said, "Finally."

"Okay, let's wrap it up," I said as the group dispersed, convinced Gran was doing okay.

As we moved to the fitting room to change back into our own clothes, I looked up to see Ryker standing in the hallway, leaned against the door frame, with his hands wrapped around his chest and shaking his head at the scene before him.

## Chapter Sixteen

As soon as we entered Gran's house, we dropped the shopping bags on the floor. Somehow, Edie had convinced us to buy those damn dresses. Especially after the commotion and people thinking Gran was going to die in that store, Edie said it was only fair for us to take the dresses home with us.

"Where's the next charity?" Gran asked. "I'm bringing my dress there. 'Cause no way I'm going to wear it in public or even at the house."

"You can't go to the party in jeans, Dorothy," Edie said, taking her usual seat at the kitchen table.

"Watch me," Gran said, while getting a cold beer out of the fridge.

Edie only rolled her eyes. "Bring me a beer too?"

"Me too," I said and let out a long breath as we gathered at the kitchen table.

What I didn't get was why Gran and I had to try on and buy those fancy dresses that were absolutely so not us, and Edie didn't do any of those things.

"Well, duh," Edie said, "we didn't have time what with the sneaking into the back. The moment was over after you came back. And besides, you think I don't have enough pretty dresses in my closet?"

Gran and I painfully looked Edie up and down while seeing all that polka-dot pattern on her summer dress. Then we chugged down some beer.

"Okay, Piper," Edie said, rubbing the palms of her hand in excitement. "Show us what you got."

I had told them in the car on the way here about me taking pictures of the computer screen. But we didn't want to look them up in the car, since it wouldn't have been as comfortable. Most of our conversation in the car was Gran dumping on Edie about the stunts she pulled while she "had a hard time breathing" and that next time, she definitely would use her gun. Unfortunately, Gran had lost some credibility, since she's been threatening to pull out her gun most of the times, but she never did.

Now we were huddled together around the kitchen table, and I pulled my phone out. We scanned the pictures I took. It was eerily silent as we did so, and I couldn't even hear someone breathe.

As Eleanor had said, there weren't that many sales of that shirt. We had four people on the list, names, and their credit card info. Well actually, we had three names on the list and one note that there was a fourth sale that occurred with cash. So we had no name for that.

I didn't recognize the other three names, but Edie did. They were all the friends of Dr. Curtis. And they were all present at the funeral. They were the "Casa Nostra" people. It was the attorney, the surgeon, and the accountant. Which made sense that friends of the Curtis' would support Eleanor's clothing business and shop there. Eleanor must have probably told them she got a new shirt line, and they all went to shop there.

We Googled the names because I wanted to see their faces and their statures. I thought maybe we'd be in luck, and I would recognize the shape of the intruder this way. Since all three were successful members of the Bitter End community, we found for each a website and a corresponding picture. The attorney was a bit chubby and was going bald. The surgeon was handsome with a strong jaw and short sandy blonde hair. The accountant looked slim as well with brown-ish short hair.

Hmm. Unfortunately, I didn't get a good look at out intruder; all I knew was that he was not chubby. So we ruled out the attorney. His body shape did not match the intruder's.

I also looked up how much the shirt cost. $298. Not exactly cheap. So why would anybody pay that in cash instead of credit card? We still had a fourth unknown player and that bugged me a bit. But nothing I could do about that. There was no way to track that person down. Unless we asked Eleanor, but she would never tell us.

When we finished our beer, we collectively let out a breath. We analyzed the situation from all possible angles. Well, not all of them. Since Edie was in on it too, we couldn't talk about the possibility that Lola had been one of the Falcons. That was still in the back of my mind.

"So what do we do now?" Edie said, leaning in her seat.

"I'm not sure," I said. "We can consider these three men as suspects. What their motive was, I have no idea. But I'd venture a guess that they used Lola's services, to put it nicely. From there, all possible ramifications occur. I'm assuming they're all married?"

Edie nodded.

"Well, there you have it," I said. "Maybe Lola blackmailed one of them. Maybe she fell in love with one of them and threatened to break up the family or tell the wife." I thought about it. "Although, I'm really not sure about the latter. I didn't know Lola personally, but if you get into this business, then you're probably not the softer kind. Falling in love with the client would be my last guess, actually."

"What about Dr. Curtis's stationery in Lola's room?" Edie asked. "How does that fit into it?"

"Well, the only explanation is that Dr. Curtis also used her services," I said. "But he couldn't have murdered her since he died before her. That leaves us with Eleanor too. She would be our prime suspect."

"Yeah, but the intruder wasn't female," Edie reminded us. "And we already are assuming that the intruder is also the murderer, right?"

I sighed. My brain was almost on fire. "Yes, that's what we are assuming, because that would be the most logical explanation. But maybe we have it all wrong. Maybe Eleanor was involved in Lola's death and she was in cahoots with one of his buddies."

Edie seemed to think about it. "That could be. But unfortunately, I don't know anything about that. I didn't hear any rumors about Eleanor being in cahoots with anybody. Which doesn't mean that she wasn't."

"Exactly," I said. "Anything is possible. What I do know, though, is that Eleanor lied and she did know who Lola was."

"How do you know?" Edie asked.

"Her reaction to your questions today," I said and stretched out my arms. "Her facial expressions mostly. Trust me, she knew who Lola was even before her husband's death and while we're at it, she's not that much of a grieving widow either. It's more like she needs to keep up appearances. Have you noticed how she responded to you inviting her to the party? Her reason was, it's not appropriate and not she's so sad, she can't even leave her bedroom."

"I don't know how to do it but it's fascinating," Edie said to me, all beaming. "Now that you mention it, yes, there was something off with her reaction."

"And by the way, you are amazing," I said to Edie. "You interrogated her like a real pro. You flawlessly executed the whole socially acceptable condolences crap and really nailed it."

Edie blushed a bit. "I do what I can."

"Do you know what we should do?" Gran finally spoke as she leaned in her seat. "We should get them all to that stupid prom party."

"What do you mean?" Edie asked but I already knew where Gran was heading with this.

"You don't know these people personally, the ones who bought the shirt," Gran said in her let's-get-down-to-business tone. "Piper can't go and talk to them because they're never gonna open up. You could go down that route again as you did today with Edie in tow, expressing condolences and whatnot and talk to them one at a time but that takes a while. And it's no guarantee you'll find out anything." She paused before she said, "You need to get them all together in the same room."

"And then what?" Edie frowned.

"And then we improvise," I said as Gran nodded at me. "Gran is right. We need to get them all together and see from there."

Silence fell over us as we let that sink in.

"Okay, but why the prom?" Edie asked but then she answered her own question. "Oh, I get it. Because that's the perfect place to get them all together. The party is already happening, we don't have to fake a party."

"Bingo," Gran said.

"But how do we get them there?" Edie asked.

"Just say it's a charity thing of some kind," Gran said. "We know what kind of world they belong to, and rich people love that crap. Tell them they can donate for something. New oxygen tanks or whatever."

"New oxygen tanks?" Edie asked, wincing. "What kind of a fundraiser is that?"

"I don't know, that's not really my area of expertise, that's yours. You think of something. Just extend the invitation to the wife and the guys who bought the shirt and a couple of more people, like the dentist's staff members, maybe also people from the funeral home, then you have them all here together and the perfect opportunity to talk to them. Look also for a knife wound on his skin, a graze of some sort or a Band-Aid. Piper got him with her knife."

"Dorothy, that's genius, really," Edie said.

Gran looked pleased. "Of course it is."

"I like it when you get involved," Edie winked at her.

"Let's not get carried away, okay?" Gran said without sketching even a tiny smile.

I got up and brought us some water.

"Then I'll think of something to make it more urgent since the prom is only a couple of days away," Edie said. "Maybe people already have plans, so we need to move fast." Edie then straightened her shoulders and put on a serious face and looked us in the eye then said in a grave voice, "I need to make them an offer they can't refuse."

Gran and I blinked at Edie.

"Yes . . . we already got that, Edie," I said.

Edie stared at me expectantly and then at Gran. Then she put out her chin and changed her voice a little bit deeper and more breathier and repeated, "Like I said, I would make them an offer they can't refuse."

Gran turned to me. "Is she okay? Is she losing her marbles?"

Edie threw her hands up in the air. "Are you kidding me? That's the famous line from the Godfather. What did you not get?"

"The Godfather?" I said. "Is that like a movie or something?"

"Of course it's a movie," Edie said and her voice got an octave higher. "You've never seen the Godfather?"

Gran and I both shook our heads.

"Did you live under a rock or something?" Edie said. "You have to see the Godfather. It's a must. It's a classic. You two would enjoy it more than anyone I know."

"Well gee, we had a life, you know," Gran retorted. "Not everybody has time for movies and stuff."

Of course Gran and I knew the movie The Godfather. It was like our mantra back in Oregon. We were just joshing Edie.

"Why do you say we would enjoy it most?" I asked Edie out of curiosity.

"I don't know, it just seems like you would, it's about the mafia and all," Edie said, and I almost spit out my water.

"Well, if that makes you spit out your drink then wait until you see the movie," Edie said.

"Fine, we'll see the movie," I said. "Now can we get back to our situation at hand please?

In that moment, my phone rang. I looked at the screen. Leonardi. Damn it. I forgot about him. Which was funny, since he was the one that got me into this situation in the first place. I told him I'd call and report what we found out after going to Eleanor's store which I didn't do.

"Why the hell didn't you call back?" Leonardi barked into the phone.

"Now hold your horses," I said. "I was just about to call you."

"Liar," Leonardi said. "I'll be there in five minutes."

***

One hour later we were all up to date and exhausted.

Gran and Edie were sitting in the dining nook and Leonardi and I were on the couch, with our heads against the headrest.

It was shortly after four in the afternoon, and I felt so exhausted, I could have gone to bed right away.

Before Leonardi came, the three of us needed to figure out quick what we would tell him about the intruder in the morgue. We couldn't tell him we were there to check out Lola. And we couldn't tell Edie that we were there to actually see about the tattoo. Good god, I felt like we were knitting ourselves into deeper and deeper lies. One of these days, I was afraid Gran or I was going to slip out something we shouldn't. It got harder to keep track of the lies we told. We told something to Edie but had to tell something different to Leonardi, then another completely different thing to Ryker. Ugh.

Dillon had briefed us on this aspect when preparing us for our new lives. Hmph. Prepare. As if anybody could ever be prepared for changing identities. But Dillon had made it clear that we'd be living a life of perpetual lies, something we had to deal with. Considering our criminal past, that shouldn't be super hard, he'd said. We stood a better chance of not going complete nutso while living a continuous lie compared to individuals with no criminal background, who were forced into constant dishonesty.

I could have punched Dillon square in the face. Better chance my butt.

Truth was, in our past lives, we were the ones to choose when we told the lies and when not. Now it was our constant companion.

We told Leonardi that we used Edie as the connection to Eleanor and she confided in us what she found out from the cops. That fabrics were found in Dr. Curtis's casket that match the shirts she was selling in her boutique. So the cops had reason to believe whoever killed Lola also wore one of those shirts. Leonardi looked confused at first since this was completely new information for him. He still thought our plan was to visit Dr. Curtis's medical practice and the funeral home. But we were skipping that for now.

Leonardi had no reason to question our lie. Chances were low to none that Leonardi would speak to Eleanor to corroborate this story.

But as for me and Gran, we would have to keep track of whom we've told what lie.

We also informed Leonardi about our plan to invite all those people to the prom so we could check them out.

Leonardi looked at us in a stupor. "So you three decided that? Just like that?"

I knew what he meant. His ego was bruised because we kind of took charge and left him out of it. I would have felt the same way.

"Look at it this way," I said. "They're doing your work for free." I pointed to Gran and Edie.

Leonardi flashed us his tooth gap. "Still, I brought this case in. It would be nice to be more involved in it. And also, you thought it's a good idea to invite a potential murderer to a senior's party?"

There was silence. Indeed, nobody thought of that. Yap, I was so losing my touch.

"Well, um . . . if you put it like that . . ." Edie started.

"We just want to gather some information out of them without being conspicuous," I said. "Having them all at the party is the perfect place to do that. We could strike up conversations mentioning the Curtis guy, then gradually move up and mention Lola, see how they react, at least. You're a PI, you should be good at reading reactions."

Leonardi smirked. "Way to turn it around on me."

I smiled. "I'm that good."

"And the person paying with cash?" Leonardi asked. "What about him?"

"We can't track that," I said. "But we still have the other three. It's the best we can do, and you know it."

Leonardi studied us for a couple of beats. Then he grinned. "So, what time does this shindig start?"

## Chapter Seventeen

EDIE'S HOUSE WAS GET READY CENTRAL. It was Saturday and we were getting ready for the prom. Yup. From outlaws on bikes to witness protection, to prom night.

*Shoot me now.*

Gran was there—reluctantly—and Beatrice was there, and I was there too. Gran was currently hiding in the bathroom.

Beatrice wore a glitzy mid-calf cream dress that made her purple hair stand out. Edie still wore her bathrobe over the dress we haven't seen yet. But the tiara was right there in her curls. It had become a consistent accessory in the past few days. She wore pink heels, that had that 1920s vibe. To be honest, I was kind of afraid of what might be hiding underneath that bathrobe.

Gran and I forcibly wore the new dresses we bought from Eleanor's store. If someone had told me that a septuagenarian would make us wear dresses to go to a senior prom night, I would have never believed it.

Edie styled my hair in an elegant updo with some curls cascading down the side of my face that she cemented in place using a turbo hairspray. Only thing that worked in the Florida humidity. She loaned me three-inch gold summer heels to go with my red dress that her daughter had left at her house. Not that I had asked for it. I was hoping to wear my white sneakers with the dress because I didn't care. But as soon as I stood in front of the mirror with the heels on, I didn't dislike the whole package. A small gold clutch completed my outfit.

"She's smiling," Beatrice whispered to Edie behind me. "She likes it."

"Of course she likes it," Edie said, proudly. "She looks amazing in that dress. I picked it out for her, you know? She should wear that more often."

"Where would I wear this more often?" I asked. "For breakfast at the dining hall or for driving around in the golf cart?"

"Why not both?" Edie said.

"I can't even walk in these shoes," I said, moving around Edie's antique furniture like a penguin trying not to smash anything down.

"You'll get used to it," Edie said.

"In the next half an hour?" I asked.

It took longer to handle knife throwing properly and this seemed like an even more dangerous task.

Gran trudged out of the bathroom, and I could see she put on a bit of makeup. She wasn't as unhappy about the situation as she stated. Beatrice stared at Gran in her black leather bodice and black tulle. "You're going to be the bombshell of the retirement complex." Then she looked down. "But not in those godawful boots. You know I like your style, Dorothy, but not for tonight."

"She refuses to wear heels," Edie said as way of explaining.

"But why?" Beatrice asked. "It's not like you have to wear six-inch heels. Just one or two will do." She showed off her foot in a shiny silver heel.

"I don't have to do anything," Gran said, and plopped on Edie's couch right next to her freakish looking dolls. That was a sight! Gran couldn't have been more in contrast with the dolls.

I was sure she wore the infamous garter, and the gun was tucked in it. Which made me feel even more nervous because I couldn't hide my knife anywhere in this outfit. I contemplated getting a pocketknife for the future. It was smaller and the blades were tucked in when it was closed. And I could squish it in between my boobs just like I did with the cell phone.

"Is this the way you think people will vote for you?" Beatrice asked Gran.

"I don't care about that either," Gran said.

"Yes, she does," Edie said. "She just won't admit it."

"Well then maybe this is exactly what the people need," Gran said. "Someone who's different and doesn't give a sh—"

In that exact moment Edie took off her bathrobe and we almost went blind. She was wearing a hot pink multi-layer taffeta dress, with puffy built-in shoulders, like a baby doll dress with lots of ruffles.

She looked like someone puked out Pepto Bismol.

"I'll take it back," Gran said.

"What in the world is that?" I asked.

"Now that's a dress for a Prom queen," Beatrice said, with sparkling eyes behind those thick glasses of hers.

"What?" Edie said. "I need people to spot me."

"Astronauts can spot you from outer space," I said.

"Well, then, good," Edie said and moved in front of the mirror. "Astronauts can vote for me too."

"You know, with her looking like that, we could probably just stay at the house, and nobody would notice," Gran said to me.

There was a knock at the door.

"Could you get that?" Edie asked.

We all looked at each other.

Finally, Gran stood and headed for the door. "Might as well be me. This way I don't see that hot pink mess straight in my eyes."

Gran swung the door open and instantly tensed up.

"Theodore," she said. "Hello."

Edie had told Theodore and Ryker that we were at her house, and they should pick us up there. Obviously, I put up resistance first. Since I somehow got tricked into being a part of this blowout, I didn't need to be handled like a baby. I could drive to the rec hall by myself. But as usual, there was no arguing with Edie about that.

Theodore looked Gran up and down and held his gaze on her leather bodice a second longer. He grinned. "I like your dress," he said.

"Thanks," Gran deadpanned.

Theodore stepped inside and we were all speechless. He wore a sleek, fitted black tuxedo, a black bow complimenting a crisp white shirt. His hair was neatly slicked back and even from afar I could sense the faint smell of a fine cologne. He had black shiny shoes on that screamed high quality.

"You clean up nice, Theodore," I said to him, smiling wide.

"Why thank you so much, Piper," he said and adjusted his bow. "You ladies all look very lovely."

Theodore got some more brownie points for not commenting on Edie's outfit.

He took us all in, then his gaze landed on Gran again. He was virtually beaming. Poor guy. He would be so much better off with someone who was not Gran.

Gran also gave him the once-over and said, "Nice tux." Which in her world is like the best remark you could get out of her, compliment-wise.

Theodore produced a corsage out of nowhere. A single, elegant red rose surrounded by small greenery, tied together with a ribbon. He approached Gran holding the corsage in front of him.

Gran took a step back. "What are you doing?"

Theodore smiled. "Just let it happen, Dorothy."

He was so suave, and his voice was almost hypnotizing, Gran stood still and let Theodore put on the corsage around her wrist.

"See?" Theodore said. "Looks way better now."

Gran looked down at her hand. For a moment there was silence, and I thought a flash of sadness crossed Gran's eyes. For a second, she let down her guard. But then she put it back on.

"If you say so," she said.

Edie rolled her eyes. "Your grandmother really has some issues, Piper."

"Oh, I know," I said with a smile.

Then there was another knock. Theodore, who was closest to the door, peeked outside through the window and said, "It's Ryker."

Edie cut her eyes to me. "Now don't you pull off the same thing Dorothy did, you hear me?"

There was something threatening and demanding in Edie's voice, so I complied.

I felt all eyes on me as I half walked, half stumbled to the door in those heels. I straightened my posture, and adjusted the chest pouch, while checking to see if everything was still tucked in, then I opened the door.

Ryker instinctively took a step back when he saw me. "Piper . . ." he said then cleared his throat. "You look . . . even better than you did at the store."

I shifted from one heal to another uncomfortably and I felt that blush again. There were too many blushes lately. This new life here in Florida really screwed me over.

I smiled. "You don't look so bad yourself." Then I looked at Edie and she nodded approvingly. I took to mean I did better than Gran.

Ryker stepped inside and positioned himself right next to Theodore. He was practically Theodore's younger version. Black tux, white shirt, awesome physique, and a lot of hotness. Ryker nodded at us then his gaze landed on Edie, and he flinched. I could see his lower lip started to tremble, but he coughed to mask it.

Just when I thought I was off the hook, Ryker produced a corsage as well. I was stunned as Gran started laughing.

I got delicate orchid blooms with small filler flowers around them that went very well with the red dress I was wearing. Gran's corsage matched with her black dress too.

Ryker wrapped the corsage on my wrist and told me again how nice I looked.

"Don't get your hopes up," I said to him. "I can barely walk in these heels."

Ryker smiled. "No worries, you can lean on me."

I swear, I almost melted right then and there. I felt really hot all of a sudden even though I was in a very revealing dress and the AC was on.

"Finally some young love around here," I heard Beatrice whispering to Edie. I just hoped Ryker didn't hear it. There was no love here. And there would never be. If anything, Ryker would sniff out my real identity and then it would all be over. I had my own internal struggles about how to ever form a genuine connection with a potential romantic partner while constantly hiding my true self. Besides, how could anyone on the right side of the law ever love me if they knew who I was?

"Why aren't you having dates, if we're on the subject?" I asked Beatrice and Edie.

They shrugged.

"Don't really care about that," Edie said.

"I think you're the only ones going to the prom with a plus one," Beatrice said.

Well, wasn't that great? Gran and me, the two people around here who were least excited about the party, had dates. It was like the universe had it all backwards since we got here.

"Grams," Ryker said to Edie, giving her a hug. "You look . . . breathtaking."

Indeed, it made us stop breathing there for a second.

"Thank you, but do you think I went too far with it?" Edie asked looking down at herself.

"It wouldn't be you if you didn't raise the bar high enough," Ryker said, smiling warmly at his grandmother. She smiled back and snuggled into Ryker's chest as he squeezed her tight.

That made my heart melt just a little and I felt a ping of jealousy that Gran and I weren't as heartfelt with each other. We bonded more over ammo and shooting practice and the latest tricks to launder money properly.

"So how are we getting to the prom?" I asked Ryker. "On your bike?"

The image of me in this dress and heels, hopping on Ryker's bike made me warm inside again.

"No, I arranged for something better for all of us," he said and opened the door.

A black stretch limo was parked outside Edie's house.

"Shut up!" Edie said, playfully hitting Ryker in the arm.

Okay, I had to admit, I was impressed. A black shiny stretch limo looked extremely sexy. And then I saw the contrast with Gran's naughty looking gnomes not too far from it and changed my mind.

"So, everybody ready?" Edie asked. "Then let's get this party started."

\*\*\*

We were crammed into the limo, Edie already blasting party music. I couldn't really believe my life right then. Managing to sit gracefully in that dress was a challenge, especially with the sunken seats. Ryker was sitting next to me, which made me a tad uneasy. Our knees brushed against each other, and I struggled to find a comfortable way to keep my legs together.

Gran, on the other hand, couldn't care less. Her dress came up to her calves, but she sat there with her legs spread apart like she owned the car. Theodore sat next to her and was too cheerful for Gran's somber demeanor. Then there were Edie and Beatrice who seemed somehow way more chipper than usual. I mean, it was just a party. Since they're having parties here almost every week, this one shouldn't have been special.

"Say, have you been taking something that you shouldn't have?" I asked.

Gran perked up.

Edie and Beatrice did an innocent face.

"Who, we?" Edie said. "We would never take more than the regular dosage."

Just like always, I had no idea if she was joking or actually telling the truth. I decided to just let it go. But I did hear Gran mumbling something about how she never gets asked to take even the regular dosage with them.

I was studying Edie and I wished I could have traded places with her. She was having a lot more fun than I did or would have. I still had the Lola murder and the Falcons thing on my mind. Especially since the party we were going to was also kind of business.

In the last couple of days, Edie had worked almost overtime to get the people we were interested in coming to the party as well. Thankfully, Edie knew her way around this social stuff and she managed to get affirmative RSVP's from the people we wanted there. The attorney, the surgeon, the accountant, Eleanor of course, who deemed it as un-tacky all of a sudden. Eleanor's sister would come— the-too-inappropriate-tight-pants-at-a-funeral-chick—along with Dr. Curtis's employees and other people from the dentist's social world.

Edie had made it seem like they were throwing an impromptu fundraiser for supplying seniors in need of an . . . oxygen tank.

Yup. She did. She put a really good spin on it too, and some checks already flew in.

I wasn't sure how we would approach these people and find out who had a connection with Lola and a motive for wanting her dead. A couple of days before, I found out from Leonardi that the ME did the autopsy on Lola but as of now, they were still investigating.

On top of it all, I dreaded the moment Leonardi and Ryker would bump into each other at the party. Then again, they were grown men and they just had to deal with it. It was not my problem.

Then we had Sourpuss. As if we didn't have enough on our plate. Both she and Edie were less active in their Prom queen campaigns in the last few days. Gran was zero active in her campaign. I half-anticipated a retaliatory move from Sourpuss directed at Edie, stemming from her belief that Edie switched her campaign buttons. It was unclear if Sourpuss just gave up or if revenge was still coming.

The good news was that there were no more incidents in the last couple of days involving foot powder.

As I counted all the various probable disruptions and clashes expected tonight, it seemed we were heading towards a potential disaster. It was the perfect storm of so many things going south.

I just hoped everyone came out of it alive.

## Chapter Eighteen

AFTER THE WOO-HOOS AND ADMIRATION over our limo from fellow residents, we entered the rec hall. The tables were draped in lively tablecloths. Balloons floated about and the disco ball glittered from above. There were voting boxes for the Prom queen and king and the whole place was packed. Everybody was dressed to the aces, which kind of made sense, given they were all from a generation that knew how to dress up even for a routine flight.

Edie was in her element. She navigated the room, exchanging handshakes, greetings, and engaging in conversations with ease. She should have gone into politics.

Gran was greeted by her poker playing gang and admiration ensued about her outfit. Gran managed again to set a trend here and now it was about the combination of wearing boots and a cocktail dress. Theodore remained at Gran's side, even during discussions about poker, that didn't seem to interest him much. Gran seemed slightly irritated but Theodore was totally unfazed and was the perfect gentleman.

Beatrice mingled with other groups and Ryker, and I made our way to the bar. I already felt a toe going numb in those heels. I struggled to maintain grace in my stride and felt unusually self-conscious. Given my past life, that was saying a lot.

I crossed paths with two other residents, whom I had nicknamed Belly Man and Raspy. Their eyes widened when they saw me, and they both whistled and gave Ryker hearty back-slaps as if he was doing the heavy lifting tonight. How about slap me on my back because I was the one walking in these shoes and didn't fall on my nose yet. Then again, a slap on my back might just cause me to do that.

One of the staffers of the retirement complex stood behind the bar together with two others. "Piper, it's so good to see you," he said then suddenly stopped. "My, you look absolutely breathtaking tonight."

I hoped not as breathtaking as Edie looked.

"Thank you so much, Jim," I said, setting my clutch down on the bar surface, then self-consciously fumbling with my dress again.

Jim was one of the nicer staffers here in the complex. He was about in his forties and had the most piercing blue eyes I've ever seen.

Ryker positioned himself next to me and shook Jim's hand. "We'll have two martinis."

I snapped my head at Ryker. "So now you're ordering for me? Like I'm some kid?"

"Well, if you were a kid, then I wouldn't have ordered a martini for you," Ryker said.

"That's a good joke," I said with a hint of sarcasm. Then I turned and saw Jim doing the ping-pong between the two of us. "Are you two an item?" he asked, then slapped a hand over his mouth. "I apologize, that's none of my business. It just slipped out."

Poor Jim. I was pretty sure he had a crush on me and now seeing me here with Ryker must have him thinking.

"No, we're not an item," I said to Jim and made sure it was loud enough for Ryker to hear. The music was already getting loud. "It's just a stupid thing that happened and we ended up here at the party." I turned to Ryker. "Right?"

He flinched for just a mini-second, and I thought a slight disappointment crossed his face. But I was sure I was just imagining things. He cleared his throat. "Right. We're not an item. I just convinced her to be my date for the prom."

"And I accepted the challenge because backing out is not my style," I said and stared intently into Ryker's eyes.

He inched closer to me and I could feel the warmth radiating from his body. "So I'm a challenge, huh?" he asked smiling.

I stepped even closer to him and said, "I've faced far tougher challenges that I have conquered."

We were almost pressed nose to nose, thanks to my heels that propped me up a couple of inches. We stood in a silent standoff for a few seconds, the tension palpable. Jim's fake cough broke the silence and he said, "Sorry, here are your martinis." Then he nodded and moved on to another resident who had his arm raised at the bar.

Ryker took one martini glass and handed it to me.

"That guy really likes you," he said.

We clinked glasses and I replied, "Who doesn't?" Then I took a sip.

Ryker laughed and I laughed with him.

I hated to admit that Ryker was right. A martini was exactly what I needed right now.

We both leaned against the bar, surveying the crowd around us. I felt my second toe getting numb.

More guests streamed in, and I even spotted Sourpuss somewhere with her posse. Maybe I should tell her Gran was packing so she wouldn't rattle her.

In the crowd, I spotted Samuel Appleby, the director of the retirement complex, standing out like a sore thumb. He wore his usual khakis and Hawaiian shirt and made his five seconds tops appearance before leaving. He never butted into anything around here and sometimes I forgot he even existed. It was as if the seniors were running the place, not him.

Jim came back around and asked if we liked our drinks. We nodded and then he said, "I could use one as well."

"Don't mind us," I said with a snort. "Mix yourself a drink."

"I can't," he said. "I'm on the job. And I'm working at a retirement complex. It really wouldn't be professional if I drank alcohol while working. Besides, someone has to take care of all that powder in the back."

"Say what?" I asked with a frown.

"There's like ten cases of foot powder in the storeroom behind the kitchen," Jim said. "Mrs.

Barnett needed it stored in a cooler place. Something to do with this party, I guess."

Holy crap. What was she up to?

"Why would she store that many cases here?" I asked Jim, pinching the bridge of my nose.

"I'm not sure," he said. "She said it was a surprise or something. If she gets voted Prom queen or something. Then she would give out free foot powder."

Oh, goodie. Who on earth would want that foot powder after people had a rash last time it was in her hands?

I sighed. "I may need a second martini," I said to Jim. Then I said to Ryker, "Let's sit at a table, I can't stand much longer in these heels."

I clutched Ryker's arm as we moved to a table. There went toe number three and four. Ryker pulled out a chair for me, and an unfamiliar sensation washed over me—it felt like a date. Except, instead of my usual gear like a knife and bike, I was in heels and driving a golf cart.

The table was set for four and other residents sat there already. The music began to get even louder, and people started moving to the dance floor. I recognized the man playing DJ. He often assumed this role at these parties.

Two women and one man that sat at the table next to us glanced over and nodded approvingly. "You two look so sweet together," one of the women shouted over the loud music.

"We needed some young love around here," the man spoke loudly.

This was going to be an exhausting night. I just smiled and waved it away while Ryker only smiled. At me.

Then he leaned in and whispered in my ear—while I felt like melting in a puddle—, "I know your feet hurt but let's dance."

"Dance?" I frowned. "It's not even a slow song." Then I regretted saying that the minute it came out of my mouth.

"Oh, a slow song?" Ryker nodded wickedly. "So you would like to dance with me to a slow song?"

I shook my head vigorously. "No, no, that's not what I meant. What I meant was . . ."

What did I mean?

Ryker bobbed his head up and down like he was waiting for a reply. "I'm waiting."

He was so loving this. I pulled myself together. He was no match for me. I was just having some weak moments around him that apparently just kept on coming more often. "I meant people usually

311

dance together to a slow song. Not to this jumpy pop music."

"Well, I thought we'd try something new," Ryker said and winked at me.

"Not tonight we won't," I said in a determined tone.

"I see," Ryker said and leaned into his chair. "That's too bad. I thought we could have some fun before the night gets too serious."

I frowned. "Have some fun? Before the night gets too serious? What is that supposed to mean?"

Ryker studied me for a second. "I know you're up to something. I know Dr. Curtis's people are coming tonight and that you and Grams and Dorothy have something to do with it."

Oh yes. I was expecting this. Obviously, it was no secret that we invited all those people, but it was all under the pretense of them making a donation. For oxygen tanks.

"I have no idea what you're talking about," I said to Ryker. But what response did he expect? "The residents here thought it was a good idea for the good people of the community to join us in our party and make a donation." That was such a phony lie I cringed inside.

"Did you just hear yourself?" Ryker asked, already knowing me too well.

"Yeah, I just heard myself," I said. "But I stand by it."

"You can stay by it all you want but it doesn't make it truer," Ryker said. "You are investigating the Lola case with Leonardi and now all of a sudden, all the people from Dr. Curtis's clique are coming here. It's so you can snoop around better, isn't it? You can talk to them more freely here in this situation, right?"

I hated it that Ryker wasn't just a lousy PI. I also kind of hated that it turned from Ryker being all nice and holding out my chair and complimenting my looks to serious talk. I've had enough seriousness lately to last a lifetime.

I took another sip of my martini. "Do you really want to have this discussion? You know I'm not going to admit to anything except for yes, I already told you I'm investigating this with Leonardi. That's still ongoing and to be honest, the way we do it is really our own decision and you have nothing—"

In that moment, Leonardi appeared by our side. We both looked up.

"Speaking of the devil," Ryker said with a tone of disappointment in his voice.

"What?" Leonardi said, hands in his pocket, like he was out for a stroll. "I was invited."

"I kinda figured that already," Ryker said, but he was looking at me. He stood and clutched his tuxedo jacket tighter. Leonardi sized him up, then let out a laugh, like he was mocking him. "What are you? An extra in a spy movie?"

Ryker narrowed his eyes at him. "No more than you are one in a bad reality TV show."

Leonardi's grin vanished. But Ryker was right. Leonardi wore a suit jacket over a shirt with an even busier colorful pattern than usual, his hair was slicked back even greasier than usual, making him look like an oil tycoon caught in a disco fever dream.

"Okay, break it up," I said, moving in between them. "You're making me move and I can barely stand on these shoes." I looked at Ryker. "You. Go and mingle." Then I looked at Leonardi. "You. Let me show you the bar."

"That's a good call," Leonardi said, still eyeing Ryker.

"I was just leaving anyhow," Ryker said, backing away and disappearing into the crowd.

I wiped some sweat from my forehead. My to-do list of this evening was just getting longer and longer. Okay, keep Ryker and Leonardi far away

314

from each other. Keep Gran and Sourpuss far away from each other. Hoping that foot powder in the back was not going to be responsible for rash epidemic number two. Walk heel to toe, so I wouldn't fall on my nose.

On the way to the bar, I saw Leonardi checking me out.

"What?" I said, a bit on edge.

He put his hands up in defense. "Nothing, nothing. I just wouldn't have pegged you for someone wearing this kind of outfit. You seemed more like a . . . biker chick."

Oh, how right he was.

"Yeah, well, I got roped into it," I said.

"You just can't say no to the old-timers here, huh?" he said, laughing.

"If only you knew," I said, then ordered Leonardi a martini as well.

"What am I? A kid?" he said, and I had to laugh.

"Trust me, you're gonna love it," I said and handed him his drink, as Jim was eyeing him confused.

"It's alright," I said to Jim. "He's with me."

"O-kay," he said, with an even more confused look on his face.

Maybe I should have expressed myself better. Jim's eyes were so wide, they almost popped out of their socket. But I didn't have time to explain and honestly, as sweet as Jim was, I didn't have to.

Leonardi and I moved to the side so we could talk privately for a bit. Privately meant in a crowd of people and shouting at each other over the loud music. Also, toe number five just said goodbye and left the party without any parting gifts. On top of that, I felt a stabbing pain around my foot arch that was growing in intensity the more I walked.

"Man, do these people ever get out?" Leonardi asked, with a twisted look on his face. His gaze was directed at all the wrinkles that were bobbing on the dance floor. I saw Theodore asking Gran to dance and as expected Gran shook her head and put two fingers at her temple and made the sign that she would rather shoot herself. Theodore laughed but didn't move from her side. He was a tough one. Just like Gran. Only someone from the military could handle her.

I had to crane my neck and look around for Sourpuss but I saw her on the other side of the room still talking to her people. But soon I would lose track of both of them since they were all smushed in the crowd and I really had business to attend to here.

Leonardi took a chug of his martini and drank half of it. I watched him set the glass on the counter.

"Could you maybe not act like a brute tonight?" I asked him. "How do you want to blend in and talk to the finest people of Bitter End like this?"

He flashed me his tooth gap. "Don't worry, I can change it up in a second."

Whatever.

"Speaking of the finest people, I just passed them all outside so it's not long till they make an entrance," Leonardi said.

I strengthened my back and perked up. "They're here?"

Just then I saw a shy Eleanor step into the room and was immediately caught in the sway of overly exuberant partygoers. She stumbled backward, colliding into a man who looked to be the chubby attorney. I had memorized the faces from their websites. The attorney steadied Eleanor as she apologized for stumbling into him. Then they made their way into the crowd.

Another batch of people came in, all looking sharp as well. I spotted the surgeon and the accountant too. Everyone was with their spouses here. Every face seemed familiar since they were also at the funeral. So basically, we had almost the whole funeral crowd here. I was worried that we couldn't fit that many people in the rec hall, but we managed somehow. Just hoped nobody from the fire department was here to lecture us about safety rules.

Leonardi and I locked eyes, and I felt a surge of adrenaline running through my body. These were the times where I got the excitement of my old life back. The thrill, the suspense, and the risk of getting caught were all the perfect concoction that made me feel like on cloud nine and truly alive.

Leonardi and I both knew what to do. He downed the rest of his martini, slammed the glass on the counter and said, "It's showtime."

\*\*\*

One hour and a half later I had found out a lot of information but none that was pertinent to Lola and the dentist.

Leonardi and I had split up. I talked to the accountant and the surgeon, and he talked to the attorney and a few other people that were at the funeral. I had to admit my outfit proved beneficial in these conversations. Breaking the ice required much less effort than it did with my usual attire. Men were really easy. While they found me somewhat intimidating as a biker chick, they now seemed to underestimate me in my current red dress and heels.

Both the accountant and the surgeon seemed genuinely upset about their friend, Dr. Stephen Curtis, passing away, and also genuinely surprised by "that girl's appearance" in his casket. None of them gave me either kind of indication that they were hiding information. And none of them made the impression that they might have known Lola.

I played the naïve and curious guest and asked them if Dr. Curtis might have known Lola and they both smirked. Which led me to believe the good dentist had been using her services. Unfortunately, I couldn't find out more.

I made a mental note to thank Gran later for her ingenious idea. It was clear that engaging in conversation with these individuals in any other setting besides this party would have been impossible. If Leonardi and I had approached them in their offices as a private investigator and consultant, they would have likely thrown us out.

Leonardi held onto his word and surprisingly connected with the people he talked to. I even saw him raising beer glasses with the attorney and then chugging them down like a contest. Then Leonardi and I regrouped back to the side of the bar to tell each other that we basically didn't find out much.

"Let's mingle again and see what we can find out," Leonardi said, already swinging to the music and disappearing into the crowd.

Did he actually have fun?

I kind of felt like I was doing the splits, swinging across the dance floor with the older residents, catching Ryker's eye as he conversed with either Eleanor or his grandmother and other residents, all while keeping an eye on me and Leonardi. Simultaneously, I kept watch for Sourpuss; she didn't collide with Gran or Edie. Yet.

Meanwhile, Edie was totally in her element, dancing with everybody and blinding everybody in her hot pink dress. In between moves, she had asked me how it was going and I told her I was still on it, talking to our suspects. She offered to help but I refused. This was her night. She had other things to do. She campaigned for Prom queen, for crying out loud. She deserved to win and deserved to have fun. Edie-style.

I inquired about the timing for the final Prom king and queen results, and she informed me that they would be announced in approximately an hour by the five members of the Prom committee.

"So you're not the host this evening?" I asked Edie, smiling. Edie was usually the host and the MVP of every party.

"Well, apparently you can't be the host and the contestant," Edie said, adjusting her tiara.

"But if anyone can change that, that's you," I said.

"Damn straight it is," Edie said, and we both laughed.

I stopped by the bar again just as toe number six drifted off to dreamland. I drank a glass of water because I felt like just being at a marathon. I cut my eyes to the back and was glad the foot powder didn't explode yet, so at least there was that.

There was a donation booth set up in a corner and a huge picture of an oxygen tank hung in front of it. The people from the dentist's side all stopped by with their checks.

Leonardi and I were at an impasse.

"I'm telling you, we're missing the fourth person who bought the shirt in cash," he shouted in my ear.

I finished my water. "Well, unless you're telepathic, there's nothing we can do about that." In that moment, Eleanor walked past me, and squished through the masses of people to get to the bar. I put my glass down. "You know what?" I said to Leonardi. "Let's give it one more try. I'll be right back." I left him frowning, and moved next to Eleanor just as she got a drink.

"Eleanor!" I shouted over the music and gave her a stuck-up hug, just like Edie had done when we were at her store.

She looked startled. "Oh, do I know you—?" Then she squinted at me. "Oh. Piper Harris. You bought this dress from me. You look . . . I mean, I almost didn't recognize you." Funny what a new hairdo, some makeup, and some shoes could do to change you, although I was wearing the exact same dress she already saw me in.

I channeled my inner Edie and started the conversation with chit-chat. Mind-numbing chit-chat and complimenting her for this and for that. But I had a plan. I needed to know who bought that shirt. So I diverted the conversation towards that.

"You know, my date decided to wear a tux tonight," I said. I nodded towards Ryker in the crowd. "Isn't he a sweetheart?"

Eleanor looked in his direction. "Oh, Ryker is your date?"

I realized she had no idea about that, since neither I, nor Gran or Edie mentioned Ryker's name as my date when we were talking about outfits at Eleanor's store.

"Yes, a fine man that is," I said. I didn't mention her being Ryker's client, that was not the direction I wanted to steer this conversation to.

In that second, a man elbowed me from behind. It was Cyrus. He winked at me. "I knew you two were falling for each other!" he shouted.

Oh crap. Cyrus was wearing his hearing device tonight.

"No, Cyrus, that's not . . ." But Eleanor was standing right there. I had to keep up appearances. "I mean, um . . . Ryker is a good guy. That's all."

"Sure, a fine man and a sweetheart, right?" Cyrus laughed and moved away from us.

Damn it. I hoped he wouldn't tell Ryker that. But that was not something I had time for right now.

I turned back to Eleanor who was sipping her drink from a straw.

"Anyway," I continued, "I was kind of bummed my date didn't buy one of your beautiful shirts. You know, the ones with the gold trim. I mean, you should start a trend with those, right?"

Eleanor nodded, still sipping. I was glad that she was, since me asking about those shirts again after she eyed me suspiciously in the store was not your regular small talk.

"Maybe a marketing campaign would work?" I said, thinking out loud. "Some advertisements? Are you advertising right now? I'm guessing the first people to buy a new clothing line would be people you know, friends maybe, right?" I gestured toward the crowd. "Like your acquaintances that also came here tonight, right?"

Eleanor stopped sipping and said, "Of course, my friends always shop at my store. Especially when I have a new line out." She paused before she said, "And then there's my brother. Obviously, I sent him a shirt as well. He lives near Atlanta."

My jaw almost dropped on the floor. Her brother! Why of course! The brother who lived near Atlanta, who also was at the funeral.

"So you sent your brother one of the shirts? One of the checkered shorts with the gold trim?"

Eleanor frowned and tilted her head to the side. "Yes, I did. I shipped it there. Is that some kind of problem?"

"No . . . of course not," I said. "You sent your brother a shirt. That only makes sense because he's family."

"Indeed," she said, shaking her head.

The moment was over. I'd push it too far if I'd ask anything else.

"Well, then, I'll let you . . ." I looked down at her drink, "attend the party."

I left Eleanor and searched for Leonardi to give him this juicy piece of information. I found him on the dancefloor with . . . Beatrice? They were tearing up the dance floor. O-M-G. Not Edie's hot pink dress was going to get me blind tonight. *This* was!

I made my way to them, moving past dancing people. My seventh toe was hanging in there still. "What are you two doing?" I shouted over the music.

"What?" Beatrice said, shaking her hip against Leonardi with her hands up in the air. Her purple hair was bouncing, and her eyes were huge behind her glasses. "We're dancing."

"I can see that." Unfortunately. "But . . . you two?"

"So what?" Beatrice said. "You already have a date. You can't have two dates."

Cringe.

"Do you want Leonardi as your date?" I asked loudly, holding in laughter.

"Wait, what?" Leonardi stopped shaking his upper body and perked up.

"Come on," Beatrice said to him. "I love this song." She shook the other side of her hip as well.

"Um, I need to talk to him for a sec," I said to Beatrice. "I'll bring him right back."

Beatrice looked disappointed. "Fine, I'll be waiting." Then she winked at Leonardi and turned around and found other people to dance with.

Leonardi followed me out of the dancing crowd. We passed by Ryker, who was talking to one of the residents and his gaze was following us.

We moved into a somewhat quiet corner and I told Leonardi what I just found out from Eleanor.

"Her brother?" he asked, scratching his head. "In Atlanta?"

"Well, near Atlanta, but yeah, that's a bit of a problem," I said. We now had another man who owned one of those shirts and he was not local. Although if he lived near Atlanta, then would he have come back to break into the ME's office? Probably yes, if he was the murderer.

Only driving all the way to Atlanta to talk to a stranger was complicating things right now.

Leonardi let out a sigh. "So what do we do now?"

I looked around us. It was so crowded, and I really started sweating. The party was definitely a winner although we still had a long way to go. The collision between the queen bees hasn't happened yet. They still had to announce the winners of the prom. Which reminded me I didn't put in my vote yet. Couldn't they have just been more like the guys? You didn't hear a peep out of the men's nominees for Prom king.

"We could try talking to some other people," I said to Leonardi. "Or you could just go back to your dance partner and have some fun."

Leonardi grinned. "Or I can do both."

I laughed. "Fine, you go. I'll head to the bar first. I need hydration urgently."

I pushed my way to the bar just as toe number seven decided to quit its job. Not to mention, I had a sensation like my calf muscles were burning. I saw Jim and the other two staffers were really busy giving out drinks to the people. I knew they were keeping the water bottles in the storeroom fridge in the back, so I decided to slip in there and just grab a few. I would be near the foot powder cases and I hoped they wouldn't implode while I was there.

As I moved around the corner of the bar, I bumped into someone. At first, I didn't recognize him but then it dawned on me. It was the funeral director from the funeral home that handled Dr. Curtis's demise. I had seen him at the funeral too.

We smiled at each other. "Oh, by all means," he said and bowed like a gentleman to let me pass first.

"Thank you, I was just going to the back to get some water," I said to him.

"Water?" he said and wiped some sweat off his forehead. "Do you mind if I come with you? I am absolutely parched."

He seemed to be in his fifties and was wearing a light sweater over shirt and black slacks. Yeah. I would be parched too if I was wearing that.

"Of course," I said, and he followed me around the bar and into the hallway that led to the back. It was so full of people, nobody noticed.

I thought this wasn't bad, actually. I could talk to the funeral director as well, since the funeral home had been on our list of potential investigation. And bonus point, he was the funeral director. It was under his direction that someone had managed to slip Lola's body into another man's casket.

We walked down the narrow and dark hallway, and I asked him, "Are you having a good time?"

"I am, actually," he said. "I didn't think I'd be partying at all anymore at my age, but since it's for a good cause, I decided to do it."

I swung the storeroom door open, and we stepped inside. It was pitch black, so I flipped the light switch. The music from outside dulled in here. Stacks of water bottles filled the right side of the room, neatly arranged in boxes. On the opposite end, an array of household cleaning supplies cluttered the shelves. But my attention was drawn to the infamous containers of foot powder on the left. I made a mental note to steer clear of them. Who knew what Sourpuss did to them? I considered if I should listen for any faint ticking sounds coming from that direction.

"We thank you for being here," I said as I tore the shrink wrap off the water bottles and pulled out two. "Especially since most of the guests were friends of Dr. Curtis's. It's really so sad what happened to him. I think you were at the funeral as well, weren't you? Man, I have to tell you, I had a shock when that woman was found in the casket." I handed him a bottle of water and watched his reaction.

"I was at the funeral, yes," he said. "The incident was quite shocking and let me tell you, the investigation I conducted at my funeral home was extensive. This is bad for business, you know?"

"I totally understand," I said, as he stretched his hand out to take the water bottle. "So did you—"

But as our hands drew closer for the bottle exchange, I saw a graze on the side of his wrist. It was about two inches long and definitely fresh.

I gasped.

Then I looked up and it was only then in the brighter light of the storeroom that I noticed a sparkling golden trim lining the collar of the shirt he wore beneath the sweater.

We locked eyes.

And we both knew.

My breath caught in my throat.

This was the intruder from the ME's office.

Before I could respond, he acted fast. He shoved me hard, and I bumped against the foot powder cases behind me.

Just when I hoped I didn't set off a potential foot powder bomb, everything went dark.

## Chapter Nineteen

MY HEAD WAS POUNDING, and my mouth felt dry. I lifted my hand and massaged the back of my head. Ouch. That hurt.

Where the heck was I?

I slowly opened one eye, then the other. I was lying on the floor but propped up against something. More pain emerged, but it was coming from my feet. I looked down.

Oh yeah. I was wearing heels.

Then it all started to come back to me. The party, the dress, the oxygen tanks, the dentist, Lola, the Falcons, the funeral director.

That was a twist I really didn't expect.

He was the intruder from the morgue, and I highly suspected he was Lola's murderer too.

I looked around and realized I was in the storeroom behind the kitchen in the rec hall.

Well, the only thing making this even worse was if the funeral director belonged to the Falcons too. But I doubted that. Curiously, I didn't even know his name, since Leonardi and I haven't gotten to visiting the funeral home yet. I kind of expected this evening to reveal the real intruder. Which it did. I shook my head about the irony of the situation.

Okay, it was time to get the hell out of there and take that sweater-wearing doofus down.

I got up to my feet somehow and realized everything hurt. Sometime in the process, toe number eight went to sleep too.

The heck with the heels. I took them off and felt relieved, although the arch of my foot still hurt.

I looked down at myself and checked if everything was still tucked into that dress. Yup. I was good.

I realized I was leaning on containers of some sort next to me and my heart skipped a beat.

The foot powder! Luckily, they were still intact, given that the back of my head must have hit them when the guy pushed me. He got lucky. I must have hit the one spot on my head that knocked me out altogether.

I would have expected my fall against the foot powder to cause it to explode or something, but everything was good. For now, at least.

I headed to the door, but it was locked.

Seriously?

What kind of door was this, that locked from the outside but not from the inside?

I tried to pull harder, but nothing. The storeroom was windowless and had only a small vent opening but it was clear I wouldn't fit through it. I banged on the door and called for help and waited. Nothing. No movement. All I could hear was the muted music from outside.

Really now? Someone had to come in here for something.

*Jim, where are you?*

I took a step back from the door and placed my hands on my hips then I pulled at the chest pouch. It was really starting to get on my nerves. Or maybe everything was starting to get on my nerves. Especially a rookie guy having the upper hand over me. He just got lucky with me hitting my head, or else, he would have been in a great deal of pain right now.

What was he up to now, though? I just assumed he would scramble after knocking me out cold. Sure, he shut the door to win some extra time but now what? How far did he make it?

I looked around for my clutch. My cell phone was in there and I should have had signal in the storeroom. I moved around the small room but couldn't find it. Of course. The guy took it with him. Maybe he wasn't such a rookie after all. Or maybe he learned this was the way to go after getting rid of Lola's stuff.

The music in the background stopped and I heard the sound of a microphone screeching. I pressed my ear to the door. An unknown voice said into the microphone, "How is everybody doing?"

Cheers erupted.

Then the voice continued, "Are you ready for your Prom king and Prom queen?"

More cheers erupted.

"Then get yourself another drink, we'll be announcing the winners in a few minutes," the voice said. Then the music started up again. That must have been one of the women from the prom committee.

I shook my head. I couldn't believe the party was in full swing out there and I was locked up in here and nobody knew. But at least now I had somewhat of a sense of time. If they were announcing the winners now, then about forty to fifty minutes have passed since I last talked to Edie.

I banged on the door some more and called out for help. I felt defeated and a whole lot of scenarios for revenge appeared in my mind. What would he do? Would he get a fake passport and leave the country? Or would he just continue to live his life and pretend nothing happened? Then it dawned on me. It would be his word against mine. I would have to go to the cops and not only that but also admit that I, myself was in the morgue at the ME's office and that was how I knew about the funeral director. Obviously, I would leave Gran and Edie out of it, but I would get myself into it. The question was, would I do that even?

As I was starting to hyperventilate that the guy would get away because I wouldn't put myself in the line of fire, I heard a click on the door and the funeral director stepped inside.

Okay, this was unexpected.

But never mind the unexpected, he was here now, and this was my chance. Just as I revved up to jump on him, he quickly shut the door behind him and aimed a gun at me. I stopped in my tracks.

Ouch.

My foot hit the floor weirdly, since they were still recovering from the position in the heels and toe number nine just went on strike.

Now I was really pissed. More about my toes than about this guy aiming a gun at me. Nevertheless, I remained still. I needed to see how he'd proceed and then decide on the best way to take him down. Either way, he chose the third option of coming back with a gun, which was the worst option of all. He had no idea I was in witness protection and not exactly a fan of the cops and I wouldn't put myself into danger to testify against him. He decided he couldn't leave someone alive who knew what he did. That I understood.

"Are you insane?" I asked, putting my hands up. "We're at a party. You really think you can get away with this?"

He smirked and I saw his crooked teeth. "As long as I have this," he gestured at his gun, "I'll be alright. Just had to grab it from my car. What're you going to do? Get yourself killed? Or get anyone else killed?"

"If you shoot me, they'll hear the shot," I said, although I wasn't so sure about that. The music outside was extremely loud.

"No, they won't," the director said. "They won't hear a thing."

"Okay, so then what?" I asked, a bit annoyed and with nine non-functional toes, a huge headache, the feeling that I had to pull my chest pouch up all the time, and the returning shoulder pain I got from jumping on this guy at the ME's morgue, I was a bit on edge. "You came back to kill me?"

He loosened his shirt collar with one hand, then returned to holding the gun with both hands. "I will shoot you, but not here. We'll go somewhere else where they won't ever find you. I've made the mistake once of not disposing properly of someone, I won't do it again."

"Ah, Lola," I said.

He nodded and put on a wild grin. "Exactly, Lola. That tramp had it coming. Thought she could mess with me. Nobody messes with me. I own a funeral home, for crying out loud. I decide who gets in the casket and who doesn't."

I refrained from letting him know that he did not have the power to decide about that, but I could sense he was turning into a madman right there before my eyes. Better to let him talk and stall for time until I knew what to do next.

"So you placed Lola in Curtis's casket," I said. "Making the body disappear. It would have been the perfect crime."

He nodded again and shifted from one leg to the other while more sweat beads fell from his forehead.

"Everything would have been okay if those idiots hadn't let that casket slip down," he barked.

337

Then it dawned on me that at the funeral it was the director who also went ahead and helped the other guys carry the casket. I realized only then it was not actually in the tasks of a funeral director to do that but this one did. Because he knew the casket was heavier because Lola was inside, and he offered to help because he wanted to avoid the exact thing that happened. He knew he would have been in trouble if the body appeared.

Why didn't I think of that before? Of course the funeral director was the perfect person to hide a body in a casket. He had full, unrestricted access to the caskets. But there was no potential motive that we found for him murdering Lola.

"So why did you do it?" I asked. "Why are you calling Lola a tramp?"

"Because she was!" he said and his nostrils started flaring. "She told me she loved me, but she lied. She lied!"

Oh wow. Nutty much? So love was the reason. This was the guy Ruby had talked about. Lola was seeing this guy.

Music kept thumping outside while I was inside held at gunpoint by a crazy person.

"Did you know what she did for a living?" I asked him, hoping he would talk more. Then I had more time. Someone might pop in here and then...and then what? They would risk getting shot by this maniac. It surprised me again that I did give a damn, more than a damn, about the people here. What if Jim came? What if Edie came in? What if Beatrice came in?

No, I had to do this without involving them and without putting their lives on the line.

The only people who I wished would come were Gran and Ryker. Although even with them I didn't want them to get hurt.

"Of course I knew what she did," he sputtered. "I was not one of her guys. That was despicable. We met at a party about two months ago. A guy had her as an escort there. But we hit it off and started seeing each other. It was wonderful."

Okay, that he was in love with Lola I could believe. But what about Lola? Did she really have feelings for . . . this guy? Sweater Nutso?

"Did Lola feel the same way?" I asked.

His face reddened, and the gun trembled in his hand. I took a step back with my hands still up. I tried to scan out of the corner of my eye if there was something I could use as a weapon. God, I missed my knife so much.

But I was too far away from the household supplies, I would have to bend for my heels, and the only thing next to me was the questionable foot powder.

Oh.

The foot powder. Now I really hoped it had a bomb attached to it.

"Of course she felt the same way," he said. "Our connection was special. It was unique. I wanted to marry her, to gift her my love, but she let me down."

"How so?"

"She promised she'd leave her job behind," he said looking mad again. "But she didn't. She wouldn't." A sadness crossed his face, but I had zero pity with him.

He was holding me at gunpoint, he knocked Edie down at the morgue and now he was ruining the senior's party. Leonardi was right. We invited a murderer amongst us.

"She came to you last week on Sunday and you talked," I said, trying to make sense of this, since there was nothing else I could do. Except for inching slowly toward the foot powder containers. "And she told you she won't be leaving her job and you got mad at her."

He nodded and the gun trembled some more, and he sweated some more. That shirt beneath the sweater must have been soaked by now.

"She was so nonchalant about it too," he continued. "As if we hadn't discussed it at all. The plan was for her to quit doing that nasty thing she did and get herself a real job. I would have provided her with a job at my place."

I winced. Call girl versus corpse observer? I'd take the first one any time of day, thank you very much.

"And you had plans to marry?" I asked. I wondered why Lola was keeping this on the down low that not even Ruby knew who her guy was.

"We did," Sweating-In-A-Sweater said, then he paused and shrugged. "After I'd get a divorce."

Ah. There it was. The secret.

"So you . . . were mad at Lola for not going through her part of the deal but you were . . . still married?" I asked. Was he even serious?

"What's that gotta do with anything?" he sputtered, and I got startled. "I told you I would have gotten a divorce. That was the plan."

Sure. 'Cause that always works out fine.

"Anyway," he said. "Lola came by. She always did when my wife was out of town. And then that night . . ." he tried to compose himself, but more sweat pearls were running down his neck. "That night when we were in bed and she casually told me she landed two other guys and would go out with them, I lost it. I was madly in love with her, and she just stood there, breaking my heart. I don't know what came over me but suddenly, I had her delicate neck in my fingers and . . ." He seemed to be looking at nothing in particular behind my shoulders. Then he snapped out of it and focused again. "She got what she deserved."

I let out a breath. Now this was passion. I needed to be careful here. This man was obviously deranged.

Also, now my arms started to hurt on account of me still holding them up. I moved another inch closer to the foot powder and still stalled for time.

I could understand his options after he strangled her. What was done was done. He needed to get rid of the body somehow and I could respect that out of the perspective of Falcon Piper.

Now we also had the explanation why Lola came out of the casket naked, wrapped in a sheet. She was in bed with this guy when he killed her.

The sheet. That was another thing that the cops could have traced back to him with the help of the forensics department, since I was assuming it was the sheet from his own bed. Only the director was counting on making Lola disappear a total success. She would be gone, and his sheet would be gone too.

"And then you decided to place her in the dentist's casket," I said, shifting from one numb toe to the other. "Did you even know him?"

He shrugged. "Not personally. I knew of him. Knew he was a pillar in the medical community in town. He was just there when I needed to put Lola somewhere."

So it was a coincidence that Lola shared the casket with the good dentist. If only this guy knew that Lola was also offering her services to the dentist as well. What irony. I decided not to share this bit of information with this guy. Who knew what he'd do then? He didn't seem to be the most stable one.

I wondered how he had functioned in his own life. Was he normal and this Lola episode just brought out the ugliness in him?

"Those morons!" he repeated. "I should have made more men carry that piece of cheap wood. Let me tell you something, for a man that was rich, he got the cheapest quality casket I had in my catalogue. There was no love lost between him and that wife of his. Being in this business, you know these things.

You know when your family wants only the best funeral stuff for you, you were important."

Hmph. That didn't really surprise me about Eleanor. It was just as I suspected. She didn't care much for her husband. Which brought me to think about the checkered shirts.

I zeroed in on this guy's soaking shirt underneath the sweater. "Just out of curiosity, where did you get that shirt from?"

He looked down at himself but then back up. I could see he was straining to hold that gun straight.

"The shirt?" he said, and again, a sadness crossed his eyes. "I got it from Lola. She bought it for me not too long ago."

Oh. It was Lola. Lola was our fourth sale! But of course. Lola paid for the shirt in cash. In her line of work, cash was king. But if she went to Eleanor's boutique, then . . . that might be the connection between Eleanor and Lola. Either Eleanor knew about Lola and her husband from sometime before or she realized that when Lola was in the store. Might have been something Lola was wearing that Eleanor could connect with her husband. It could have been anything, really.

My whole body really started to ache, and I wanted to finish this already. There was still loud music coming from the outside and people seemed to be having a lot of fun.

The funeral director watched me and smirked. "You in pain?"

I nodded.

"Suits you well. You did this to me, didn't you?" He flashed his graze on his wrist.

I nodded again. "You mean that scratch?" I said with a tone of sarcasm. "Yeah, that was me. You should be glad you're still alive."

How was he to think so little of me? I told Gran to spare his life. I could have stabbed him dead myself. And now he thought he was the big guy? My fists clenched up in the air.

He sneered. "Like you can hurt me. Hello?" He waved his gun. "I'm holding this. But I have to say, I didn't expect you and those other broads in the morgue the other day. A guy can't even dispose of a body properly. That was my second chance and you ruined it. Too bad it was too dark to see any faces, but I had a feeling you three would be here tonight."

Even if he'd seen Edie in bright light at the morgue, he still wouldn't have recognized her in the hot pink candy outfit tonight.

I scrambled my brain for something to keep him talking, as I inched even closer to the foot powder area.

Then the music stopped, and a voice rang out from the microphone again. "This is it, ladies and gentlemen, the moment you've all been waiting for."

Cheers erupted again.

"We got your votes and we're ready to declare our winners!"

Woo-hoos blasted out.

The funeral director raised an eyebrow. "What the heck is going on out there?"

The voice continued. "I'm holding here in my hand the envelope with the names of the Prom king and queen!"

Clap, clap, clap.

"Prom king and queen?" Funeral Director twisted his face in a disgusted look. "What kind of sick games are you playing around here?"

Sick? That was sick? Coming from him?

"The seniors at the complex here are living their best life," I said. "Which is not what I can say about you."

He smirked again but listened in.

It was then that I identified a feeling of regret. Regret I wasn't out there with the others, with Gran,

Edie, Theodore, Beatrice and even Ryker and not only I didn't put my vote in, but I would miss the moment my neighbors worked so hard for—well, Gran not so much—the climax of some very intensive weeks we had.

There was the sound of a drum roll over the speakers. Even here in the back, I could sense the tension from outside.

"Starting with the men," the voice said, "if I could just open this envelope." There were some static sounds over the mic, and I could tell the person was struggling to open the piece of paper.

"Here, let me help you," a male voice said, a bit farther away from the mic.

It was all muffled, but I recognized Ryker's voice. I felt a slight sadness that he was out there, and I was here, in total dishevelment and pain and one second away from this guy to lose his temper and pull the trigger.

"Oh, thank you," the voice returned. "And now, you voted for him, your Prom king is . . ." More drum roll. I held in my breath and leaned in forward as if to hear better and I could tell Funeral Director Guy was also listening intently.

". . .Theodore Lawrence!"

Hoots and hollers ensued and on cue, the song *We Are the Champions* by Queen spilled through the speakers.

I smiled.

*Way to go, Theodore.*

The funeral director rolled his eyes. "What a load of crap. You know what? We've been here long enough. It's time to go." He motioned for me to move forward. "Listen, we're going out and I will shoot you the second you're trying to pull something funny. You got that?"

I nodded and clenched my fist even harder. This guy had no idea who he was up against.

"Did you just say something about a load of crap?" I asked him in my softest voice.

He frowned. "Yeah. This here. That out there. A load of crap."

"Ahem," was all I said then sprang into action and hoped he was a lousy shooter.

In one second, I turned and grabbed one of the foot powder containers and pressed really hard on it, aiming it at Funeral Director Guy. A whole mass of white flew out and hit him straight in the face.

"What the—" he said and coughed.

His finger hit the trigger and a bullet whizzed by my head and landed behind me in the wall.

Phew. Close one.

I had to take that gun away from him and I opted for a roundhouse kick instead of a frontal attack. To be honest, I was a bit worried he would shoot me involuntarily if we'd struggle body on body. I was at the optimal distance for a kick, so I quickly pulled up my dress—never ever in my life did I have to pull up a dress to fight—lifted my knee while turning sideways, extended my leg and kicked the gun out of his hand with the lower part of my shin.

Might as well have aching pains all over my legs, not just the feet.

The gun flew against the water bottle boxes and clapped on the ground. I thought I had him then but unfortunately, as soon as I let go of my dress and jumped forward, I stumbled in it and lost my balance.

Funeral Director Guy, blinking awkwardly through all the powder, took advantage of that moment, turned, swung the door open and bailed.

Loud music spilled inside the room and the same voice as before said into the mic, "Let's hear it again for Theodore, ladies and gentlemen!"

More clapping.

I regained my balance and started running out after Funeral Director Guy.

I ran through the hallway, past the bar and collided into a wall of people. They were all positioned facing the dance floor, where the woman from the prom committee was speaking on the mic.

"And now, now it's time to announce the name of our Prom queen," she said, and cheers exploded.

My eyes were darting all around as I elbowed my way through the crowd, looking for my prey. I would not let him get away with this.

In that second, I spotted him, working his way through the crowd on the left. I elbowed my way even harder, ignoring the "Hey, watch it," comments from the seniors. I knew a simple cry of "That's the guy, get him," wouldn't do without further explanation on my part. Then he would get away.

I was so close behind him, breathing hard and sweaty, with my feet throbbing, my arms and shoulder aching, hair strands falling all over my face, but my focus was so sharp, it could have cut a grass in half.

I was fifteen feet away from him, then ten feet, then . . . I passed a bun that looked like an antenna. Sourpuss. Nope. No time for that. I kept going. Seven feet . . . I passed hot pink ruffled. Edie. Nope. No time for that either. Six feet . . .

# CLOSED CASKET

"Our new Prom queen is—" the woman on the mic said while everyone was holding their breath.

Just then, I sprang on Funeral Director Guy and we both landed with a thud on the dance floor at the feet of the committee woman. She yelped and jumped aside, microphone screeching sound causing a collective grunt.

Funeral Director Guy was flailing with his arms and hands, but I held him down this time, at the same time trying not to come in contact with the powder on his face.

"What are you doing?" he screamed. "She's crazy! Someone get her off me!"

A collective gasp filled the whole room. All I could hear was the guy's and my breathing hard.

The familiar click of a gun echoed and made us both stop struggling.

I looked up and there was a gun pointing at us. I shook my head. No, it was not pointed at us. It was pointed at him.

Gran hovered over us, a mean look on her face, hands clutching her gun steadily in front of her and her black dress standing up on one leg, making her garter visible.

"Move one inch and I'll shoot you," she said to Funeral Director Guy in a deep voice.

In that moment, Beatrice, who was standing not too far from us in the first row, fainted and landed square on my foot.

Toe number ten just resigned and joined the others on their beach vacation.

# Chapter Twenty

I WAS SIPPING MY COFFEE at the kitchen table with Gran and Edie by my side. Edie had brought a peach pie that was delicious, as it always was.

It was two days since the Prom ended in disaster. It was the kind of a disaster I longed for, although now I was living with the consequences. My body was in full aching-mode, and I hoped my toes would recover in this lifetime.

After we caught Funeral Director Guy, the cops came and stopped short. They were most probably shocked at the mass of people at the retirement complex, partying like there was no tomorrow.

They took Funeral Director Guy away and I, once again, had to give the dreaded statement to them. They already knew me by now, which I found frightening.

Everything else that happened after that was a blur.

Edie and the others were in shock when I had told them I was in the storeroom the whole time. She had wondered where I was and why I wasn't there for the big reveal.

Ryker had rushed by my side and made sure I was okay. Well, I had asked him to define okay. When everything was over, my adrenaline rush abruptly came down and I semi-crashed into his arms. He carried me in his arms to a nearby table and ordered me to go to the hospital to get checked out.

I refused. I knew why I was in pain; I knew nothing was broken and I only needed time for everything to heal. Who knew what they would want to check in the hospital, my fingerprints probably not, but still. I didn't need to worry about that now.

Ryker informed me he would be stopping by very soon. On account of lecturing me again or really just checking up on me, I didn't know.

The seniors wanted a party, so they got one. The talk that ensued after Lola came out of the dentist's casket was nothing compared to the talk there was now.

Gran and I were their heroes.

Just what we needed. To be in the center of attention.

Since then, Gran and I locked ourselves into the house until things would start to die down. Edie was our only visitor.

"This is good rum," Edie said, taking another sip of her coffee with a splash of rum inside. Caribbean coffee, as she titled it.

"It's not the best I have, but it's okay," Gran said. I gave our best bottle to Leonardi and I made a mental note to remind him to thank me for that.

"So when are you coming to the dining hall for your meals?" Edie asked.

I shrugged. "I don't know. I can't take another handshake, and another hug, and another talk about what happened at the party."

"But you saved the day," Edie said. "What do you expect?"

"Ignorance and bliss?" I said with a grin.

"You're not going to get either one of those here, that's for sure," Edie said.

"So how come you gave up the tiara?" I asked her.

Edie shrugged, then leaned in her seat. "The moment's over, you know?"

Me colliding into Funeral Director Guy came at the worst timing ever. There was no Prom queen announced and with all the commotion, the party was obviously cancelled. We were waiting for a new date but haven't heard anything yet.

"I'm sorry you're disappointed," I said to Edie. "I know how much you wanted to win."

She waved it away. "Oh well, they already had a winner, they just didn't tell us who it was." She seemed to think about it. "You know, the winner's name was in that envelope. Assuming they didn't just throw it away, do you think—"

I held my hand up. "No. I know where this is going and no. Just no. We are not going to sneak into someone's house to get the envelope."

Edie pouted. "But this time, we wouldn't be dealing with killers."

"Still, no," I said. "Who knows what mishaps we'd be getting ourselves into?"

"Especially with you around," Gran finally chimed in.

Edie gave her a look. "I know you're disappointed about the prom too. Just admit it."

"I admit it was a helluva fun thing to point my gun at someone," Gran said.

I was thankful that Gran sprang into action at the party and pulled out her gun. That was all Gran needed. In only a couple of seconds, after I pounced on Funeral Director Guy, she knew something was wrong, and she immediately acted. I was sure her status at the complex grew even higher now. And if not, she could always wear the dominatrix dress with the boots again.

Edie took our prom night outfits and said she would store them at her house. The clothes were too pretty to get ruined, and Edie didn't trust us with them.

"We're not going to burn them or anything," I had said.

Edie had gestured towards Gran. "Maybe you wouldn't, but she would."

Okay, Edie was right. We couldn't be trusted with them.

I poured some more rum into my coffee.

"Where was Leonardi the whole time you were in the back?" Gran asked.

"Leonardi was outside, flirting with Eleanor's sister, that's where he was," I said, rolling my eyes. "He was in total party mode."

"Wow, what timing," Edie said.

"Indeed," I said and rubbed my feet. "What a great partner I had. There I was, held at gunpoint while he was off flirting."

Leonardi had called me the day before, wanting to wrap up this case. We were on the phone for about half an hour while I told him details about my super evening in the storeroom. When the cops came, Leonardi made sure I was okay, but then he split. He was just as much of a fan of the cops as I was.

He reported that Ruby was sending her compliments for finding out who murdered Lola. She would be sending the rest of the fee this week. I still had to sign the paperwork with Leonardi to get my share of the money.

After that, I didn't know what to do. Being Leonardi's consultant gave me the freedom to work whenever I wanted and also to refuse work whenever I wanted. I didn't have to take every case he offered. That was a huge advantage.

But for now, my body needed to heal first.

We haven't heard much about Eleanor and Funeral Director Guy, whose name was Harold Daugherty. Edie planned another trip to Eleanor's boutique, but I already told her I was out of this one. And Gran too. We concluded our business with Eleanor, and I couldn't do another round of meaningless small talk with her. In the end, we didn't have confirmation about whether she knew about her husband and Lola, and it didn't matter. She had her own life to live.

Gran and me had our own lives to live too. What did matter to us was if Lola was a Falcon or not, but that was another thing we wouldn't find out. We were just glad that the murder got solved, there was no Falcon involved, at least, no Falcon that wasn't us, and there haven't been any hitmen knocking at our door.

"So how about that powder?" Edie said, starting to laugh. "I still can't believe you took that guy down with Lucretia's foot powder."

"Me either," I said. "Did we hear anything back? Did the guy get boils on his face or something?"

Edie had tears of laughter in her eyes. "No, nothing yet, but I'm crossing my fingers."

"Do we even know why Sourpuss had so much foot powder stashed in there?" I asked.

Edie shrugged. "Couldn't find that out either. She says it would have been a gift for her voters. You know, she campaigned for it too. But you'd have to be out of your mind to accept foot powder from her after everything that happened."

"People are gullible," Gran said, "and they'll believe everything you tell them eventually."

Both Edie and I stared at Gran.

"What?" she said. "It's true."

"So did you switch Sourpuss' campaign buttons with the funny ones?" Edie asked her and leaned forward.

"I don't know what you're talking about," Gran said and looked away. "I think you poured too much rum into your coffee."

"She didn't really answer the question, did she?" Edie asked me.

I chuckled. "No, she didn't."

"So I'm not that gullible," Edie said and sipped more coffee.

I laughed. "You? Never."

"Besides, if Gran really switched the buttons, she would have gotten rid of the original ones, you know, burn them, bring them to the landfill, or shoot them up into space, so we'll never find the evidence," I said.

Edie nodded along. "Oh yeah, you're right. She would cover her tracks. I can totally see that. Probably held the operator at the landfill at gunpoint and made him crush the buttons in the machine."

"Um, hello?" Gran said. "I'm sitting right here."

"Yes, Dorothy, we know," Edie said. "But since you're not telling us anything, we have to speculate."

"There's nothing to tell," Gran said. "I was not at any landfill."

Edie's eyes cut to the corner of the living room. "Maybe you should?"

"What do you mean?" Gran asked.

"When are you going to throw away those foot powder baskets?" Edie asked.

Oh, yeah. Those.

Gran glanced at the covered-up blob of gift baskets in the corner of the living room.

"I'd have thought you wouldn't even want to be near that dubious stuff," Edie said with a wince.

"You're right," I said. "I can't believe we're living with Sourpuss's foot powder under our roof."

"Not only that, but you're sleeping in the same room with it," Edie said.

Yuck.

I shuddered and tried not to think about that. Better to focus on my Caribbean coffee. That was always the best option. I pondered about drinking a second cup when I heard the familiar sound of a roaring motorcycle outside. Involuntarily, my heart skipped a beat, and I got goosebumps. I knew who that was. My mind went straight to Ryker and how good he looked on that bike of his.

Ryker.

The bike.

Ryker again.

The bike again.

I couldn't choose which one was sexier.

I tried to push those images out of my mind, when I looked up and saw Gran and Edie grinning at me.

"What?" I said, taken aback.

"He's here for you," Gran said.

"What are you talking about?" I asked.

"You know what I'm talking about," Gran said. "Actually, who I'm talking about."

"You mean Ryker?" I said. "He's here to see Edie, not me."

Edie laughed. "Ryker never came over to 'check on me'," she air-quoted, "as often as he does since you got here."

I shifted in my seat. "That's nonsense," was all that came out, but the goosebumps got more intense.

I decided I was going to have another Caribbean coffee. Just as I was pouring the cup full to the brim, there was a knock at the door.

Gran and Edie looked at me expectantly.

"What is it now?" I asked, feeling a bit more on edge after the week I've had.

"*You* should open the door," Edie said. "He wants to see *you*."

"I don't think so," I said. "He's probably here to see you; you're his grandmother, after all."

"But how does he know I'm here and not at my house?" Edie asked.

"Because you're always here," I said.

Gran cackled. "Isn't that the truth?"

Edie gave Gran her version of the death stare.

I let out a breath. "Fine, let's get this over with."

I marched to the door, swung it open and was face to face with Ryker.

He stood there, wearing light denim jeans and a blue T-shirt that stretched comfortably across his chiseled upper body, a wink in his sparkling dark eyes directed at me. His healthy sun-kissed tan adorned his skin and was in contrast to my pasty-white, never-lay-in-the-sun complexion.

All of a sudden, I couldn't feel the aching in my body anymore.

I shook out of it. "Ryker," I said. "You here to see Edie?"

"Her too," Ryker said.

I moved to the side as a sign for Ryker to come in.

He stepped inside and Edie asked, "How did you know I was here?"

"Because you're always here," Ryker said.

Gran laughed again and Edie pouted.

Ryker looked around. "You know, this is the first time you've asked me to come in."

"I didn't technically ask you," I said, wobbling back to my seat.

Ryker smiled. "You're right, you didn't. Let me rephrase it then. You *allowed* me to come in."

"Well, my feet hurt just standing in the doorway," I said.

Ryker pulled up the fourth chair and took a seat at the table. He glanced at our coffee cups and then at the rum bottle. "Why wasn't I invited to the party?"

"Because you'd probably lecture us about how we should be careful and what not," I said.

"So you're saying I'm a party pooper?" Ryker asked with a grin.

I shifted in my seat. "You can be."

Ryker's grin grew even wider.

Gran brought Ryker an empty cup and placed it in front of him, along with the coffee pot and the rum bottle. Then we all stared at him.

"This is worse than being held at gunpoint," Ryker mumbled and mixed himself a drink. "It's been ages since I've had a Carajillo. Although its preparation is widely different."

Gran, Edie and I exchanged confused glances.

Ryker took a big gulp, then laughed. "Not so much a party pooper after all, right?"

"I have to admit, I'm impressed," I said.

"You should be." Ryker winked at me. Then he said on a more serious note, "As I am with you."

I almost choked on my Carajillo. I did not expect that.

"You were exceptional the other night in apprehending Daugherty," Ryker continued. "It was dangerous, but you did it. Once again."

"Thank you," I said. Then I waited for what would come next. But nothing came. "No questions about me being a spy or an agent or something?"

Ryker smiled wryly. "Oh no, I'm convinced you're something, I just don't know yet what exactly."

"Ryker," Edie said, slightly slapping his arm. "She's my neighbor, and my friend. Stop being suspicious of everybody."

Warmth filled my chest. Two and a half months into my new life in witness protection and I found someone that called me a friend. Yeah, okay, she was a septuagenarian who had been wearing a tiara in her curls all last week, but still. I felt like this was making progress.

Nevertheless, I studied Edie and wasn't sure how much to buy her defending me. She came off as naïve, but I swear, sometimes I had the feeling she knew something was up with Gran and me. Even worse, sometimes I had the feeling she knew *exactly* what was up with me and Gran. But I was certain, it was all in my head and I was just being paranoid.

Ryker put his hands up in defense. "Sorry, Grams. What can I say? It's the flaw of my job."

I almost added it was also his refined instinct, but I refrained.

"So do we have a closed case?" Gran finally said something. "Is that Daugherty guy behind bars? Can we end this conversation now?"

Ryker nodded. "Yes, Dorothy. We can all move on with our lives now."

I cut my eyes to Gran. *Move on with our lives.* What an interesting way to put it. Little did Ryker know about our struggles to do just that.

"Is that why you came here?" Gran asked Ryker. "To tell us it's wrapped up?"

Ryker waited a beat, then said, "Sure. And to see how you all are."

"You mean how Piper is?" Edie wiggled her eyebrows up and down.

I rubbed the bridge of my nose. "Good god."

"Actually, yes," Ryker said, taking another gulp of his spiked coffee. "She was the one in the guy's line of fire, she was held in that storeroom, and she brought him down. It could have gone down much, much worse."

I nodded. "Guess I got lucky."

"I don't think luck has anything to do with it," Ryker said. "It's your skill. Nonetheless, I know you must be beat after what happened and I'm glad to see you're doing okay, considering the circumstances."

Whoa. What was that? I wasn't sure if that was raw honesty or if Ryker had an agenda. But I was too exhausted to even try to decipher his intentions, so I said, "Thanks, Ryker, I appreciate it. And I'm good."

"I'm glad," Ryker said with a warm smile.

Edie leaned into Gran and whispered, "Should we leave them alone?"

"No!" I said, snapping out of it. "I mean, what for? We're good, everything's good."

Ryker laughed. "What are you afraid of?"

I narrowed my eyes at him. "Me? I'm not afraid of anything. But it's like you've just said. The case is wrapped up."

"Then I guess we better drink to that," he said and raised his cup of spiked coffee.

We all clinked mugs and took a big gulp.

"This is really good," Ryker said.

"Of course it is," Gran replied. "I bought the rum."

Ryker nodded in awe towards her then he glanced around the living room. "You have a very . . . nice place here."

Gran and I burst out laughing.

"Are you kidding me?"

"This place sucks."

Gran and I spoke at the same time.

The closest Ryker has gotten to Gran's house was on the doorstep, so I knew he already got a good snapshot of the I'd-rather-pull-out-my-eyelashes interior design but now he took it all in for the first time.

And he was a diplomat about it too, which made him even more appealing.

Ugh.

*Come on, Piper, snap out of it!*

"Then why don't you just change it?" Ryker asked.

Edie snorted. "Yeah, right. As if Piper and Dorothy are such fans of change."

Yeah, she knew us too well.

"We'll do it when we feel like it," Gran said.

"I could help you move stuff around, if you want to," Ryker said.

I raised my eyebrow. "Really?"

"Yes, really," Ryker said and grinned. "I'm a nice person, in case you haven't noticed."

I felt those goosebumps again.

"Well, then . . .," I cleared my throat. "We may take you up on that."

Ryker nodded. "I'll be at your disposal. Whenever you—" His gaze landed somewhere behind my shoulder. He frowned. "What is that?"

I turned and saw he was staring at the covered-up heap in the corner.

"That's our gift basket extravaganza," I said, shaking my head and drinking some more Carajillo.

Ryker winced. "Do I want to know what that is?"

"No," Gran deadpanned.

"Oh, it's this thing we had with—" Edie let out a long sigh and put her head in the palms of her hand. "You know what? I'm too tired to explain. The short version is: that's foot powder. Probably good to build explosives too."

Ryker shook his head. "Like I said, I don't want to know."

369

I thought about the foot powder some more. "You know what? I'm starting to think it could develop some kind of super toxic mold if we let it sit there longer."

I slowly got up from the chair.

"What are you doing?" Gran asked, and I sensed a touch of alarm in her voice.

"I'm thinking we really should get rid of that foot powder, once and for all," I said, making my way slowly to the dusted gift basket area. We should at least put a no enter band around it.

"What? Now?" Gran stood straighter. "Now's not the time. You can barely walk. Besides, we need that powder for potential retaliation missions."

Ryker shook his head again and covered up his ears.

"She's right, you know," Edie said. "Besides, you'd need a hazmat team to dispose of that. You'd be polluting the environment just throwing it away like that."

I ignored them both and pulled the sheet off the baskets, bracing myself for any implosions.

But nothing blew up in my face.

Phew.

Instead, something shiny caught my eye. A small bag was wedged in between the baskets and there was something in it, something that was not foot powder.

"Piper, would you please come back to the table?" Gran said, a bit more alarmed now.

I grabbed the bag and looked inside. Then I looked up and grinned wide.

"What is it?" Edie asked. "What do you have there? Is it worse than the powder?"

I displayed the contents of the bag as everyone was leaning in curiously.

Edie gasped. "No!" Then she whipped her head at Gran. "Lucretia's campaign buttons. So it *was* you!"

Busted!

Apparently, Gran decided to hide the buttons direct under our noses. Smart move. No landfill was involved.

Gran just rolled her eyes and poured herself some more rum in her coffee.

Ryker most probably already knew about the buttons, since he was at the dining hall when we were speculating who the culprit was. He said teasingly, "Dorothy, I had high hopes for you that you wouldn't get sucked into the drama around here."

Gran sipped her coffee and ignored him.

"But what else is there to do around here?" Edie said.

"You mean, besides you three going after murderers and somehow managing to avoid a breaking and entering charge?" Ryker asked.

"Again with that," I said, throwing my hands up in the air. "We did not break into the medical examiner's office."

"Oh yeah?" Ryker said. "The cops found tinsel all over the place."

Silence filled the room.

"So?" Edie said, shifting in her seat. "Does the police know where it came from?"

Ryker looked us all in the eye, then he said, "Nope, that clue was a dead end."

Edie raised her mug. "To dead ends."

"I'll drink to that," I said, and we all took a nice gulp of the Caribbean coffee.

# About the Author

Born and raised in Romania (Transylvania, to be exact), Deany Ray moved to Germany when she was 21 years old and since then calls Cologne her home. She keeps hearing some mentions about vampires and Dracula and whatnot, but she thinks that's all just a bunch of hooey.

Just keep any wooden stakes far away from her, okay?

She's not a native English speaker, so her editor and proofreader make sure her books don't sound like baloney. You could come across some typos in her emails (this is a sneaky way of asking you to join her newsletter), but hey, she just wants to put some good, entertaining stories out there.

She hopes you enjoyed this Piper Harris mystery story.

DeanyRay.com (for that newsletter she mentioned)

Facebook.com/DeanyRayBooks

Made in the USA
Las Vegas, NV
21 January 2024

84696284R10218